D0777350

tangled up
IN YOU

By Rachel Gibson

RACHEL GIBSON

tangled up IN YOU

AVON

An Imprint of HarperCollinsPublishers

This is a work of fiction. Names, characters, places, and incidents are products of the author's imagination or are used fictitiously and are not to be construed as real. Any resemblance to actual events, locales, organizations, or persons, living or dead, is entirely coincidental.

AVON BOOKS
An Imprint of HarperCollins*Publishers*
10 East 53rd Street
New York, New York 10022-5299

Chapter 1

The glowing white neon above Mort's Bar pulsed and vibrated and attracted the thirsty masses of Truly, Idaho, like a bug light. But Mort's was more than a beer magnet. More than just a place to drink cold Coors and get into a fight on Friday nights. Mort's had historical significance—kind of like the Alamo. While other establishments came and went in the small town, Mort's had always stayed the same.

Until about a year ago when the new owner had spruced the place up with gallons of Lysol and paint and had instituted a strict no-panty-tossing policy. Before that, throwing undies like a ring-toss up onto the row of antlers above the bar had been encouraged as a sort of indoor sporting event. Now, if a woman felt the urge to toss, she got tossed out on her bare ass.

Ah, the good old days.

Maddie Jones stood on the sidewalk in front of Mort's and stared up at the sign, completely immune to the subliminal lure that the light sent out through the impending darkness. An indistinguishable hum of voices and music leached through the cracks in the old building sandwiched between Ace Hardware and the Panda Restaurant.

A couple in jeans and tank tops brushed past Maddie. The door opened and the sound of voices and the unmistakable twang of country music spilled out onto Main Street. The door closed and Maddie remained standing outside. She adjusted the purse strap on her shoulder, then pulled up the zipper on her bulky blue sweater. She hadn't lived in Truly for twenty-nine years, and she'd forgotten how cool it got at night. Even in July.

Her hand lifted toward the old door, then dropped to her side. A surprising rush of apprehension raised the hair on the back of her neck and tilted her stomach. She'd done this dozens of times. So why the apprehension? Why now? she asked herself, even though she knew the answer. Because it was personal this time, and once she opened that door, once she took the first step, there was no going back.

If her friends could see her, standing there as if her feet were set in the concrete, they'd be shocked. She'd interviewed serial killers and cold-blooded murderers, but chatting up nut jobs with anti-social personality disorders was a piece of cake compared to what waited for her inside Mort's. Beyond the NO ONE UNDER 21 sign, her past waited for her, and as she'd learned recently, digging into other people's pasts was a hell of a lot easier than digging into her own.

"For God's sake," she muttered and reached for the door. She was a little disgusted with herself for being such a wimp and a weenie, and she squelched her apprehension under the heavy fist of her strong will. Nothing was going to happen that she did not want to happen. She was in control. As always.

The heavy thump of the jukebox and the smell of hops and tobacco assaulted her as she stepped inside. The door shut behind her and she paused to let her eyes adjust to the dim light. Mort's was just a bar. Like a thousand others she'd been in across the country. Nothing special, not even the array of antlers hanging above the long mahogany bar was anything out of the ordinary.

Maddie didn't like bars. Especially cowboy bars. The smoke, the music, the steady stream of beer. She didn't particularly care for cowboys either. As far as she was concerned, a pair of snug Wranglers on a tight cowboy butt couldn't quite make up for the boots, the buckles, the wads of chew. She liked her men in suits and Italian leather shoes. Not that she'd had a man, or even a date, in about four years.

She studied the crowd as she wove her way to the middle of the long oak bar and the only empty stool. Her gaze took in cowboy hats and trucker caps, a few crew cuts, and a mullet or two. She noticed ponytails, shoulder-length bobs, and some of the worst perms and flipped bangs to ever come out of the eighties. What she didn't see was the one person she'd come searching for, although she didn't really expect to see him sitting at one of the tables.

She wedged herself onto the stool between a man in a blue T-shirt and a woman with overprocessed hair. Behind the cash register and bottles of alcohol, a mirror ran the length of the bar while two bartenders pulled beers and blended drinks. Neither was the owner of this fine establishment.

"That little gal was into AC/DC, if you know what I mean," said the man on her left, and

Maddie figured he wasn't talking about *Back in Black* or *Highway to Hell*. The guy in question was about sixty, sported a battered trucker's hat and a beer belly the size of a pony keg. Through the mirror Maddie watched several men down the row nod, paying rapt attention to beer-belly guy.

One of the bartenders set a napkin in front of her and asked what she'd like to drink. He looked to be about nineteen, although she supposed he had to be at least twenty-one. Old enough to pour liquor within the layers of tobacco smoke and knee-deep bullshit.

"Sapphire martini. Extra dry, three olives," she said, calculating the carbs in the olives. She pulled her purse into her lap and watched the bartender turn and reach for the good gin and vermouth.

"I told that little gal she could keep her girl-friend, so long as she brought her over once in a while," the guy on her left added.

"Damn right!"

"That's what I'm talking about!"

Then again, this was small-town Idaho, where things like liquor laws were sometimes overlooked and some people considered a good bullshit story a form of literature.

Maddie rolled her eyes and bit her lip to keep her comments to herself. She had a habit of saying what she thought. She didn't necessarily consider it a *bad* habit, but not everyone appreciated it.

Through the mirror, her gaze moved up, then down the bar, searching for the owner, not that she thought she'd see him plopped down on a stool any more than sitting at a table. When she'd called the other bar he owned in town, she'd been told that he would be here tonight, and she figured he was probably in his office examining his books or, if he was like his father, the inner thigh of a barmaid.

"I pay for everything," the woman on Maddie's opposite side wailed to her friend. "I even bought my own birthday card and had J.W. sign it, thinking he'd feel bad and get the hint."

"Oh, geez," Maddie couldn't help but mutter and looked at the woman through the mirror. Between bottles of Absolut and Skyy vodka, she could make out big blond hair falling to chubby shoulders and breasts spilling out of a red tank top with rhinestones on it.

"He didn't feel bad at all! Just complained that he didn't like mushy cards like the one I bought." She took a drink of something with an umbrella in it. "He wants me to come over when his mother goes out of town next weekend and make him dinner." She brushed moisture from beneath her eyes and sniffed. "I'm thinking of telling him no."

Maddie's brows drew together and a stunned, "Are you shitting me?" escaped her mouth before she knew she'd uttered a word.

"Excuse me?" the bartender asked as he set the drink in front of her.

She shook her head. "Nothing." She reached into her purse and paid for her drink as a song about a Honky Tonk Badonkadonk, whatever the hell that meant, thumped from the glowing neon jukebox and coalesced with the steady hum of conversation.

She pulled back the sleeve of her sweater and reached for her martini. She read the glowing hands of her watch as she raised the glass to her lips. Nine o'clock. The owner was bound to show his face sooner or later. If not tonight, there was always to-morrow. She took a sip and the gin and vermouth warmed a path all the way to her stomach.

She really hoped he'd showed up sooner rather than later. Before she had too many martinis and forgot why she was sitting on a barstool eavesdrop-ping on needy passive-aggressive women and de-lusional men. Not that listening in on people with lives more pathetic than hers couldn't be highly entertaining at times.

She set the glass back on the bar. Eavesdrop-ping wasn't her first choice. She much preferred the straightforward approach: digging into people's lives and plumbing their dirty little secrets without distraction. Some people gave up their secrets without protest, eager to tell all. Others forced her to reach deep, rattle them loose or rip them out by the roots. Her work was sometimes messy, always gritty, but she loved writing about serial killers, mass murderers, and your everyday run-of-the-mill psychopaths.

Really, a girl had to excel at something, and Maddie, writing as Madeline Dupree, was one of the best true crime writers in the genre. She wrote blood and gore. About the sick and disturbed, and there were those who thought, her friends among them, that what she wrote warped her personality. She liked to think it added to her charm.

The truth was somewhere in the middle. The things she'd seen and written about did affect her. No matter the barrier she placed between her sanity and the people she interviewed and researched, their sickness sometimes seeped through the cracks, leaving behind a black tacky film that was hard as hell to scrub clean.

Her job made her see the world a little differently than those who'd never sat across from a serial killer while he got off on the retelling of his "work." But those same things also made her a strong woman who didn't take crap from anyone. Very little intimidated her, and she didn't have any illusions about mankind. In her head, she knew that most people were decent. That given the choice, they would do the right thing, but she also knew about the others. The fifteen percent who were only interested in their own selfish and warped pleasure. Out of that fifteen percent, only about two percent were actual serial killers. The other social deviants were just your everyday rapists, murderers, thugs, and corporate executives secretly plundering their employees' 401(k) accounts.

And if there was one thing she knew as certainly as she knew the sun would rise in the east and set in the west, it was that everyone had secrets. She had a few of her own. She just held hers closer to the vest than most people.

She raised the glass to her lips and her gaze was drawn to the end of the bar. A door in the back opened and a man stepped from the lit alley and into the dark hall.

Maddie knew him. Knew him before he walked from the shadows. Before the shadows slid up the wide chest and shoulders of his black T-shirt. Knew him before the light slipped across his chin and nose and shone in his hair as black as the night from which he'd come.

He moved behind the bar, wrapping a red bar apron around his hips and tying the strings above his fly. She'd never met him. Never been in the same room, but she knew he was thirty-five, a year older than herself. She knew he was six-two, one hundred and ninety pounds. For twelve years he'd served in the army, flying helicopters and raining Hellfire missiles. He'd been named after his father, Lochlyn Michael Hennessy, but he went by Mick. Like his father, he was an obscenely good-looking man. The kind of good-looking that turned heads, stopped hearts, and gave women bad thoughts. Thoughts of hot mouths and hands and tangled clothes. The whisper of warm breath against the arch of a woman's throat and the touch of flesh in the backseat of a car.

Not that Maddie was susceptible to those thoughts.

He had an older sister, Meg, and he owned two bars in town, Mort's and Hennessy's. The latter had been in his family longer than he'd been alive. Hennessy's, the bar where Maddie's mother had worked. Where she'd met Loch Hennessy and where she'd died.

As if he felt her gaze, he glanced up from the strings of the apron. He stopped a few feet from Maddie and his eyes met hers. She choked on the gin that refused to go down her throat. From his driver's license, she knew his eyes were blue, but they were more a deep turquoise. Like the Caribbean Sea, and seeing them looking back at her was a shock. She lowered her glass and raised a hand to her mouth.

The last strains of the honky-tonk song died out as he finished tying the strings, and he stepped closer until only a few feet of mahogany separated his gaze from hers. "You going to live?" His deep voice cut through the noise around them.

She swallowed and coughed one last time. "I believe so."

"Hey, Mick," the blonde on the next stool called out.

"Hey, Darla. How're things?"

"Could be better."

"Isn't that always the case?" he said as he gazed at the woman. "Are you planning on behaving yourself?"

"You know me." Darla laughed. "I always plan on it. Course, I can always be persuaded to misbehave."

"You're going to keep your underwear on tonight, though. Right?" he asked with a lift of one dark brow.

"You never can tell about me." She leaned

forward. "You never know what I might do. Sometimes I'm crazy."

Just sometimes? Buying her own birthday card
for her boyfriend to sign suggested a passive/
aggressive disorder that bordered on crazy as hell.

"Just keep your panties on so I don't have to
toss you out on your bare butt again."

Again? Meaning it had happened before? Maddie took a drink and slid her gaze to Darla's consid-
erable behind squeezed into a pair of Wranglers.

"I just bet you all would love to see that!" Darla
said with a toss of her hair.

For the second time that night, Maddie choked
on her drink.

Mick's deep chuckle drew Maddie's attention to
the amusement shining through his startling blue
eyes. "Honey, do you need some water?" he asked.

She shook her head and cleared her throat.

"That drink too strong for you?"

"No. It's fine." She coughed one last time and
set her glass on the bar. "I just got a horrifying
visual."

The corners of his lips turned up into a knowing smile that made two dents in his tan cheeks.
"I haven't seen you in here before. You just passing through?"

She forced the image of Darla's big bare butt

from her head and her mind back on the reason she was in Mort's. She'd expected to dislike Mick Hennessy on sight. She didn't. "No. I bought a house out on Red Squirrel Road."

"Nice area. Are you on the lake?"

"Yes." She wondered if Mick had inherited his father's charm along with his looks. From what Maddie had been able to gather, Loch Hennessy had charmed women into the sack with little more than a look in their direction. He'd certainly charmed her mother.

"Are you here for the summer, then?"

"Yes."

He tilted his head to one side and studied her face. His gaze slid from her eyes to her mouth and lingered for several heartbeats before he looked back up. "What's your name, brown eyes?"

"Maddie," she answered, holding a breath as she waited for him to connect her with the past. His past.

"Just Maddie?"

"Dupree," she answered, using her pen name.

Someone down the bar called his name and he glanced away for a moment before returning his attention to her. He gave her an easy smile. One that brought out those dimples of his and softened his masculine face. He didn't recognize her. "I'm

Mick Hennessy." The music started once more and he said, "Welcome to Truly. Maybe I'll see you around."

She watched him walk away without telling him the reason she was in town and why she was sitting in Mort's. Now wasn't the best time or place, but there was no "maybe" about it. He didn't know it yet, but Mick Hennessy would be seeing a lot of her. Next time he might not be so welcoming.

The sounds and smells of the bar pressed in on her and she hung her purse over her shoulder. She slid from the stool and wove her way through the dimly lit crowd. At the door, she looked over her shoulder toward the bar and Mick. Beneath the lights above him, he tilted his head back a little and smiled. She paused and her grasp on the handle tightened as he turned and poured a beer from a row of spigots.

While she stood there, the juke playing something about whiskey for men and beer for horses, her gaze took in his dark hair at the back of his neck and his wide shoulders in his black T-shirt. He turned and placed a glass on the bar. As she watched him, he laughed at something, and until that moment Maddie hadn't known what she'd expected of Mick Hennessy, but whatever it had been, this living, breathing man who laughed and smiled hadn't been it.

Through the dark bar and cigarette haze, his gaze landed on her. She could almost feel it reach across the room and touch her, which she knew was pure illusion. She stood in the darkened entrance and it would be near impossible for him to distinguish her from the crowd. She opened the door and stepped outside into the cool evening air. While she'd been in Mort's, night had descended on Truly like a heavy black curtain, the only relief a few lit business signs and the occasional streetlamp.

Her black Mercedes was parked across the street in front of Tina's Mountain Skivvies and the Rock Hound Art Gallery. She waited for a yellow Hummer to pass before she stepped from the curb and walked from beneath the glow of Mort's neon sign.

A keyless transponder in her purse unlocked the driver's-side door as she approached, and she opened it and slid inside the cool leather interior. Normally, she wasn't materialistic. She didn't care about clothes or shoes. Since no one ever saw her underwear these days, she didn't care if her bra matched her panties and she didn't own expensive jewelry. Before purchasing the Mercedes two months ago, Maddie had put over two hundred thousand miles on her Nissan Sentra. She'd needed a new vehicle and had been looking at a Volvo SUV when she'd turned around and locked eyes on the black S600 sedan. The showroom lights had been shining down on the car like a signal from God, and she could have sworn she heard angels singing hallelujahs like the Mormon Tabernacle Choir. Who was she to ignore a message from the Lord? A few hours after walking into the dealership, she'd driven the car out of the showroom and into the garage of her home down in Boise.

She pressed the start button on the shifter and hit the lights. The CD in her stereo system filled the Mercedes with Warren Zevon's *Excitable Boy*. She pulled away from the curb and flipped a U in the middle of Main Street. There was something brilliant and disturbing about Warren Zevon's lyrics. A little like looking into the mind of someone who stood at the line between crazy and sane and occasionally pushed one toe over. Toying with the line, testing it, then pulling back just before getting sucked into looneyville. In Maddie's line of work, there weren't many who pulled back in time.

The Mercedes' headlights cut through the inky night as she turned left at the only traffic signal in town. The very first car she'd ever owned had been a Volkswagen Rabbit, so battered the seats had been held together with duct tape. She'd come a long way since then. A long way from the Roundup Trailer Court where she'd lived with her mother, and the cramped little house in Boise where she'd been raised by her great-aunt Martha.

Until the day of her retirement, Martha had worked the front counter at Rexall Drug, and they'd lived off her small paycheck and Maddie's Social Security checks. Money had always been tight, but Martha kept half a dozen cats at any given time. The house had always smelled like Friskies and litter boxes. To this day, Maddie hated cats. Well, maybe not her good friend Lucy's cat, Mr. Snookums. Snookie was cool. For a cat.

She drove for a mile around the east side of the lake before turning into her driveway lined with thick towering pines and pulling to stop in front of the two-story home she'd bought a few months ago. She didn't know how long she'd keep the house. One year. Three. Five. She'd bought rather than leased for the investment. Property around Truly was hot, and when or if she sold the place, she stood to make a nice profit.

Maddie cut the Mercedes' headlights and the darkness pressed in on her. She ignored the apprehension in her chest as she got out of the car and walked up the steps and onto the wraparound porch lit up with numerous sixty-watt bulbs. She wasn't afraid of anything. Certainly not the dark, but she knew bad things did happen to women who weren't as aware and as cautious as Maddie. Women who didn't have a small arsenal of safety devices in their shoulder bags. Things like a Taser, Mace, a personal alarm, and brass knuckles, just to name a few. A girl could never be too careful, especially at night in a town where it was difficult to see your hand in front of your face. In a town set smack-dab in the middle of dense forest where wildlife rustled from trees and underbrush. Where rodents with beady little eyes waited for a girl to go to bed before ransacking the pantry. Maddie had never had to use any of her personal safety devices, but lately she'd been wondering if she was a good enough shot to zap a marauding mouse with her Taser.

Lights burned from within the house as Maddie unlocked the forest-green door, stepped inside, and flipped the deadbolt behind her. Nothing scurried from the corners as she tossed her purse on a red velvet chair by the door. A large fireplace dominated the middle of the big living room and divided it into what was meant to be the dining room but what Maddie used as her office.

On a coffee table in front of the velvet sofa sat Maddie's research files and an old five-by-seven photograph in a silver frame. She reached for the picture and looked into the face of her mother, at her blond hair, blue eyes, and big smile. It had been taken a few months before Alice Jones had died. A photo of a happy twenty-four-year-old, so vibrant and alive, and like the yellowed photograph in the expensive frame, most of Maddie's memories had faded too. She recalled bits of this and snatches of that. She had a faint memory of watching her mother put on makeup and brush her hair before leaving for work. She recalled her old blue Samsonite suitcase and moving from place to place. Through the watery prism of twenty-nine years, she had a very faint memory of the last time her mother had packed up their Chevy Maverick and the two-hour drive north to Truly. Moving into their trailer house with orange shag carpet.

The clearest memory Maddie had of her mother was the scent of her skin. She'd smelled like almond lotion. But mostly she recalled the morning her great-aunt had arrived at the Roundup Trailer Court to tell her that her mother was dead.

Maddie set the photo back on the table and moved across the hardwood floor into the kitchen. She grabbed a Diet Coke out of the refrigerator and unscrewed the cap. Martha had always said that Alice was flighty. Flitting like a butterfly from place to place, from man to man, searching for somewhere to belong and looking for love. Finding both for a time before moving on to the next place or newest man.

Maddie drank from the bottle, then replaced the cap. She was nothing like her mother. She knew her place in the world. She was comfortable with who she was, and she certainly didn't need a man to love her. In fact, she'd never been in love. Not the romantic kind that her good friend Clare wrote about for a living. And not the foolish, mad-for-the-man kind that had ruled and ultimately taken her mother's life.

No, Maddie had no interest in a man's *love*. His body was a different matter, and she did want an occasional boyfriend. A man to come over several times a week to have sex. He didn't have to be a great conversationalist. Hell, he didn't even have to take her to dinner. Her ideal man would just take her to bed, then leave. But there were two problems with finding her ideal man. First, any man who just wanted sex from a woman was most likely a jerk. Second, it was difficult to find a willing man who was good in bed rather than who just thought he was good. The chore of sorting through men to find what she wanted had become such a hassle, she'd given up four years ago.

She hooked the top of the Coke bottle between two fingers and moved from the kitchen. Her flip-flops slapped the bottoms of her feet as she walked through the living room and passed the fireplace to her office. Her laptop sat on an L-shaped desk shoved up against the wall and she flipped on the lamp clamped to the hutch of her desk. Two sixty-watt bulbs lit up a stack of diaries, her laptop, and her "Taking Names and Kicking Ass" sticky notes. Altogether there were ten diaries in various shapes and colors. Red. Blue. Pink. Two of the diaries had locks, while one of the others was nothing more than a yellow spiral notebook with the word "Diary" written in black marker. All of them had belonged to her mother.

Maddie tapped the Diet Coke bottle against her thigh as she gazed at the top white book. She hadn't known they'd even existed until her great-aunt Martha's death a few months ago. She didn't believe Martha had purposely kept the diaries from her. More than likely she'd intended to give them to Maddie someday but had completely forgotten. Alice hadn't been the only flighty female on the Jones family tree.

As Martha's only living relative, it had been up

to Maddie to settle her affairs, see to her funeral, and clean out her house. She'd managed to find homes for her aunt's cats and had planned to donate most everything else to Goodwill. In one of the last cartons she'd sorted through, she'd come across old shoes, outdated purses, and a battered boot box. She'd almost tossed the battered box without lifting the top. A part of her almost wished that she had. Wished she'd spared herself the pain of staring down into the box and feeling her heart shoved into her throat. As a child she'd longed for a connection with her mother. Some little something that she could have and hold. She'd dreamed of having something she could take out from time to time that tied her to the woman who'd given her life. She'd spent her childhood longing for something . . . something that had been a few feet away in the top of a closet the whole time. Waiting for her in a Tony Lama box.

The box had contained the diaries, her mother's obituary, and newspaper articles about her death. It had also held a satin bag filled with jewelry. Cheep stuff, mostly. A Foxy Lady necklace, several turquoise rings, a pair of silver hoop earrings, and a tiny pink band from St. Luke's Hospital with the words "Baby Jones" printed on it.

Standing in her old bedroom that day, unable to

breathe as her chest imploded, she'd felt like a kid again. Scared and alone. Afraid to reach out and make the connection, but at the same time excited to finally have something tangible that had belonged to a mother she hardly remembered.

Maddie set her Coke on the top of her desk and spun her office chair around. That day, she'd taken the boot box home and placed the silk bag in her jewelry box. Then she'd sat down and read the diaries. She'd read every word, devouring them in one day. The diaries had started on her mother's twelfth birthday. Some of them had been bigger and taken her mother longer to fill. Through them she'd gotten to know Alice Jones.

She'd gotten to know her as a child of twelve who'd longed to grow up and be an actress like Anne Francis. A teen who longed to find true love on *The Dating Game*, and a woman who looked for love in all the wrong places.

Maddie had found something to connect her to her mother, but the more she'd read, the more she'd felt at loose ends. She'd gotten her childhood wish and she'd never felt so alone.

Chapter 2

Mick Hennessy slipped a rubber band about a stack of cash and set it next to a pile of credit card and debit receipts. The sound of the electric coin sorter sitting on his desk filled the small office in the back of Mort's. Everyone but Mick had gone home for the evening and he was just balancing the tills before he headed that way himself.

Owning and running bars was in Mick's blood. Mick's great-grandfather had made and sold cheap grain alcohol during Prohibition and opened Hennessy's two months after the Eighteenth Amendment was repealed and the spigots once again flowed in the United States. The bar had been in his family ever since.

Mick didn't particularly care for belligerent

drunks, but he did like the flexible hours that came with being his own boss. He didn't have to take orders or answer to anyone, and when he walked into one of his bars, he had a feeling of possession that he'd never felt with anything else in his life. His bars were loud and raucous and chaotic, but it was a chaos he controlled.

More than the hours and feeling of possession, Mick liked making money. During the summer months, he made tons of money from tourists and from the people who lived in Boise but owned cabins on the lake in Truly.

The coin sorter stopped and Mick slid stacks of coins into paper sleeves. An image of a dark-haired, red-lipped woman entered his head. He wasn't surprised that he'd noticed Maddie Dupree within seconds of stepping behind the bar. It only would have surprised him if he hadn't noticed her. With her beautiful smooth skin and seductive brown eyes, she was just the sort of woman who drew his attention. That small mole at the corner of her full lips had reminded him just how long it had been since he'd kissed a mouth like hers and worked his way south. Down her chin and the arch of her throat to all the soft places and sweet parts.

Since his move back to Truly two years ago, his sex life had suffered more than he liked. Which sucked. Truly was a small town where people went to church on Sundays and married young. They tended to stay married and if not, looked to remarry real quick. Mick never messed with married women or women with marriage on their minds. Never even thought twice about it.

Not that there weren't plenty of unmarried women in Truly. Owning two bars in town, he came in contact with a lot of available women. A good share of them let him know they were interested in more than his cocktail list. Some of them he'd known all of his life. They knew the stories and gossip and thought they knew him too. They didn't, or they would know he preferred to spend time with women who didn't know him or the past. Who didn't know the sordid details of his parents' lives.

Mick shoved the money and receipts into deposit bags and zipped them closed. The clock on the wall above his desk read 2:05. Travis's latest school photograph sat on a polished oak desk; a sprinkling of brown freckles scattered across the boy's cheeks and nose. Mick's nephew was seven going on fourteen and had too much Hennessy in him for his own good. The innocent smile didn't fool Mick one bit. Travis had his ancestors' dark hair and blue eyes and wild ways. If left

unchecked, he'd inherit their fondness for fighting, booze, and women. Any one of those traits
by themselves wasn't necessarily bad in moderation, but generations of Hennessys had never
cared squat about moderation, and the combination had sometimes proved lethal.

He moved across the office and set the money
on the top shelf of the safe, next to the printout of
that night's transactions. He swung the heavy
door shut, pushed down the steel handle, and
spun the combination lock. The tick-tick of the
lock filled the silence of the small office in the back
of Mort's.

Travis was giving Meg hell, that was for sure,
and Mick's sister had little understanding of boys.
She just didn't get why boys threw rocks, made
weapons out of everything they touched, and
punched each other for no apparent reason. It was
up to Mick to be the buffer in Travis's life and to
help Meg raise him. To give the boy someone to
talk to and to teach him how to be a good man.
Not that Mick was an expert or a shining example
of what made a good man. But he did have firsthand knowledge and some experience in what
made an asshole.

He grabbed a set of keys off the desktop and
headed out of the office. The heels of his boots

thudded against the hardwood floor, sounding inordinately loud in the empty bar.

When he was a kid, no one had been around for him to talk to or teach him how to be a man. He'd been raised by his grandmother and sister, and he'd had to learn for himself. More often than not, he learned the hard way. He didn't want the same for Travis.

Mick flipped the light switches off and headed out the back door. The cold morning air brushed his face and neck as he stuck a key in the deadbolt and locked it behind him. Right out of high school he'd left Truly to attend Boise State down in the capital city. But after three years of aimless pursuits and a rotten attitude, he'd enlisted in the army. At the time, seeing the world from the inside of a tank had sounded like a real smart plan.

A red Dodge Ram was parked next to the Dumpster and he climbed inside. He'd certainly seen the world. Sometimes more of it than he cared to remember, but not from the inside of a tank. Instead he'd viewed it from thousands of feet in the air within the cockpits of Apache helicopters. He'd flown birds for the U.S government before getting out and moving back to Truly. The army had given him more than a kick-ass career and a chance to live a good life. It had taught him how to be a man in a way that living in a house of women had not. When to stand up and when to shut the hell up. When to fight and when to walk away. What mattered and what wasn't worth his time.

Mick started the truck and waited a few moments for the vehicle to warm up. He owned two bars, and he figured it was a very good thing that he'd learned to deal with belligerent drunks and assorted dipshits in a way that didn't require throwing fists and cracking heads. Otherwise, he'd get little else done. He'd be in one fight after another, walking around with a black eye and busted lip like he had growing up. Back then he hadn't known how to handle the dipshits of the world. Back then he'd been forced to live with the scandal his parents had created. He'd had to live with the whispers when he walked into a room. The sideways glances at church or the Valley Grocery Store. The taunts from other children at school or, worse, the birthday parties he and Meg had not been invited to. Back then, he'd handled every slight with his fists. Meg had retreated within herself.

Mick flipped on the headlights and shoved the truck into reverse. The Ram's taillights lit up the alley as he looked over his shoulder and backed out of the parking space. In a larger town, the salacious lives of Loch and Rose Hennessy would have been forgotten within a few weeks. Front-page news for a day or two, then eclipsed by something more shocking. Something bigger to talk about over morning coffee. But in a town the size of Truly, where the juiciest scandal usually involved such nefarious deeds as a stolen bicycle or Sid Grimes poaching out of season, the sordidness of Loch and Rose Hennessy had kept the town talking for years. Speculating and rehashing every tragic detail had become a favorite pastime. Right up there with holiday parades, the ice-sculpting contest, and raising money for the town's various causes. But unlike decorating floats and instituting after-school just-say-no-to-drugs programs, what everyone seemed to forget, or perhaps didn't care about, was that within the wreckage that Rose and Loch had created, there had been two innocent children just trying to live it all down.

He shoved the truck into drive and rolled out of the alley and onto a dimly lit street. A lot of his childhood memories were old and faded and thankfully forgotten. Others were so crystal clear he could recall every detail. Like the night he and

Meg had been woken up by a county sheriff, told to grab a few things, and taken to their grandmother Loraine's house. He remembered sitting in the back of the squad car in his T-shirt, underwear, and sneakers, holding his Tonka truck, while Meg sat next to him, crying as if their world had just ended. And it had. He remembered all the squawk and adrenaline-laced voices on the police radio, and he remembered something about someone checking up on the other little girl.

Leaving the few city lights behind, Mick drove through the pitch-darkness for two miles before turning onto his dirt street. He drove past the house where he and Meg had been raised after the death of their parents. His grandmother Loraine Hennessy had been affectionate and loving in her own way. She'd made sure he and Meg had things like winter boots and gloves and were always filled with comfort food. But she'd completely neglected what they'd really needed. The most normal life possible.

She'd refused to sell the old farmhouse where he and Meg had lived with their parents. For years it sat abandoned on the outskirts of town, becoming a haven for mice and a constant reminder of the family that had once lived there. A person couldn't enter town without seeing it. Without seeing the overgrown weeds, the peeling white paint, and the sagging clothesline.

And Monday through Friday, for nine months out of every year, Mick and Meg had been forced to pass it on their way to school. While the other children on the bus chatted about the latest episode of *The Dukes Of Hazzard* or checked out the contents of their lunch boxes, he and Meg turned their heads away from the window. Their stomachs got heavy and they held their breath, praying to God no one noticed their old house. God hadn't always answered and the bus would fill with the latest gossip the kids had overheard about Mick's parents.

The bus trip to school had been a daily hell. A routine torture—until a cold October night in 1986 when the farmhouse erupted in a huge orange fireball and burned completely to the ground. Arson had been determined as the cause of the fire, and there'd been a big investigation. Almost everyone in town had been questioned, but the person responsible for dousing the place with kerosene had never been caught. Everyone in town thought they knew who'd done it, but no one had known for sure.

After Loraine's death three years ago, Mick sold

the property to the Allegrezza boys and he'd thought about selling the family bar too, but in the end he decided to move back and run the place. Meg needed him. Travis needed him, and to his surprise, when he'd returned to Truly, no one really talked about the scandal anymore. Whispers no longer followed him, or if they did, he no longer heard them.

He slowed the truck and made another left, turning into his long driveway and heading up a hill seated at the base of Shaw Mountain. He'd bought the two-story house shortly after he'd moved back to Truly. It had a great view of the town and the rugged mountains surrounding the lake. He parked in the garage next to his twenty-one-foot ski boat and entered the house through the laundry room. The light in his office was on and he turned it off as he passed. He moved through the dark living room and took the stairs two at a time.

For the most part, Mick didn't really think of the past that had been such a focus in his child-hood. Truly didn't talk about it anymore, which was ironic as hell, because he just didn't give a shit what people said and thought about him these days. He walked into his bedroom at the far end of the hall and moved through the moonlight pouring through the open slats of his wooden blinds. Shadow and muted strips of light touched his face and chest as he reached into his back pocket. He tossed his wallet on his dresser, then grabbed two fistfuls of his T-shirt and pulled it over his head. But just because he didn't give a shit about the past didn't mean that Meg was over it. She had her good days and bad days. Since the death of their grandmother, her bad days were getting worse, and that was just no way for Travis to live.

Moonlight and shadow spilled across the green quilt and solid oak posts of Mick's bed. He dropped the shirt by his feet, then walked across the room. Sometimes he felt that moving back to Truly had been a mistake. It felt as if he were standing in one place, unable to move forward, and he didn't know why he felt that way. He'd bought a new bar and was thinking of starting a helicopter service with his friend Steve. He had money and success and he belonged in Truly with his family. The only family he had. The only family he was ever likely to have, but sometimes . . . sometimes he couldn't shake the feeling that he was waiting for something.

The mattress dipped as he sat on the edge and pulled off his boots and socks. Meg thought all he needed was to meet a nice woman to make him a good wife, but he just couldn't see himself married. Not now. He'd had a few good relationships in his life. Good right up until the moment that they weren't. None had lasted more than a year or two. Partly because he'd been gone so much. Mostly because he didn't want to buy a ring and walk down the aisle.

He stood and stripped to his underwear. Meg thought he was afraid of marriage because their parents' had been so bad, but that wasn't true. The truth was that he didn't remember his parents all that much. Just a few watery memories of family picnics at the lake and his parents cuddling on the sofa. His mother crying at the kitchen table and an old heavy telephone thrown through the television screen.

No, the problem wasn't the memories of his parents' fucked-up relationship. He'd just never loved one woman enough to want to spend the rest of his life with her. Which he didn't consider a problem at all.

He pulled back the quilt and lay between the cool sheets. For the second time that night, he thought about Maddie Dupree, and he laughed into the darkness. She'd been a smart-ass, but he'd never held that against a woman. If fact, he liked a woman who could stand up to a man. Who gave as good as she got and didn't need a man to take care of her. Who wasn't needy or weepy or crazy as hell. Whose moods didn't swing like a pendulum.

Mick turned on his side and glanced at the clock on his nightstand. He'd set his alarm for ten A.M. and was ready for a full seven hours of uninterrupted shut-eye. Unfortunately, he didn't get it.

The next morning, the ringing of the telephone brought him out of a deep sleep. He opened his eyes and squinted against the morning sun pouring across his bed. He glanced at the caller ID and reached for the cordless receiver.

"You better be spurting blood," he said and pushed the covers down his naked chest. "I told you not to call before ten unless it's an emergency."

"Mom's at work and I need some fireworks," his nephew informed him.

"At eight-thirty in the morning?" He sat up and ran his fingers through one side of his hair. "Is your sitter there with you?"

"Yeah. Tomorrow's the Fourth of July and I don't got no fireworks."

"You just realized this?" There was more to the

story. With Travis, there was always more to the story. "Why didn't your mom get you your fireworks?" There was a long pause and Mick added, "You might as well tell me the truth because I'm going to ask Meg."

"She said I have a potty mouth."

Mick stood and his feet sank into thick beige carpeting as he walked across the room toward a dresser. He was almost afraid to ask. "Why?"

"Well . . . she made meatloaf again. She knows I hate meatloaf."

He didn't blame the kid there. The Hennessy women were notorious for their shitty meatloaf. He opened the second dresser drawer and prompted, "And?"

"I said it tasted like shit. I said you thought so too."

Mick paused in the act of pulling out a white T-shirt and glanced into his reflection above the dresser. "Did you use the real *s*-word?"

"Uh-huh, and she said I can't have fireworks, but you say the *s*-word all the dang time."

That was true. He hung the shirt over one shoulder and leaned forward to look into his bloodshot eyes. "We talked about words I can say and words you can say."

"I know, but it just slipped out."

"You need to watch what slips out of your mouth."

Travis sighed. "I know. I said I was sorry, even though I'm not really. Just like you said I should say to girls. Even the stupid ones. Even when I'm right and they're wrong."

That wasn't quite what he'd said. "You didn't tell Meg I said that, though." He pulled a pair of Levi's out of the dresser and added, "Right?"

"Right."

He couldn't countermand his sister, but at the same time, a boy shouldn't be punished for speaking the truth. "I can't buy you fireworks if your mom says no, but we'll see if we can't work something out."

An hour later, Mick shoved a bag of fireworks behind the driver's seat of his truck. He'd bought a small variety pack as well as a few sparklers and snakes from the Safe and Sane stand in the parking lot of Handy Man Hardware. He hadn't bought them for Travis. He'd bought them to take to Louie Allegrezza's Fourth of July barbeque. If anyone asked, that was the story, but he doubted anyone would believe him. Like all other residents of the pyrotechnically obsessed town, he had a big box of illegals just waiting to be shot over the lake. Adults didn't buy Safe and Sanes unless they had kids. Legal fireworks were kind of like training wheels.

Louie's son Pete Allegrezza and Travis were buddies, and days ago, Meg had agreed that Travis could go to the barbeque with Mick if he stayed out of trouble. The barbeque was tomorrow, and Mick figured Travis should be able to control his behavior for one more day. Mick shut the door to his truck, and he and Travis headed across the parking lot toward the hardware store. "If you behave yourself, maybe you can hold a sparkler."

"Man," Travis whined. "Sparklers are for little kids."

"With your track record, you'll be lucky if you're not in bed before dark." Sunlight shone in his nephew's short black hair and across the shoulders of his red Spider-Man T-shirt. "You're having a hard time controlling yourself lately." He opened the door and waved to the owner standing behind the counter. "Meg's still pretty mad at us both, but I have a plan." For several months, Meg had complained about a leaky pipe beneath her kitchen sink. If he and Travis fixed her S-trap so that she didn't have to keep emptying a pan of water, maybe she'd be in a more forgiving mood. But with Meg, a person never knew. She wasn't always the most forgiving person.

The soles of Travis's sneakers scuffed alongside Mick's boots as they walked to the plumbing section. The store was quiet except for a couple looking at garden hoses and Mrs. Vaughn, his first-grade teacher, rooting through a bin of assorted drawer handles. He was always amazed to see Laverne Vaughn still alive and walking around. She had to be older than dirt.

While Mick grabbed a PVC pipe and plastic washers, his nephew picked up a caulking gun and aimed it at a bird feeder at the end of the aisle as if it were a .45 Magnum.

"We don't need that," Mick told him as he reached for some plumber's tape.

Travis popped off a few rounds, then tossed the gun back onto the shelf. "I'm gonna go look at the deer," he said and disappeared around the corner of the aisle. Handy Man's had a big selection of plastic animals that people could display in their yards. Although why you would want to do that when the real thing was likely to roam through was beyond Mick.

He stuck the pipe beneath one arm and went in search of his nephew, who didn't usually go looking for trouble, but like most seven-year-old boys seemed to find it anyway. He moved through the store, glanced down each crammed row, and paused next to a display of mops.

A smile of pure male appreciation curved the corners of his mouth. Maddie Dupree stood in the middle of aisle six, a neon-yellow box in her hands. Her brown hair was in one of those claws and looked like someone had stuck a dark feather duster on the back of her head. His gaze moved down her smooth profile, past her throat and shoulder, and stopped dead on her black T-shirt. Last night, he hadn't been able to get a good look at her. Today, the fluorescent lighting of Handy Man Hardware lit her up like a walking, talking, breathing centerfold. Like an old-school playmate before eating disorders and silicone. Desire stirred in the pit of his stomach. He didn't even know her well enough to be feeling a thing. Didn't know if she was married or single, had a man in her life and ten kids waiting at home. Apparently it didn't matter, because she drew him down the aisle like a magnet.

"Looks like you got problems with some mice," he said.

"What?" Her head snapped up and her gaze flew to his like he'd caught her doing something she shouldn't. "Christ almighty." Her lips parted and she sucked in a breath, drawing his attention to the mole at the corner of her mouth. "You startled me."

"Sorry," he said, but he really wasn't. She looked good all wide-eyed and breathy and a little off balance. He glanced up and pointed with the PVC to the box in her hand. "Mice troubles?"

"One actually ran across my foot this morning while I was making coffee." She crinkled her nose. "It slid under the pantry door and disappeared. It's probably in there right now feasting on my granola bars."

"Don't worry." Mick laughed. "He probably won't eat much."

"I don't want him to eat anything at all. Except maybe some poison." She turned her attention back to the box in her hand. Fine dark hairs clung to the side of her neck and Mick thought he smelled strawberries.

At the far end of the aisle, Travis turned the corner and stopped in his tracks. His mouth got a little slack as he stared at Maddie. Mick knew the feeling.

"It says here that odor problems can occur if rodents expire in inaccessible areas. I really don't want to have to search for stinking mice." She looked up at him out of the corners of her eyes. "I wonder if there isn't something better I could use."

"I wouldn't recommend the tape." He pointed to a box of glue boards. "Mice get stuck on it and squeak a lot." There it was again. Strawberries, and he wondered if Handy's had some scented feeders for hummingbirds. "You could use traps," he suggested.

"Really? Aren't traps kind of . . . violent?"

"They can snap a mouse in half," Travis said as he came to stand beside Mick. He rocked back on his heels and grinned. "Sometimes their head pops off when they go for the cheese."

"Good Lord, kid." Maddie's brows drew together as she lowered her gaze to Travis. "That's gruesome."

"Uh-huh."

Mick stuck the pipe under his arm and placed his free hand on top of Travis's head. "This gruesome guy is my nephew, Travis Hennessy. Travis, say hello to Maddie Dupree."

Maddie stuck out her palm and shook Travis's hand. "It's a pleasure to meet you, Travis."

"Yeah. You too."

"And thanks for telling me about the traps," she continued and released him. "I'll keep them in mind if I decide on decapitation."

Travis's smile grew to show off his missing front tooth. "Last year I killed tons of mice," he boasted, employing his special brand of seven-year-old charm. "Call me."

Mick glanced down at his nephew and wasn't sure, but he thought Travis was puffing up his skinny chest. "The best way to get rid of mice," he said, saving Travis from embarrassing himself further, "is to get a cat."

Maddie shook her head and her brown eyes looked into his, all warm and soft and liquid. "Cats and I don't get along." His gaze slid to her mouth and he again wondered how long it had been since he'd kissed a mouth that good. "I'd rather have severed heads in my kitchen or hidden carcasses stinking up the place."

She was talking about severed heads and stinking carcasses and he was getting turned on. Right there in Handy Man Hardware, like he was sixteen again and couldn't control himself. He'd been with a lot of beautiful women and wasn't a kid. He'd saved Travis from embarrassing himself, but who was going to save him?

"We've got some plumbing to do." He held up the sealant and took a step back. "Good luck with those mice."

"See you boys around."

"Yeah," Travis said and followed him to the checkout counter. "She was nice," he whispered. "I like the color of her hair."

Mick chuckled and set the PVC next to the register. The kid was only seven, but he was a Hennessy.

Chapter 3

September 5, 1976

Dan said he was going to leave his wife for me!! He said he'd been sleeping on the couch since May. I just found out she got pregnant in June. I've been cheated and lied to!! When is it my turn for happiness? The only person who loves me is my baby girl. She's three now and tells me every day that she loves me. She deserves a better life.

Why can't Jesus drop-kick us somewhere nice?

Maddie closed her eyes and leaned her head back in her office chair. In reading the diaries, not only had Maddie discovered her mother's passion for exclamation marks, but her fondness for other women's husbands as well. Counting Loch Hennessy, she'd had three of them in her twenty-four years. Not counting Loch, each had vowed to leave his wife for her, but in the end, they'd all *cheated and lied!!*

Maddie tossed the diary on her desk and stretched her arms above her head. Besides the husbands, Alice had dated single men also. In the end, they'd all cheated and lied and left her for someone else. All except Loch. Although, if the affair hadn't been cut short, Maddie was sure Loch would have cheated and lied like all the others. Single or married, her mother had chosen men who left her heartbroken.

Through the open windows, the noise from her neighbors' barbeque carried on a slight breeze. It was the Fourth of July, and Truly was in full celebration mode. In town, buildings were decked out in red, white, and blue bunting, and that morning there'd been a parade down Main Street. Maddie had read in the local paper about the big celebration planned in Shaw Park and the town's "impressive fireworks show" to begin "at full dark."

Maddie stood and walked into the bathroom. Although really, how "impressive" could the show be in such a small town? Boise, the capital city, hadn't had a decent show in years.

She plugged the drain in the deep jetted tub and turned on the water. As she undressed, her neighbors' laughter carried though the small window above the toilet. Earlier in the day, Louie and Lisa Allegrezza had come over to invite her to their barbeque, but even at her best, she wasn't very good at making polite conversation with people she didn't know. And lately, Maddie had not been at her best. Finding the diaries had been a real mixed blessing. The diaries had answered some important questions for her. Questions that most people knew from birth. She'd learned that her father was from Madrid and that her mother had become pregnant with Maddie the summer after graduating from high school. Her father had been in the States visiting family, and they'd both fallen madly in "luv." At the end of the summer, Alejandro had returned to Spain. Alice had written him several letters to tell him about her pregnancy, but she'd never heard from him. Apparently, their "luv" had been one-sided.

Maddie swept her hair up and clamped it on top of her head with a big claw. She'd come to terms with the fact long ago that she would never know her father. That she would never know his face or the sound of his voice. That he'd never teach her to ride a bike or drive a car, but like everything else, reading the diaries had brought it all to the surface again and she wondered if Alejandro was dead or alive and what he might think of her. Not that she would ever know.

Maddie poured German chocolate cake bubble bath into the running water and set a tube of chocolate-cake-scented body scrub on the side of the tub. She might not care about matching underwear or the brand name on her shoes, but she loved bath products. Scented potions and lotions were her passion. Give her a creamy scrub and body butter over designer clothes any day.

Naked, she stepped into the tub and lowered herself into the warm scented water. "Ahh," she sighed as she slid beneath the suds. She leaned back against the cool porcelain and closed her eyes. She owned every scent imaginable. Everything from roses to apples, espresso to cake, and years ago she'd made peace and learned how to live with her inner hedonist.

There'd been a time in her life when she'd binged on almost anything that gave her pleasure. Men, dessert, and expensive lotions had featured high on her list. As a result of all that bingeing she'd developed a narrow view of men and a large behind. A very soft and smooth behind, but a big butt nonetheless. As a child, she'd been over-weight and the horrors of once again hauling a wide load had forced her to change her life. The realization that she needed to change had hap-pened on the morning of her thirtieth birthday when she'd woken up with a cheesecake hangover and a guy named Derrick. The cheesecake had been mediocre and Derrick a real disappointment.

These days she was still a hedonist at heart, but she was a *nonpracticing* hedonist. She still over-indulged on lotions and bath products, but she needed those to relax and destress and to stave off dry, flaky skin.

She sank farther beneath the water and at-tempted to find a little peace for herself. Her body succumbed to the bubbles and warm water, but her mind wasn't so easily quieted and continued to roam over the past few weeks. She was making real progress on her timeline and notes. She had a list of people mentioned in her mother's last diary, the few friends she'd made in Truly and people with whom she'd worked. The county coroner from 1978 had died, but the sheriff still lived in Truly. He was retired, but Maddie was sure he could provide valuable information. She had news-paper accounts, police reports, the coroner's findings, and as much information on the Hennessy family as she could possibly dig up. Now all she had to do was talk to anyone connected to her mother's life and death.

She'd discovered that two women her mother had worked with still lived in town and she planned to start with them tomorrow morning. It was past time she talked to people in town and unearthed information.

The warm water and scented bubbles slid over her stomach and the bottom swell of her breasts. Reading those diaries, she could almost hear her mother's voice for the first time in twenty-nine years. Alice wrote about her fear at finding herself alone and pregnant and her excitement over Maddie's birth. Reading about her hopes and dreams for herself and her baby had been heartbreaking and so bittersweet. But with the heartbreaking and bittersweet discoveries, she'd learned that her mother wasn't the blond-haired, blue-eyed angel she'd created in her child's head and heart. Alice had been the sort of woman who had to have a man in her life or she'd felt worthless. She'd been needy and naive and eternally optimistic. Maddie had never been needy, nor could she recall a time when she'd been naive or overly optimistic about anything. Not even as a child. Discovering that she had absolutely nothing in common with the woman who'd given her birth, nothing that tied her to her mother, left her empty inside.

Early in life, Maddie had developed a hard shell around her soul. Her tough exterior had always been an asset while doing her job, but she didn't feel so tough today. She felt raw and vulnerable. Vulnerable to what, she didn't know, but she hated the feeling. It would be so much easier if she tossed the diaries and wrote about a psychopath by the name of Roddy Durban. She'd been writing about the nasty little bastard who'd killed more than twenty-three prostitutes right before she'd found the diaries. Writing about Roddy would be a hell of a lot easier than writing about her mother, but the night that Maddie had taken the diaries home and read them, she knew there was no turning back. Her career, while not always carefully calculated, had not been random. She was a true crime writer for a reason, and as she'd pored over her mother's overly feminine hand-writing, she knew the time had come to sit down and write about the crime that had left her mother dead.

She turned off the water with her foot and reached for the body scrub on the side of the tub. She squirted the thick sugar scrub into her palm and the scent of chocolate cake filled her nose. With it came the unbidden memory of standing on a chair next to her mother and stirring chocolate pudding on the stove. She didn't know how old she'd been or where they'd lived. The memory was as tangible as a wisp of smoke, but it managed to deliver a punch to the lonely place next to her heart.

Bubbles clung to her breasts as she sat up and lifted her feet over the side of the tub. Obviously, she'd failed to find the calm and comfort she usually found in her bath, and she quickly exfoliated her arms and legs. When she was through, she got out of the tub and dried off, then she rubbed chocolate-scented lotion into her skin.

She tossed her clothes in the hamper and walked into her bedroom. Her three closest friends lived in Boise, and she missed meeting them for lunch or dinner or impromptu bitch sessions. Her friends Lucy, Clare, and Adele were the closest thing she had to a family, and the only people to whom she would consider giving a kidney or loaning money. She was fairly certain they would return the favor.

Last year when her friend Clare had discovered her fiancé with another man, the other three friends had rushed to her house to talk her off the ledge. Out of the four women, Clare was the most kindhearted and easily hurt. She was also a romance writer who'd always believed in true love. For a time after her fiancé's betrayal, she'd lost her faith in the happy-ever-after until a reporter by the name of Sebastian Vaughan came into her life and restored her faith. He was her very own romance hero, and the two were getting married in September. Maddie had to drive to Boise in a few days to be fitted for her bridesmaid dress.

Once again she was allowing one of her friends to deck her out in a ridiculous dress and make her stand up at the front of a church. The year before she'd been a bridesmaid at Lucy's wedding. Lucy was a mystery writer and had met her husband Quinn when he'd mistaken her for a serial killer. Long story short, he hadn't let a little thing like homicide stand in the way of his pursuit of Lucy.

Out of the four friends, that left herself and Adele still single. Maddie pulled on a pair of black cotton panties and tossed the towel on the bed. Adele wrote fantasy novels for a living, and although she had her own man troubles, Maddie figured it was a lot more likely that Adele would marry before she would herself.

Maddie fit the large cups of her bra over her breasts and fastened it in back. In fact, she just didn't see herself getting married. She wanted a kid about as much as she wanted a cat. The only time a man came in handy was when she needed someone to do some heavy lifting or when she desired a warm naked body next to hers. But she owned a sturdy hand truck and big Carlos, and when she had need of heavy lifting or sexual release she reached for one of them. Admittedly, neither was as good as the real thing, but the hand truck went back in the garage when she was through, and big Carlos got shoved back into her bedside table. Both of them stayed put and didn't give her crap, play games with her heart, or cheat on her. Pretty much a win-win.

She stepped into a pair of jeans and then shoved her arms through the sleeves of her most comfortable hooded sweatshirt. She just didn't have the same burning desires, or instincts, or clocks that drove other women into matrimony and childbirth. Which wasn't to say that she didn't get lonely sometimes. She absolutely did.

Shoving her feet into a pair of flip-flops, she moved from the bedroom, though the living room, to the kitchen. The noise from the neighbors' party grew louder and she reached into the refrigerator. Voices floated in through her open windows as she pulled out a bottle of carb-reduced merlot.

She was alone and lonely and apparently feeling quite sorry for herself too. Which really wasn't like her. She never felt sorry for herself. There were too many people in the world with real problems.

The shrill screech of at least a half dozen Piccolo Petes sliced through the air, and Maddie almost dropped the corkscrew. "Damn it," she cursed and placed her free hand over her heart. Beyond the French doors leading out to her deck, she could see the pale shadows of dusk and the darkening surface of the usually emerald-green lake. She poured red wine into a glass and carried it outside to the deck and set it on the railing. A dozen or so people stood on the neighbors' deck and the beach below. Along the water's edge three mortar tubes stuck out of the sand and pointed toward the sky. Several children held sparklers while men supervised, lit more Piccolo Petes and something that flashed like little strobe lights. Smoke from bombs of every color clouded the beach, and the children ran through the paisley haze like genies from a bottle.

Against the smoke and chaos, Mick Hennessy stood in profile with a punk between his teeth like a long thin cigarette. She recognized his wide shoulders and black hair and the boy who stood gazing up at him. He handed his nephew a lit sparkler and Travis spun on one foot and waved it about. Mick took the punk from between his teeth, said something, and Travis immediately stopped and held the firework in front of him like a statue.

Maddie took a sip of her wine. Yesterday, see-ing him at the hardware store had been a real shock. She'd been so intent on her box of poison that she hadn't noticed him until he'd stood right next to her. Looking up into those blue eyes so close and so much like his father's had forced a stunned "Christ almighty" out of her.

She lowered the glass and set it on the railing as she watched Mick with his nephew. She really didn't know what to think about him. Not that she knew enough to form an opinion or that it even mattered. The book she planned to write had nothing to do with him and everything to do with the love triangle between Loch, Rose, and Alice. Like Maddie, Mick had been just another inno-cent victim.

Louie Allegrezza and two other men knelt close to the water and stuck bottle rockets into several soda bottles. They lit one fuse right after the other, and Maddie watched the rockets fly up high over the water and explode with soft pop-pop-pops.

"Be careful with those around the kids," Lisa called down to her husband.

"These never hurt anyone," he called back as he once again loaded up the bottles. Four of the rockets flew straight up, while the fifth flew straight at Maddie. She hit the deck as it whizzed past her head.

"Shit!"

The rocket landed behind her and exploded. With her heart pounding in her ears, she straightened to peer over the railing.

"Sorry about that," Louie called out.

Through the light wash of gray night, Mick Hennessy looked up and stared at her for several seconds. His dark brows lifted as if surprised to see her. Then he rocked back on his heels and laughed like the whole thing was horribly funny. The dimples denting his cheeks and the amusement in his shining blue eyes gave the illusion that he was as trustworthy and harmless as a Boy Scout. But harmless Boy Scouts wore their beige shirts buttoned and tucked into their pants. A Boy Scout didn't leave his shirt hanging open, showing off washboard abs and a lickable happy trail running down his sternum, circling his navel, and disappearing behind the waistband of his Levi's. Not that she was in any danger of licking any part of him. But just because he was who he was and she was who she was didn't mean she was blind.

"Louie, warn us before you set those things off," Lisa said above the noise. "Maddie, come over here. You'll be safer."

Maddie tore her gaze from Mick's chest and looked across the ten feet of yard at her neighbor. When it came to safety, trading her deck for theirs didn't make a bit of sense, but since staring at Mick's chest was the biggest thrill she'd had in weeks, she was obviously bored and sick of her own company.

She stood, grabbed her glass, and walked the short distance. She was quickly introduced to Louie's daughter Sofie and her friends who lived in Boise and attended BSU but were in Truly for the weekend. She met several neighbors from farther down the beach, Tanya King, a petite blonde who looked like she hung from her heels and did crunches all day, and Suzanne Porter, whose husband Glenn and teenage son Donald were on the beach setting off fireworks. After that, she lost track of names and couldn't remember who was whom, where they lived, or how long they'd lived in town. They all blurred together except for Louie's mother and his aunt Narcisa, who sat at a table wearing equally disarming scowls of disapproval and speaking to each other in rapid Basque. No way could she forget those women.

"Would you like more wine?" Lisa asked. "I've got Basque Red and Chablis. Or you can have beer or a Coke."

"No, thanks." She held up her half-full glass and looked at it. "I'm a cheap date tonight." She needed to get up early and get to work, and wine tended to give her a headache.

"Before I married Louie and had Pete, these Fourth of July barbeques were out of control. Lots of drunks and dangerous fireworks."

As far as Maddie could see, not a lot had changed.

The last person she was introduced to was Lisa's sister-in-law, Delaney, who looked about twelve months pregnant.

"I'm not due until September," Delaney said as if she'd read Maddie's mind.

"You're joking."

"No." Delaney laughed and her blond ponytail brushed her shoulder as she shook her head. "I'm having twin girls." She pointed toward the beach. "That's my husband, Nick, down there with Louie. He's going to be a great dad."

As if on cue, the great dad-to-be turned and his gaze sought his wife. He was tall and unbelievably handsome, and the only other guy around who gave Mick Hennessy any competition whatsoever in the looks department. Then his intense gaze found his wife and the competition was over. There was just nothing sexier than a man who only had eyes for one woman. Especially when that woman looked like Buddha.

"Are you okay?" Nick Allegrezza called out.

"For goodness' sake," Delaney grumbled, then yelled, "Yes."

"Maybe you should sit down," Nick suggested.

She spread her arms. "I'm fine."

Maddie's gaze slid to Mick, who knelt on one knee as he helped Travis light a flashing strobe. She wondered if he had ever looked that way at any one woman, or if he was more like his father and had eyes for a lot of women.

"Fire in the hole," Louie yelled, and Maddie's gaze flew to the bottle rockets whizzing upward. This time none of the rockets buzzed Maddie's head and instead exploded above the lake. Relief calmed her beating heart. A few years ago, she'd volunteered to be Tasered in one of her self-defense classes. She wasn't a chicken, but those flying missiles worried her.

"Last week I started to have a few contractions, and the doctor said the babies are probably going to come early," Delaney said, drawing Maddie's attention. "Nick's totally freaking out about it, but I'm not worried. We've been through hell to have these girls. The hard part is over and everything else will be fine."

Maddie had spent her adult life trying *not* to get pregnant and wondered what Delaney had been through, but she didn't know her well enough to ask.

"You two did go through hell." Lisa rubbed her sister-in-law's belly, then dropped her hands to her sides. "But I have a feeling that having two thirteen-year-old girls in the same house at the same time is going to give new meaning to the word hell."

"Not a problem. Nick's not going to let the girls out of his sight until they're twenty-one for fear they'll run into boys like him."

Suzanne raised a glass of white wine and laughed. "I never thought Nick would settle down and get married. Growing up, he was as wild as Louie was crazy."

"Louie wasn't crazy," Lisa defended her husband, and her brows lowered over her blue eyes.

"Everyone called him Crazy Louie for a reason," Delaney reminded her sister-in-law. "He stole his first car when he was, what? Ten?"

"Yeah, well, Nick was right there in the passenger seat with Louie." Lisa sniffed. "And he really didn't steal cars. He just borrowed them for a few hours."

Delaney's brows lowered. "Are you listening to yourself?"

Lisa shrugged. "It's true. Besides, Nick came up with lots of bad ideas all on his own. Remember those horrid snowball fights?"

"Of course, but Nick doesn't have to throw things at me to get my attention these days." Delaney smiled and rested her hands on top of her big belly. "He's still a little wild sometimes, but nothing like he was in school."

"Every class had at least one bad boy. Class of 1990 it was Mick Hennessy," Suzanne said. "He was always in trouble. In the eighth grade, he punched Mr. Shockey in the face."

Maddie casually took a sip of her wine as if her ears hadn't perked up.

"I'm sure Mr. Shockey deserved it," Lisa defended Mick. "He used to make us run track even when we had period cramps. Sadistic bastard."

"Lisa, you were always having cramps," Delaney reminded Lisa. "Even in the first grade. And I swear you'd defend the devil."

Lisa shrugged. "All I'm saying is that considering

what Mick had to deal with growing up, he turned out pretty good."

Maddie didn't know what Mick had dealt with as a child, but she could guess.

"I didn't know Mick growing up, but I've heard the stories." Tanya raised her glass and took a drink. "And he turned out *real* good." Behind the glass, one corner of Tanya's lips lifted, leaving little doubt that she knew just how "real good" Mick was.

"Be careful, Tanya, Mick is like his daddy," Suzanne warned. "He isn't the kind of guy to stay with one woman. Last year Cinda Larson thought she had him all to herself, but he was seeing a few other women at the same time."

The difference being, Maddie thought, Mick wasn't married like his daddy had been.

"I just got divorced last year." Tanya wore a strapless sundress on her tiny body, and she shrugged one bare shoulder. "I'm not looking for an exclusive relationship."

Maddie took a drink of her wine and made a mental note. Not that Mick's relationships with women were of interest to her, personally or professionally. His and Meg's personal relationships would not end up in the book any more than hers, but she was curious. Curious if their childhood had been any better than hers. From the little she'd just heard, she'd say no.

Suzanne moved to the rail and yelled down, "Donald, make sure you point the big ones over the lake." Then she turned back and her green eyes settled on Maddie. "Do you have children?" she asked.

"No." If she hadn't been standing next to a pregnant lady, she might have added that she didn't think she'd ever want children either.

"What do you do for a living?"

If Maddie answered truthfully, she'd open herself up to questions she wasn't so sure she wanted to answer at a Fourth of July barbeque. Not yet, and especially not with Mick and Travis walking up the beach toward her. The ends of Mick's shirt slightly billowing about his chest and hips as he moved, drawing her and every other female's attention to his Levi's hanging low on his bare waist.

There was no doubt about it. Mick Hennessy was so blatantly all man that it hit a woman like a brick to the forehead. He was headed straight for her, and she'd be lying to herself if she pretended that he wasn't hot as hell. While she had no problem lying to other people, she could never lie to herself.

Chapter 4

"Fire in the hole!" Louie shouted and set off several screeching rockets, saving Maddie the effort of thinking up a half-truth or full-out lie. Four rockets flew up instead of at her head and her pulse steadied.

These rockets were a little bigger than the last and exploded in small bursts of color. Louie had broken out heavier artillery, yet still no one seemed in the least worried. No one except Maddie.

"I want to stay down there," Travis grumbled as he, Mick, and Pete moved up the steps of the deck.

"The big show's about to start," Mick said, "and you know kids have to move where it's safe."

Big show? She raised her wine and drained the glass. She wondered if Mick was going to put

Tanya out of her misery and button his shirt. Sure, it had been hot earlier, but it was getting fairly nippy now.

"Donald is a kid," Pete complained.

"Donald is fourteen," Lisa said. "If you're going to argue, you can go sit by your grandmother and Tia Narcisa."

Pete quickly plopped his behind down on the steps. "I'll sit here." Travis sat next to him, but neither appeared happy about being confined to the deck.

"Hey, Mick," Tanya called out to him.

He glanced up from Travis, but his gaze met Maddie's. His blue eyes looked into hers for several heartbeats before he turned his attention to the petite woman on Maddie's left. "Hey, there, Tanya. How's it going?"

"Good. I still have some Bushmills Malt 21. What are you doing after the show?"

"I've got to take Travis home, then head to work," he said. "Maybe some other time." He moved past them to a cooler and bent at the waist. He lifted the white lid and his shirt fell open. Naturally. "Yo, Travis and Pete," he called out. "Do you boys want a root beer?"

As one, the two boys turned at the waist. "Yeah."

"Sure."

Ice and water sloshed in the cooler as he grabbed two cans of Hires and lobbed them into the boys' waiting hands. He pulled out a Red Bull, then closed the cooler's lid.

"Maddie, have you met Mick Hennessy?" Lisa asked.

Out of habit, she held out her hand, "Yes, we've met."

He wiped his hand on his pants, then took her fingers in his cool wet palm. "Kill any mice today?"

"No." His thumb brushed her bare ring finger and he smiled. Intentional or not, she didn't know, but the light touch spread hot itchy little tingles to her wrist. It was the closest she'd come to real sex in years. "No dead mice yet, but I'm hoping they're experiencing death rattles even as we speak." She pulled her hand back before she forgot who he was and why she was in town. Once he found out, she doubted there would be any more handshakes and tingles. Not that she particularly wanted either.

"Call an exterminator," Tanya said.

Maddie had called an exterminator and he couldn't get to her house for a month.

"Be careful who you call," Lisa warned. "Carpenters and exterminators work on Miller time around here and they have a habit of just up and leaving at three o'clock."

"I take it three o'clock is Miller time."

"Pretty much." Lisa's mother-in-law called her name and she grimaced. "Excuse me."

"Better her than me," Delaney uttered as Lisa walked away.

"I could give you the number of someone who might actually arrive when he says he will." Mick popped the top to his Red Bull. "And stay until the job is finished."

"Have your husband or boyfriend take care of your mice problem," Tanya suggested.

She looked at Tanya and suddenly didn't get a nice neighborly vibe. The energy had changed since Mick had walked onto the deck. She wasn't sure, but she guessed that Tanya wasn't going to be her new B.F.F. "Don't have a boyfriend and I've never been married."

"Never?" Tanya raised a brow as if Maddie were a freak, and Maddie would have laughed if it wasn't so ridiculous.

"Hard to believe, isn't it?" she said. Tanya need not worry. The very last man on the planet she would ever get involved with was Mick Hennessy. Despite his nice abs and killer happy trail. "I'm such a great catch."

Mick chuckled and took a drink of his Red Bull. Through the darkening shadows of nightfall, she could just see the laugh lines creasing the corners of his blue eyes as he looked at her over the silver can.

She smiled back and decided it was past time to change the subject. "Did you have to toss Darla out of Mort's on her bare behind?"

He lowered the can and sucked moisture from his bottom lip. "Nah. She behaved."

"Are women still tossing their panties?" Delaney asked.

"Not as much. Thank God." Mick shook his head and grinned, a flash of white against the dark. "Believe me, tossing drunk, half-naked women from my bar isn't as fun as it sounds."

Maddie laughed. Never in a million years would she have thought she'd find Mick Hennessy so utterly likable. "How often does that happen?" Then again, he was his father's son.

Mick shrugged. "Mort's used to be a really wild place before I took over, and some people are having a hard time adjusting."

"They've never adjusted to Jackson's Texaco taking over for Grover's Gas and Go, and that was about six years ago." Delaney drew in a breath and let it out slowly. "My feet are killing me."

"Fire in the hole!" Louie yelled seconds before sending up another barrage. Maddie spun around and her gaze flew to the rockets soaring straight up.

Behind her, Mick's deep laughter was almost drowned out by the rockets' pop-pop-pops. When she turned back, he'd moved to help Delaney find a chair. Tanya trailed after them and Maddie wasn't sorry to see her go. The woman had gone from perfectly pleasant to bitchy over a man, something Maddie had never understood. There were other available men on the planet, why get all uptight over one? Especially if that one had a reputation for never getting involved. For loving and leaving. Not that Maddie ever held that against anyone. She didn't understand women who got so attached so easily. After a few dates or good sex, they were in love. How did that happen? How was that even possible?

Sofie Allegrezza and her friends moved to the railing beside Maddie for a better view of her father's fireworks show. Maddie set her glass on the railing and watched Louie load up the three big mortar tubes. She'd never needed a man in order to feel good about herself or to make her life complete. Not like her mother.

"Fire in the hole." This time there was an audible

whoosh seconds before the three rounds shot from tubes and exploded with three loud booms. Startled, Maddie jumped back and collided with something solid. A pair of big hands grabbed her arms as green, gold, and red bursts of fire rained down toward the lake. "Sorry." She turned her head and looked up into the shadows resting on Mick's face.

"Not a problem." Instead of pushing her away, he held her right where she'd landed. "Tell me something."

"What?"

He lowered his face and spoke just above her ear. "If you're a great catch, why haven't you been caught?"

His warm breath touched the side of her head and slipped down her neck. "Probably for the same reason you haven't."

"Which is?"

"You don't want to be caught."

"Honey, all women want to be caught." His hands slid to her elbows, then up again, bunching her sweatshirt. "All women want a white wedding, picket fence, and a baby maker."

"Have you met all women?"

She thought she felt him smile. "I've met my share."

"So I hear."

"You shouldn't believe everything you hear."

"And you shouldn't believe all women want you for their own personal baby maker."

"You don't want me for your own personal baby maker?"

"Shocking, isn't it?"

He laughed. A low rumble against the side of her head. "You smell good." Against her back, she felt him draw in a deep breath.

"German chocolate cake."

"What?"

"I smell like chocolate cake body scrub."

"I haven't had chocolate cake in a long time." She'd been mistaken about his handshake being like the best sex she'd had in years. This, his soft breath in her hair and his hands on her arms, was practically orgasmic. Which she figured made her particularly pathetic. "You're making me hungry," he said next to her ear.

"For cake?"

His hands slid to her shoulders, then back down to her elbows. "For starters."

"Uncle Mick," Travis called out as he stood. "When are the town fireworks going to start?"

Mick looked up. His hands tightened a fraction, then dropped to his sides. "Any minute," he answered and took a step back. As if on cue, several enormous booms shook the ground and the night sky lit up with huge bursts of color. Sofie Allegrezza pushed play on her small sound system and Jimi Hendrix's sonic guitar wailed "The Star Spangled Banner" into the night. Forest critters scrambled for cover as around the lake fireworks exploded from the beaches, competing with the town's pyrotechnic eruptions.

Welcome to Truly. The original shock and awe.

D id you have fun, Travis?"
A huge yawn came from the other side of the dark truck. "Yeah. Maybe next year I can blow off bigger fireworks."

"Maybe, if you stay out of trouble."

"Mom said if I stay out of trouble, I can get a puppy."

Mick turned the Ram into Meg's driveway and pulled to a stop next to her Ford Taurus. A dog was a good idea. A boy needed a dog. "What kind of puppy?"

"I like black ones with white spots."

Lights burned from within the house and a single bulb lit the porch. Together they climbed out of the truck and walked up the front steps. It was close to eleven-thirty and Travis's feet were dragging. "How long do you have to be good?"

"For one month."

The kid couldn't stay out of trouble with his mother for one week. "Well, just watch your mouth and you might make it." He shoved his keys into his pants pocket and opened the door for his nephew.

Meg sat on the couch in her white nightgown and pink fuzzy robe. Tears shone in her green eyes as she looked up from something she held in her hand. A forced smile curved her lips and dread settled on Mick's shoulders. It was going to be one of those nights.

"Did you see the fireworks, Mom?" If Travis noticed, he didn't seem bothered.

"No, honey, I didn't go outside. But I heard them." She stood and Travis wrapped his arms around her waist. "They were huge!"

"Did you behave yourself?" She placed her hand on her son's head and looked over at Mick.

"Yes," Travis answered, and Mick confirmed it with a nod.

"That's my good boy."

Travis looked up. "Pete said maybe I could spend the night and his mom said, 'Some other time.'"

"We'll see." Like their mother, Meg was a beau-

tiful woman, with smooth white skin and long
black hair. And as with their mother, her moods
were unpredictable as hell. "Go get your pajamas
on and get in bed. I'll be in to kiss you good night
in a minute."

"Okay," Travis said through a yawn. "Good
night, Uncle Mick."

"Night, buddy." An almost overwhelming urge
to turn away pulled at Mick and he actually took
a step back. Away from what he knew was to
come and toward the cool night air.

Meg watched her son leave the room, then she
held out her hand and opened her palm. "I found
Mom's wedding ring."

"Meg."

"She took it off and left it on her nightstand
before she went to the bar that night. She never
took it off."

"I thought you weren't going to go through her
things anymore."

"I wasn't." She closed her hand around the ring
and bit her thumbnail. "It was packed away with
Grandmother Loraine's jewelry, and I found it when
I was looking for her four leaf clover necklace. The
one she used to wear all the time because it brought
her luck. I wanted to wear it to work tomorrow."

God, he hated when his sister got like this. He

was five years younger than Meg, but he'd always felt like the older brother.

Her big green eyes looked across at him and her hand fell to her side. "Was Daddy really going to leave us?"

Hell, Mick didn't know. No one knew but Loch, and he was long dead. Dead and gone and in the past. Why couldn't Meg leave it alone?

Maybe because she'd just turned ten a few months before the night their mother had loaded a snub-nosed .38 and emptied five chambers into Mick's father and a young waitress by the name of Alice Jones. Meg remembered a hell of a lot more about that night twenty-nine years ago when their mother had killed more than Loch and his latest lover. More about the night their mother had put the short barrel into her own mouth, pulled the trigger, and killed more than herself too. She'd blown apart the lives of her two children, and Meg had never really recovered.

"I don't know, Meggie. Grandmother didn't think so." But that wasn't saying anything. Loraine had always turned a blind eye and deaf ear to her own husband's and son's many affairs and offenses and later to everything Mick had done. She lived her whole life in denial. It had been easier for her to pretend everything was wonderful. Especially when it wasn't.

"But Grandmother didn't live with us then. She didn't know what it was like. You didn't either. You were too little. You don't remember."

"I remember enough." He raised his hands and scrubbed his face. They'd had this conversation before and it never resolved anything. "What does it matter now?"

"Did he stop loving us, Mick?"

He dropped his hands to his sides and felt the back of his skull get tight. *Please stop.*

Tears streamed down her cheeks. "If he still loved us, why did she shoot him? He'd had affairs before. According to everyone in town, he'd had lots of affairs."

He walked to his sister and put his hands on the shoulders of her fuzzy pink robe. "Let it go."

"I've tried. I've tried to be like you, and sometimes I can, but . . . why wasn't she buried with her wedding ring?"

The bigger question was, why had she loaded the .38? Had she really meant to kill anyone or just scare the piss out of Loch and his young lover? Who knew? Thinking about it didn't serve any purpose but to drive a person crazy. "It doesn't matter now. Our life isn't in the past, Meg."

She took a deep breath. "You're right. I'll put the ring away and forget about it." She shook her head. "It's just that sometimes I can't turn it off."

He pulled her to his chest and held her tight. "I know."

"I get so afraid."

He got afraid too. Afraid that she'd fall into the downward spiral that had claimed their mother and that she'd never climb out. Mick had always wondered if his mother had given a second of thought to him and Meg. If she'd thought about the devastation and loss she was about to leave behind on a barroom floor. As she'd loaded the gun that night, had it crossed her mind that she was about to leave her children orphans or that her actions would force them to live within the horrible fallout? As she'd driven to Hennessy's, had she thought about them and not cared? "Have you been taking your medicine?"

"It makes me tired."

"You have to take it." He pulled back and looked down into her face. "Travis depends on you. And I depend on you too."

She sighed. "You do not, and Travis would probably be better off without me."

"Meg." He looked deep into her eyes. "You of all people know that isn't true."

"I know." She pushed her hair out of her face. "I just meant that raising a boy is so hard."

He hoped like hell that's what she meant. "That's why you have me." He smiled, even though he felt ten years older than he had before walking into the house. "I'm not going anywhere. Even though you do make the world's shittiest meatloaf."

She smiled, and just like that, her mood changed. Like someone reached into her head and flipped a switch. "I like my meatloaf."

"I know." He dropped his hands and reached into his pocket for his keys. "But you like old-lady food." Meg cooked like their grandmother had. Like she was baking a casserole for a potluck at the senior center.

"You're evil and a bad influence on Travis." She laughed and folded her arms across her chest. "But you always make me feel better."

"Good night," he said and headed for the door. Cool night air brushed across his face and neck as he walked to his truck, and he took a deep breath and let it out. He'd always made Meg feel better. Always. And afterward, he always felt like shit. She'd have a breakdown, and when it was over, she'd be fine. Never seeming to notice the broken bits and pieces she'd left in the wake of her unpredictable moods.

Having been gone for twelve years, he'd almost forgotten what those moods were like. Sometimes he wished he'd just stayed gone.

Chapter 5

M addie reached for a bottle of Diet Coke sitting on her desk and unscrewed the cap. She took a long drink, then returned the cap. The instant she'd opened her eyes that morning, she'd known where the book had to open. In the past, she'd always opened each book with chilling facts.

This time she sat down and wrote:

"I promise it's going to be different this time, Baby." Alice Jones glanced at her young daughter, then returned her gaze to the road. "You're going to love Truly. It's a little like heaven, and it's about damn time Jesus drop-kicked us into a better life."

Baby didn't say anything. She'd heard it before. The excitement in her mother's voice and the promises of a better life. The only thing that ever changed was their address.

Like always, Baby wanted to believe her mother. Really she did, but she'd just turned five. Old enough to realize that nothing ever got better. Nothing ever changed.

"We're going to live in a nice trailer house."

She unfolded her arms from across her chest as she looked out the windshield at the pine trees whizzing by. A trailer house? She'd never lived in a house.

"And a swing set in the front yard."

A swing set? She'd never had a swing set. She turned her gaze to her mother and the sunlight shining in her blond hair. Her mother looked like an angel on a Christmas card. Like she should be standing on top of a Christmas tree, and Baby let herself believe. She let herself believe in the dream of finding heaven. She let herself believe in a better life, and for five months it had been better—right up until the night an enraged wife pumped a set of .38 hollow points into Alice Jones's young body and turned the dream into a nightmare.

Maddie pushed her chair back from her desk and stood. The sleeves of her cotton pajamas slid to her elbows as she raised her arms over her head and stretched. It was a little after noon and she hadn't showered. Her good friend Clare showered and put on makeup every day before she sat down to write. Not Maddie. Of course, that meant that occasionally she got caught by FedEx looking like complete crap. Something she really didn't worry about.

She jumped in the shower and thought about the rest of her day. She had a list of names and addresses with respective relationships to the case. First on the list was a visit to Value Rite Drug, where Carleen Dawson worked. Carleen had been a waitress at Hennessy's at the same time as Maddie's mother. She wanted to set up a time to interview the woman and asking in person had advantages over asking on the telephone.

After her shower, she rubbed almond-scented lotion into her skin and put on a black dress that wrapped around and tied at the side of her waist. She pulled her hair back from her face, applied a little mascara and a deep red lipstick. She wore red sandals and slid a notebook into her slim leather briefcase. Not that she planned to use anything in the briefcase, but it gave the right impression.

Value Rite Drug was located a few blocks off

Main Street next to Helen's Hair Hut. Potted geraniums and yellow awnings gave the outside of the store splashes of color. The inside was stuffed with everything from Band-Aids and aspirin to wooden statues of elk, moose, and bear carved by locals. She asked at the front register where she might find Carleen and was pointed to the snack food aisle.

"Are you Carleen Dawson?" she asked a short woman wearing a white blouse and blue and red apron, and who was bent over a cart of marshmallows and Pop Smart.

She straightened and looked at Maddie through a pair of bifocal lenses. "Yes."

"Hello, my name is Madeline Dupree and I am a writer." She handed Carleen a business card. "I am hoping that you'll give me a few moments of your time."

"I'm not on break."

"I know." Carleen's hair was processed within an inch of its life, and Maddie wondered briefly what was up with some of the locals and bad hair. "I thought we could set up a time when you're off work."

Carleen looked down at the black and silver card, then back up. "True crime? You write true crime? Like Ann Rule?"

That hack. "Yes. Exactly."

Rachel Gibson

"I don't know how I can help you. We don't have serial killers in Truly. There was one in Boise a few years ago, a female one, of all things. If you can believe that."

Actually Maddie could believe it, since her friend Lucy had been a suspect, and since Maddie planned to write about the murderous rampage in the future.

"Nothing ever happens around here," Carleen added and stuffed a bag of marshmallows on the shelf.

"I'm not writing about a serial killer."

"What, then?"

Maddie's grasp on her briefcase tightened and she placed her other hand in the pocket of her dress. "Twenty-nine years ago you worked in Hennessy's Bar when Rose Hennessy shot and killed her husband, a cocktail waitress named Alice Jones, then turned the handgun on herself."

Carleen stilled. "I wasn't there."

"I know. You'd already gone home for the night."

"That was a long time ago. Why do you want to write about that?"

Because it's my life. "Because not all interesting true crime stories are about serial killers. Sometimes the best stories are about real people. Normal people who snap and commit horrible crimes."

"I guess."

"Did you know Alice Jones?"

"Yeah, I knew her. I knew Rose too, but I don't think I should talk about that. It was a real sad situation and people have moved on." She shoved the business card back at Maddie. "Sorry, I can't help you."

Maddie knew when to press and when to take a step back. For now. "Well, think about it." She smiled and kept one hand in her pocket and the other wrapped around the handle of her briefcase. "And if you change your mind, give me a call."

Carleen slid the card into the front pocket of her blue apron. "I won't change my mind. Some things are better left buried in the past."

Perhaps, but what Carleen didn't know but would find out was that Maddie rarely took no for an answer.

No. I can't help you."

Maddie stood on the pockmarked porch of Jewel Finley, a second cocktail waitress who had worked at Hennessy's at the time of Alice's death. "It'll just take a few moments."

"I'm busy." Jewel's hair was in pink rollers and Maddie thought she detected the aroma of Dippity-do. Lord, did they still sell Dippity-do? "Rose was my good friend and I'm not goin' to talk against her," Jewel said. "What happened to her was a tragedy. I'm not goin' to exploit her misfortune."

Her misfortune? "My purpose is not to exploit anyone, but to tell everyone's side of the story."

"Your purpose is to make money."

"Believe me, there are easier ways to make money." Maddie felt her temper rise, but she wisely held back. "Is there a better time for me to come back?"

"No."

"Perhaps when you're not quite so busy."

"I'm not goin' to talk to you about Rose, and I doubt anyone else will talk to you neither." She stepped back into her house. "Good-bye," she said and shut the door.

Maddie stuck a business card in the porch screen and walked toward her Mercedes parked at the curb. Not only did Maddie not take no for an answer, she was like the damn Terminator and she'd be back.

* * *

D o you know when he'll be back?"

"That depends on if the fish are biting. Tomorrow, if it's bad. Who knows, if it's good." Levana Potter looked at Maddie's business card and turned it over. "But I can tell you that he remembers everything about that night." The wife of the retired sheriff looked up. "It still haunts him." She'd found Levana digging in the flower bed in the front of her ranch-style home, and the good news was that the sheriff would more than likely be willing to talk to Maddie. The bad news was her interview would have to wait on the capricious lake trout. "Did you know the parties involved?"

"Sure." Levana stuck the business card in the pocket of her shirt, then shoved her hand back inside her gardening glove. "The Hennessys have lived in this valley for generations. I didn't know Alice much. Just chatted the few times she came into the little ice-cream and gift store I used to own off Third. Pretty thing and seemed kind of sweet. Looked like an angel. She had a little girl, I know that. After Alice died, her aunt came and took her. I don't know whatever happened to her."

Maddie smiled a little. "Do you remember her name?"

Levana shook her head and her white permed

hair wafted a bit in the breeze. "Heavens, no. That was twenty-nine years ago and I only saw her a few times. Heck, I have a hard time remembering my own name sometimes."

"Alice lived at the Roundup Trailer Court."

"Heck, that was torn down years ago."

"Yes, I know. But I can't find any records of people who might have lived there at the same time as Alice and her daughter." In her diaries, Alice had mentioned a few women by their first names. "Do you recall a woman named Trina who may have lived next door to Alice?"

"Hmm." Levana shook her head. "That doesn't ring any bells. Bill will know," she said referring to her husband. "He remembers everyone who ever lived in this town. I'll give him your card when he gets back from his fishing trip."

"Thank you. I'm not going to be here in town tomorrow, but I'll be back the day after."

"I'll tell him, but it might be next week."

Fabulous. "Thank you for your time."

On the way home from the Potters', Maddie stopped off at the grocery store and bought a roasted deli chicken and some Excedrin. Carleen had been guarded and uncooperative and Jewel had been openly hostile. Her head pounded, she was frustrated by her lack of progress, and she had an urge to put someone in a headlock.

With a blue basket hanging off one arm, she took her place in line at checkout number three. The next time she spoke to Carleen and Jewel, she'd try a less businesslike tactic. She'd try the nice-as-pie, friendly approach. If that didn't work, she'd go all Jerry Springer on their hillbilly asses.

"I saw you at Value Rite earlier," a woman in the next line over said.

Maddie looked up from putting her basket on the conveyor belt. "Are you talking to me?"

"Yeah." The other woman had short dark hair and wore a T-shirt with a picture of her grandkids on the front. "Carleen said you were askin' about Rose and Loch Hennessy."

Wow, word really did travel fast in small towns. "That's right."

"I grew up with Rose and she had a few problems, but she was a good person."

A few problems. Is that what they all called pumping lead into two people? Maddie would call it a psychotic breakdown. "I'm sure she was."

"That little waitress got what she deserved for messing with a married man."

Tired, frustrated, and now pissed off, Maddie said, "So you think that every woman who gets involved with a married man deserves to die on a barroom floor?"

The woman tossed a bag of potatoes on the conveyor belt in front of her. "Well, I just mean that if you mess around with another woman's man, you might get hurt. That's all."

No, that wasn't all, but Maddie wisely held her tongue.

M addie tossed her briefcase on the sofa and glanced at the photo of her mother sitting on the coffee table. "Well, that was a waste of makeup." She kicked off her shoes and put the photograph face down. She couldn't look at her mother's cheery smile when her day had been a bust.

Barefoot, she walked into the kitchen and reached into the refrigerator for the bottle of merlot she'd opened the day before. She thought better of it and grabbed the Skyy vodka, diet tonic, and a lime. Sometimes a girl needed a drink, even if she was alone. While she poured vodka into a highball glass and added the tonic, the George Thorogood song "I Drink Alone" ran through her head. She'd never liked that song. Perhaps it was the writer in her, but the chorus was redundant. Of course when you drink alone you drink with nobody else.

Just as she slid ice and a slice of lime into the glass, the doorbell rang. She grabbed her drink and raised it to her lips as she moved through the living room. She certainly wasn't expecting anyone, and the person on the other side of the door was the last person she expected.

She looked through her peephole at Mick Hennessy, and she unlocked the deadbolt and opened the door. The late afternoon sun cut across Mick's cheek and one corner of his mouth. He wore a wife beater beneath a blue plaid shirt that he'd hacked the sleeves off just above the bulge of his biceps. The pale blue in the plaids matched his eyes and set off his tan skin and black hair like he belonged on the cover of a magazine, selling sex and breaking hearts.

"Hello, Maddie," he said, his voice a low rumble. He held a business card between the fingers of one raised hand.

Shit! The last thing she needed today was a confrontation with Mick. She took another fortifying drink and waited for him to start yelling. Instead he flashed her a killer grin.

"I told you I'd give you the name of a good exterminator." He held the business card toward her. It was white, not black, and had a rat on it.

She hadn't realized she'd felt a little anxious

until relief curved the corners of her lips into a smile. She took the card from him. "You didn't have to come all the way out here to give this to me."

"I know." He handed her an orange and yellow box. "I thought you could use this until Ernie's Pest Control can get out here. It's easier than hunting for a smelly carcass."

"Thanks. No man has ever given me . . ." she paused and looked at the box. "A Mouse Motel 500."

He chuckled. "They had a Mouse Motel 200, but I thought you deserved the best."

She opened the door wide. "Would you like to come in?" She should tell him why she was in Truly, but not right now. She just wasn't in the mood for another confrontation.

"I can't stay long." He stepped past her, bringing with him the scent of the outdoors and woodsy soap. "My sister is expecting me for dinner."

"I always wanted a sister." Somewhere to go for holidays besides a friend's house.

"If you knew Meg, you might consider yourself lucky."

She shut the door and moved into the living room beside him. She had to admit, it was strange having him in her house. Not just because he was Mick Hennessy, but because it had been a long time since she'd let a man in her home. The energy seemed to change, the air to sexually charge. "Why?"

"Meg can be . . ." He smiled and glanced about the room. "A horrible cook," he said, but Maddie got the feeling that wasn't what he'd been about to say. "The kind of cook who thinks she's a lot better than she actually is, which means she'll never get better. If she's thrown peas in a casserole and calls it dinner, I'm out of there." His gaze returned to hers and he pointed to her drink. "Hard day?"

"Yeah."

"More mice feasting on your granola bars?"

She shook her head. He'd remembered that?

"What happened?"

She was fairly certain he'd hear about it soon enough. "Nothing important. Do you have time for a drink?"

"Do you have a beer?"

"Just ultra."

He made a face. "Don't tell me you count carbs."

"Oh, yeah." She moved into the kitchen and he followed close behind. "If I don't, I get a huge behind." She looked over her shoulder and watched his gaze slide down her back to her butt.

"You look pretty good to me."

"Exactly." As if he had all day, his gaze slid back up to her face. "I have vodka, gin, and Crown Royal."

His lids lowered a fraction over his eyes, making his dark lashes look very long. "Crown."

She opened a cupboard and raised onto the balls of her feet. Maddie recognized the look in his eyes. She hadn't had sex in four years, but she remembered that look.

"I'll get that," he said as he moved close behind her and reached to the top shelf.

She dropped to her heels and turned. He was so close that if she leaned forward just a little, she could bury her nose in his neck. The sides of his open shirt brushed her breasts and she held her breath.

He looked into her eyes as he handed her the old-fashioned glass. "Here you go." He took a step back.

"Thank, you." She moved around him and opened the freezer. The cold air felt good against her heated cheeks. This absolutely could not be happening. Not with him, and if he'd been any other man, she could not be held responsible for how badly she might use and abuse his body.

"Are you from Idaho?" he asked as he leaned a hip into the counter and folded his arms across his chest. "Or are you a transplant?"

"I was born and raised in Boise." Except for the five months she'd lived in Truly and the six years she'd lived in Southern California attending UCLA. She tossed a few ice cubes into the glass.

"Your folks live in Boise?"

"I never knew my father." She shut the freezer and set the glass on the counter. "I was raised by my aunt and she passed away a few months ago."

"Where's your mother?"

The same place as his. Buried about five miles away. "She died when I was young." Maddie bent at the waist and pulled the bottle of whiskey from her booze cabinet.

"I'm sorry to hear that."

"I hardly remember her." She waited for him to say something about losing his parents when he'd been a boy. He didn't and she straightened and handed him the Crown Royal. "Sorry. It isn't as good as Bushmills 21."

He took the bottle from her and unscrewed the cap. "Company is better, though." He poured three fingers of whiskey over the ice.

"You don't know me."

He put the bottle on the counter and raised the glass to his lips. "That's one of the things I like about you." He took a drink, then added, "I didn't sit next to you in second grade. Your sister isn't friends with my sister and your mama wasn't best friends with my mama."

No, but she'd been pretty good friends with your daddy. "Tanya wasn't raised around here."

"True, but she's too uptight. She can't just relax and have a good time." He lowered his glass and looked out into the living room. "This is one of the older houses on the lake."

"The realtor said it was built in the forties."

He leaned forward a little and looked down the hall toward the bathroom and bedrooms. "It looks different from the last time I was here."

"I was told that the kitchen and the bathrooms were remodeled last year." Maddie took a drink. "When were you here last?"

"Oh, I don't know." He straightened and looked down into her face. "I was probably about fifteen. So about twenty years ago."

"Did you have a friend who lived here?"

"You could say that. Although I don't know if I'd call Brandy Green a *friend.*" A smile tugged at one corner of his mouth as he added, "Her parents were at the Pendleton Rodeo in Oregon."

"And you had your own private rodeo?"

The little smile turned into a wicked grin. "You could say that."

She frowned. "Which room was Brandy's?"

He'd probably carved his initials into the ceiling beam.

"Can't say." He rattled the ice in his glass, then raised the glass to his lips. "Spent most of our time in her parents' room. Their bed was bigger."

"Oh, my God! You've had sex in my bedroom." She put her hand on her chest. "I haven't even had sex in that bedroom." The second she blurted that out, she wished the floor would open up and she would fall through. She didn't embarrass herself often, but she hated when it happened. Especially when he tipped his head back and laughed. "It's not funny."

"Yes, it is." After a few more moments of hilarity on his part, he said, "Honey, we could take care of that right now."

If his offer had felt the least bit threatening or smarmy, she would have kicked him out of her house. Instead it was simple and straightforward and made her smile even when she didn't want to. "No, thanks."

"You sure?" He took another drink, then set his glass on the counter.

"I'm sure."

"I'm a lot better at it than the last time I was here." The smile he gave her was filled with an irresistible mix of charm, confidence, and pure sin. "I've had lots of practice since then."

She hadn't had any practice lately. A fact brought home to her by the tightening in her breasts and the warm tug in her stomach. Mick was the last man on earth for whom she should fall off the sexual wagon. Her head knew that, but her body didn't seem to care.

He reached for her hand and brushed his thumb across the backs of her knuckles. "Do you know what I like best about you?"

"My Crown?"

He shook his head.

"That I don't want a white wedding, picket fence, and a baby maker?"

"Besides that." He pulled her toward him. "You smell good."

She set her glass on the counter and thought back to the lotion she'd put on earlier.

He lifted her hand and smelled the inside of her wrist. "Like cherries, maybe."

"Almonds."

"Yesterday it was chocolate. Today it's almonds. It makes me wonder what you'll smell like tomorrow." He put her hand on his shoulder.

"Peaches." Probably.

He pushed one side of her hair back and lowered his face to the side of her neck. "I like peaches about as much as I like chocolate and almonds. You make me hungry."

She knew the feeling. "Maybe you should hurry over to your sister's for some pea casserole." She felt his soft laughter against her skin a moment before he placed hot openmouthed kisses on the side of her throat. A shiver ran down her spine and her head fell to one side. She'd have to stop him, but not now. In a minute.

"Maybe I should just eat you."

Her eyes closed and she knew she was in trouble. This couldn't be happening. Mick Hennessy could not be in her house, telling her he wanted to eat her and making her have bad thoughts about where he should start. Making her want to run her hand up his chest and her fingers through his hair.

"Do you know what I'd do to you if I had more time?" His hands grasped her waist and he drew her against him. She felt the swell beneath his button fly, and she had a pretty good idea.

She swallowed hard as he lightly bit her earlobe. "Try to get another look at the master bedroom?"

He raised his head and his sexy blue eyes had gone all sleepy with desire. "Who needs a bedroom?"

That was true. Her hand slid across his shoulder and up the side of his neck. Perhaps it had been a mistake to go without sex for so long. The press of his body felt so incredible she didn't want him to stop. But he had to, of course. In a minute.

"You're a beautiful woman, Maddie." He brushed his lips lightly across hers. "If I had more time, I'd untie your dress for you."

"I can untie my own dress."

One side of his mouth lifted at the corner. "It's more fun if I do it." Then he kissed her, a soft and tantalizing press of his mouth. He teased her, drawing out the kiss until her fingers combed through his short hair to the back of his head and her lips parted. His tongue entered her mouth, wet and so good; he tasted like whiskey and lust. Liquid heat pooled between her thighs, and she slid her free hand up his flat stomach, feeling the hard contours of his chest. It had been so long. So long since she'd touched a man like this. Kissed him. Wanted to glue herself to him. Since her skin felt itchy and tight and made her want to tear at his clothes and feel the press of naked skin. It had been a long time. Partly because she'd given up on this, and partly because no man had tempted her like Mick.

His hands slipped up the sides of her waist. His grasp tightened and his thumbs pressed into her stomach just below her breasts. He tilted his head to one side and lightly sucked her tongue into his mouth, where he was warm and slick. Her fingers curled in his hair and she pressed herself against his hard body. Her nipples tightened against his hard chest and he groaned deep in his throat. This was quickly spinning out of control. A whirling cyclone of need and greed and long-denied pleasure, building deep inside and working its way out. Growing and threatening to overpower her.

She pulled back. "Stop."

He looked as dazed as she felt. "Why?"

"Because . . ." She took a deep breath and let it out slowly. *Because you don't know who I am and when you find out you'll hate me.* "Because you have to go have dinner with your sister."

He opened his mouth to argue, but then his brows lowered as if he'd forgotten. "Damn." His grasp on her tightened a fraction before he took a step back and dropped his hands to his sides. "I didn't mean to start something I can't finish."

"I didn't mean to start anything at all." Maddie licked her lips and debated whether to come clean. Right there. Right now. Before he heard it from someone in town. "This is definitely not a good idea."

"You're wrong about that." He reached for her hand and pulled her along with him toward the front door. "The only thing wrong is my timing."

"But you don't know me," she protested as she moved beside him to the entry.

"What's the rush?" He opened the door, but stopped in the threshold. He looked down into her face and let out a heavy breath. "Okay, what do I need to know?"

And she chickened out. Or rather, decided that telling him while her body still craved his wasn't the best timing. Instead she chose another approach. "I'm kind of sexually abstinent."

"Kind of?" He looked down into her face. "How can you be 'kind of sexually abstinent'?"

Yeah. How? "I just haven't had sex with a man in a very long time."

His brows drew together. "Are you a lesbian?"

"No."

"I didn't think so. You don't kiss like a lesbian."

"How do you know?"

One second she was looking up into his blue eyes, and in the next she was up against his body. His mouth closed over hers and he fed her kisses so hot she felt it in the pit of her stomach. He pulled the oxygen from her lungs and made her dizzy. Lord, she couldn't breathe or think. She was going to pass out from pleasure.

He let go of her and she fell back against the doorframe. "That's how I know," he said.

"My God, you're like a tornado," she gasped. She placed her fingers on her bottom lip. Her mouth felt numb. "Sucking up everything around you."

"Not everything." He stepped out onto the porch and into the sunlight. "And not yet."

Chapter 6

Maddie stood with her hands sticking straight out from her shoulders as Nan, the seamstress, pinned peach satin beneath her armpits. The other two bridesmaids stood on either side of her in various degrees of undress while being pinned and poked.

"You owe me," she said to her friend Clare, the blushing bride-to-be. She'd driven down from Truly that morning and planned to go out with her friends before driving back the next day.

"Look at it this way," Clare said from her position on the couch inside of Nan's Bridal. "At least the dresses aren't all froufrou like the dresses Lucy made us wear for her wedding."

"Hey. Those were beautiful," Lucy protested,

defending her choice of froufrou while a second seamstress pinned her hem.

"We looked like prom escapees," Adele argued. Adele held up her thick curly hair as a woman pinned the back of her dress. "But I've seen worse. My cousin Jolene made her bridesmaids wear purple and white toile de Jouy."

Clare, the arbiter of exquisite taste, gasped.

"Toile like the pastoral prints you see on chairs and wallpaper?" Maddie asked.

"Yep. They looked like sofas. Especially Jolene's friend who was a little roomier than the other girls."

"That's sad." Lucy turned so the seamstress could work on the back of the hem.

"Criminal," Adele added. "Some things should just be against the law. Or if not, there should be some reparation for putting a person through emotional stress."

"What did Dwayne do now?" Clare asked, referring to Adele's old boyfriend.

For two years Adele had dated Dwayne Larkin and had thought she just might end up as Mrs. Larkin. She'd overlooked his more undesirable habits, like smelling the armpits of his shirts before he put them on because he'd been buff and very hot. She'd put up with his beer-swilling, *Star*

Wars–obsessed ways, because not everyone was perfect. But the moment he'd told her she was getting a "fat ass" like her mother, she'd kicked him out of her life. No one used the *f*-word in relation to her behind or insulted her deceased mama. But Dwayne wouldn't go completely. Every few weeks, Adele would find on her porch one or two of the presents she'd given to him or things she'd left at his house. The stuff would just be lying there. No note. No Dwayne. Just random-as-hell items.

"For his birthday, I gave him a limited-edition Darth Vader." Adele dropped her hands and her thick blond hair fell down her back. "I found it on my porch with the head cut off."

Maddie could understand Dwayne's issue with the gift, but for different reasons. If she opened a birthday present and found a Darth Vader, limited edition or not, she'd get fairly pissed off. But still, any sort of violence should never be taken lightly. "You need to get an alarm system. Do you still have the stun gun I got you?"

Adele held still as the seamstress measured the circumference of her arm. "Somewhere."

"You need to find it and zap him with it." Nan moved to Maddie's bodice and she dropped her arms to her sides. "Or better yet, let me get you a

Cobra like I have, and you can Taser his ass with fifty thousand volts."

Without moving her body, Adele turned her head and looked at Maddie like she was the crazy one. "Won't that kill him?"

Maddie thought a moment. "Does he have a heart condition?"

"I don't think so."

"Then no," Maddie answered. Nan took a step back to eye her progress. "He'll convulse like you're killing him, though."

Adele's and Clare's mouths fell open in shock, as if she'd lost what little mind she had left, but Lucy nodded. She'd fought for her life against a serial killer and knew firsthand the importance of personal safety devices. "And when you have him on the ground, douse him with pepper spray."

"Dwayne is an idiot, but he's not violent," Adele said. "Although seeing the Darth Vader did remind me of something horrible."

"What?" If Dwayne had ever hit Adele, Maddie would hunt him down and zap him herself.

"He has my Princess Leia slave costume."

Clare scooted to the edge of the couch. "You have a slave costume?"

Maddie only had one question. "Are you shitting me?"

Lucy had two. "What's that?" And, "Do you mean a metal bikini?"

As if a metal slave bikini were a normal part of a woman's wardroom, Adele nodded. "Yeah. And I'd really like to have it back in one piece." She thought a moment, then added, "Well, the two pieces . . . and the armbands and collar." She must have noticed her friends' expressions, ranging from appalled to worried, because she added, "Hey, I spent a lot of money on that costume and I want it back." The seamstress stepped away to write down a measurement and Adele folded her arms under her breasts. "Don't tell me you girls have never role-played."

Lucy shook her head. "No, but I used to pretend that an old boyfriend was Jude Law. He didn't know it, though, so I don't think that counts."

Clare, who always tried to make everyone feel better, said, "Well, I told Sebastian once that I had costumes and handcuffs." She sat back on the sofa. "But I lied. Sorry."

Maddie glanced at the three seamstresses to see their reactions. They looked as poker-faced as Sunday school teachers. They'd probably heard worse. She turned her gaze to Adele, who'd tilted her head to one side as if she were waiting for something.

"What?" Maddie asked.

"I know you've done kinky stuff."

Mostly Maddie was just talk. "I've never dressed up." She thought a moment and in an effort to sooth Adele she confessed, "But if it makes you feel better, I've been tied up."

"Me too."

"Of course."

"Big deal." Adele didn't look placated. "*Everyone's* been tied up."

"That's true," Nan the seamstress added. She plucked a pin from the cushion on her wrist and glanced over at Adele. "And if it makes you feel better, every now and again I dress up as Little Red Riding Hood."

"Thank you, Nan."

"You're welcome." She made a spinning motion with her finger. "Turn, please."

After the bridesmaids were done with their fittings, the four friends drove to their favorite place to meet for lunch. Café Olé didn't have the best Mexican food in town, but it did have the best pitchers of margaritas. They were shown to one of their favorite booths, and over piped-in mariachi Muzak, they caught up. They talked about Clare's wedding and Lucy's plans to start a family with her hunk of a husband Quinn. And they wanted to hear all about Maddie's life, one hundred miles north in Truly.

"It's actually not as bad as I'd thought," she said as she raised her drink to her lips. "It's very beautiful and quiet—well, except on the Fourth. Half the women in town have really bad hair, and the other half look great. I'm trying to figure out if it's a native vs. snowbird thing, but so far I can't tell." She shrugged. "I thought spending so much time cooped up in my house would drive me insane, but it hasn't."

"You know I love you," Lucy said, which was always followed by a but. "But you are already totally insane."

Probably that was true.

"How's the book?" Clare asked as a waitress brought their food.

"Slow." She'd ordered a chicken tostada salad and picked up her fork as soon as the waitress left. She'd only told her friends about her plans to write about her mother's death a few weeks ago, long after she'd found the diaries and bought her house in Truly. She didn't know why she'd waited. She usually wasn't shy about sharing the details of her personal life with her friends, sometimes to their shock and horror, but reading her mother's diaries had left her so raw, she'd needed time to adjust and take it all in before she talked about it with anyone.

"Have you met the Hennessys?" Adele asked as she dug into an enchilada oozing with cheese and topped with sour cream. Adele worked out every day, and as a result could eat whatever she wanted. Maddie, on the other hand, hated exercise.

"I've met Mick and his nephew Travis."

"What was Mick's reaction to your writing the book?"

"Well, he doesn't know." She took a bite of her salad, then added, "The time just hasn't been right to talk to him about it."

"So." Lucy's brows drew together. "What have you talked to him about?"

That neither of them could see themselves married and that he liked her butt and the way she smelled. "Mice, mostly." Which was kind of the truth.

"Wait." Adele held up one hand. "He knows who you are, who your mother was, and he just wants to chat about mice?"

"I haven't told him who I am." All three friends paused in the act of eating to stare at her. "While he's working in his bar, or when everyone's standing around a barbeque, isn't the place to walk up to him and say, 'My name is Maddie Jones and your mother killed mine.'" Her friends nodded in agreement and went back to their meals. "And yesterday was just bad timing all around. I'd had a crappy day. He was nice and brought me the Mouse Motel and then he kissed me." She speared a piece of chicken and avocado. "After that, I just forgot."

All three friends paused once again.

"To borrow your favorite phrase," Lucy said, "are you shitting me?"

Maddie shook her head. Maybe she should have kept that one to herself. Too late now.

Now it was Clare's turn to hold up one hand. "Wait. Clear something up for me."

"Yes." Maddie answered what she thought was the next logical question. The one she would have asked. "He's really hot and he's good. My thighs about went up in flames."

"That wasn't the question." Clare glanced around, as she always tended to do when she thought Maddie was being inappropriate in a public place. "You made out with Mick Hennessy and he has no idea who you are? What do you think is going to happen when he finds out?"

"I imagine he's going to be really pissed off."

Clare leaned forward. "You imagine?"

"I don't know him well enough to predict how he'll feel." But she did. She knew he was going to be angry, and she knew she sort of deserved it. Although, to be fair to herself, there really hadn't been a good time to tell him. And she hadn't come to his house and kissed him breathless. He'd done that to her.

"When you do tell him, make sure you have your Cobra," Lucy advised.

"He's not a violent guy. I won't need to Taser him."

"You don't know him." Adele pointed her fork at Maddie and pointed out the obvious. "His mother killed yours."

"And as you are always pointing out to us, it's the sane-looking ones you have to watch out for," Clare reminded Maddie.

"And that without personal safety devices, we're all sitting ducks." Lucy laughed and lifted her drink. " 'And the next thing you know, some guy is wearing your head for a hat.' "

"Remind me again why I'm friends with you three?" Maybe because they were the only people alive who cared about her. "I'll tell him. I'm just picking my moment."

Clare sat back against the seat. "Oh, my God."

"What?"

"You're afraid."

Maddie picked up her margarita and took a long

drink until the backs of her eyeballs froze. "I call it being a little apprehensive." She placed a warm palm on her brow. "I'm not *afraid* of anything."

The black metal frame on a pair of Revo high-resolution sunglasses sat on the bridge of Mick's nose while the blue mirrored lenses shaded his eyes from the scorching six o'clock sun. As he walked across the school parking lot, his gaze was intent on player number twelve in the blue Hennessy's T-shirt and the red batter's helmet. He'd been busy going over the books and ordering beer from the distributor and he'd missed the first inning.

"Come on, Travis," he called out and sat on the bottom row of bleacher seats. He leaned forward to place his forearms on the tops of his thighs.

Travis rested the bat on one shoulder as he approached the black rubber T. He took several practice swings like his coach had shown him as the opposing team, Brooks Insurance, stood in the field, mitts at the ready. Travis got into the perfect batter's stance, swung, and completely missed.

"That's okay, buddy," Mick called out to him.

"You'll get it this time, Travis," Meg yelled down from where she sat in the top row next to her friends and fellow T-ball moms.

Mick glanced up at his sister before returning his gaze to the plate. Last night's dinner at her house had been perfectly fine. She'd made steak and baked potatoes and had been the fun-loving Meg most people knew. And the whole time, he hadn't wanted to be there. He'd wanted to be across town. In a house on the lake with a woman he knew nothing about. Talking about mice and burying his nose in the side of her neck.

There was something about Maddie Dupree. Something besides the beautiful face, the hot body, and the smell of her skin. Something that made him think about her when he should be thinking about other things. Distracted while he looked over his accounting system for errors.

Travis once again got into stance and took a swing. This time he connected and sent the ball hurling between second and third base. He dropped the bat and took off for first and his helmet slid back and forth on his head as he ran. The ball bounced and rolled past the outfielder, who took off after it. The first base coach urged Travis to keep going and he made it all the way to third before the outfielder picked up the ball and threw it a few feet. Travis took off again and did a beauty of a slider into home while the outfielder and second baseman fought over the ball.

Mick hollered and gave Travis the thumbs-up. Extremely proud as if he were the boy's daddy instead of his uncle. For the time being, he was the male in Travis's life. Travis hadn't seen his father in five years, and Meg didn't know where he was. Or, more likely, she didn't want to know where the deadbeat was. Mick had met Gavin Black one time, at Meg's wedding. He'd summed him up in one glance as a loser, and he'd been right.

Travis brushed off his pants and handed his coach the helmet. He high-fived his teammates, then took a seat on the team bench. He looked over at Mick and grinned, his one missing tooth a black shadow in his small mouth. If Gavin Black had been standing in front of Mick, he would have kicked his ass all over the schoolyard. How could any man run out on his son? Especially after raising him for two years. And how could his sister have married such a loser?

Mick placed his hands on his knees as the next batter struck out and Travis's team took the field. The best thing for Travis and Meg would be for her to find a nice dependable man. Someone who would be good to her and Travis. Someone stable.

He loved Travis and would always look out for him. Just as he'd looked out for Meg when they'd been kids. But he was tired now. It seemed to him that the more time he gave her, the more she took. In some ways, she'd become their grandmother, and he'd stayed away for twelve years to get away from Loraine. If he let Meg, he was afraid she'd become too dependent on him. He didn't want that. After a life of turmoil, whether as a child or living in war zones, he wanted some peace and calm. Well, as peaceful and calming as could be expected owning two bars.

Meg was the sort of woman who needed a man in her life, someone to balance her out, but it couldn't be him. He thought of Maddie and her assertion that she wasn't looking for a husband. He'd heard that claim before, but with her, he believed it. He didn't know what she did for a living, if anything, but she obviously didn't need a man to support her.

Mick rose and moved to the batter's cage to get a better look at Travis standing out in center field with his mitt held up in the air as if he expected a ball from heaven to land inside.

He hadn't planned to kiss Maddie yesterday. He'd brought her Ernie's card and the Mouse Motel, and he'd planned to leave. But the second she'd opened the door, his plans got shot all to hell. The black dress had clung to her sexy curves and all he'd been able to think about was untying it. Pulling the strings and unwrapping her like a birthday gift. Touching and tasting her all over.

He raised his hands and grasped the chain link in front of him. Yesterday his timing had been bad, but there wasn't a doubt in his mind. He was going to kiss Maddie again.

"Hi, Mick."

He looked across his shoulder as Jewel Finley walked toward him. Jewel had been one of his mother's friends. She had two obnoxious twin boys, Scoot and Wes, and a whiny crybaby girl named Belinda whom everyone called Boo. Growing up, Mick had hit Boo with a Nerf ball and she'd acted like she'd been mortally injured. According to Meg, Belinda wasn't quite the crybaby these days, but the twins were obnoxious as ever.

"Hello, Mrs. Finley. Do you have a grandkid playing tonight?"

Jewel pointed toward the opposing bench. "My daughter's son, Frankie, is playin' outfield for Brooks Insurance."

Ah. The boy who threw like a girl. Figured.

"What are Scoot and Wes up to these days?" he asked to be polite. Not that he gave a shit.

"Well, after their fish farm failed, they both got their commercial driver's licenses and now they drive big rigs for a movin' company."

He turned his attention to the field and Travis, who was now tossing his mitt in the air and catching it. "Which company?" If he had to move, he wanted to know who *not* to call.

"York Transfer and Storage. But they're gettin' tired of the long haul. So as soon as they save up enough money, they're thinkin' about starting one of those house-flippin' businesses. Like on TV."

Mick figured it would take the twins less than a year of working for themselves before they filed for bankruptcy. To say the boys weren't the sharpest knives in the drawer was an understatement.

"There's good money in flippin' houses."

"Uh-huh." He was going to have to talk to Travis about paying attention to the game.

"As much as fifty grand a month. That's what Scooter says."

"Uh-huh." Geez-us. Now the kid was turned completely around and watching cars drive by in the street.

"Have you talked to that writer yet?"

He probably shouldn't yell at Travis to watch the game, but he wanted to. "What writer?"

"The one who's writin' a book about your parents and that waitress, Alice Jones."

Chapter 7

Maddie tossed her overnight bag on her bed and unzipped it. She had a slight headache, and she wasn't sure if it was due to her lack of sleep, drinking too much with Adele, or listening to her friend's stories about her fractured love life.

After she'd had lunch at Café Olé, she and Adele had gone back to her house in Boise to catch up. Adele always had really funny stories about her love life—although she sometimes didn't mean for them to be quite so entertaining—and like a good friend, Maddie had listened and poured the wine. It had been a long time since Maddie had been able to reciprocate with funny and entertaining stories of her own, so mostly she'd just listened and offered occasional advice.

Before leaving Boise, she'd invited Adele to

spend the following weekend with her. Adele agreed to come and, knowing her friend, Maddie was sure she'd have several more dating horror stories to share.

Maddie took her dirty clothes from the bag and tossed them into her hamper. It was just after noon and she was starving. She ate a chicken breast and some celery with cream cheese while she checked and answered her e-mails. She checked her answering machine, but there was only one message, and that was from a carpet cleaner. No word from Sheriff Potter.

Later, she planned to find Mick and tell him who she was and why she was in town. It was the right thing to do, and she wanted him to hear it from her first. She figured she could find him at one of his two bars, and she hoped he was working at Mort's tonight. She really wasn't looking forward to walking into Hennessy's, although she would have to at some point. She'd never been inside the bar where her mother had died. To her, Hennessy's wasn't just another old crime scene. One she had to visit for her book. She would have to go to note the changes and observe the place. And while she certainly *wasn't* afraid, she was apprehensive.

As she rinsed her plate in the sink and put it in

the dishwasher, she wondered exactly how angry Mick was likely to get. Until her friends had mentioned it, she hadn't thought of packing her Taser when she told him. While he seemed perfectly nonviolent, he had shot Hellfire missiles from helicopters. And of course his mother had been a nut job, and while Maddie liked to think she had a special psycho radar, honed after years of meeting with them while they'd been chained to a table, it never hurt to err on the side of caution and a really good pepper spray.

The doorbell rang, and this time she wasn't surprised to see Mick standing on her porch. Just like last time, he held a business card between two fingers, but there was no mistaking that the card was hers.

He stared at her from behind the blue lenses of his sunglasses, and his lips were set in a flat line. He wasn't wearing a happy face, but he didn't look too angry. She probably wouldn't have to hose him with the pepper spray. Not that she even had it on her.

Maddie lowered her gaze to the card. "Where did you get that?"

"Jewel Finley."

Crap. She really hadn't meant for him to find out that way, but she wasn't surprised. "When?"

"Last night at Travis's T-ball game."

"I'm sorry you heard about it like that." Maddie didn't invite him inside, but he didn't wait for an invitation.

"Why didn't *you* tell me?" he asked as he brushed past her, six feet two, one hundred and ninety pounds, of determined man. Trying to stop him would have been as futile as trying to stop a tank.

Maddie closed the door and followed. "You didn't want to know anything about me. Remember?"

"That's a bunch of bullshit." Light from outside flowed in through the large windows, over the back of the sofa and coffee table and across the hardwood floor. Mick stopped within the spill of light and took off his sunglasses. Maddie had been wrong about his anger. It burned like blue fire in his eyes. "I didn't want to know about your old boyfriends, your favorite chocolate chip cookie recipe, or who you sat next to in the second grade." He held up the card. "This is different, and don't pretend that it's not."

She pushed her hair behind her ears. He had a right to be angry. "That first night at Mort's, I went there to introduce myself and to tell you who I was and why I was in town. But the bar was busy and it wasn't a good time. When I saw you at the hardware store and on the Fourth, Travis was with you and I didn't think it an appropriate time then either."

"And when I was here alone?" He frowned and stuck his glasses on top of his head.

"I tried to tell you that day."

"Is that so?" He slid the card in the pocket of his black Mort's Bar polo shirt. "Before or after you stuck your tongue down my throat?"

Maddie gasped. Yeah, he had a right to be angry, but not to rewrite history. "You kissed me!"

"An *appropriate time*," he said as if she hadn't protested, "might have been before you glued yourself to my chest."

"Glued? You pulled me in to your chest." Her gaze narrowed, but she wouldn't allow herself to get angry. "I told you that you didn't know me."

"And instead of you telling me the important shit like you're in town to write a book about my parents, you thought I would be more interested in knowing that you're 'kind of sexually abstinent.'" He rested his weight on one foot and tilted his head to one side as he looked down at her. "You weren't planing to tell me."

"Don't be absurd." She folded her arms beneath her breasts. "This is a small town and I knew you'd find out."

"And until I did, were you planning to fuck me for information?"

Don't get mad, she told herself. *If you get mad, you might get out the Taser.* "There are two problems with your theory." She held up a hand and raised one finger. "That I need you to give me information. I don't." She raised a second finger. "And that I was planning to fuck you. I wasn't."

He took a step toward her and smiled. Not one of his nice, charming smiles either. "If I'd had more time, you would have been flat on your back."

"You're dreaming."

"And you're lying. To me and to yourself."

"I never lie to myself." She looked into his eyes, not in the least intimidated by his size or anger. "And I never lied to you."

His gaze narrowed. "You purposely hid the truth, which is the same damn thing."

"Oh, that's rich. A morality lesson from you. Tell me, Mick, do all the women you sleep with know about each other?"

"I don't lie to women."

"No, you just bring mousetraps thinking that will get you into their pants."

"That isn't the reason I brought you the trap."

"Now who's lying?" She pointed toward the door. "It's time for you to leave."

He didn't budge. "You can't do this, Maddie. You can't write about my family."

"Yes, I can, and I'm going to." She didn't wait for him but walked to the door and opened it.

"Why? I've read all about you," he said as he moved toward her, his boot heels an angry thud across the hardwood. "You write about serial killers. My mother wasn't a serial killer. She was a housewife who'd had enough of a cheating husband. She flipped out and killed him and herself. There's no big villain here. No sick bastards like Ted Bundy or Jeffrey Dahmer. What happened to my mother and father is hardly the sensational sort of stuff that people want to read about."

"I think I'm a little more qualified to determine that than you."

He stopped on the threshold and turned to face her. "My mother was just a sad woman who snapped one night and left her children orphaned, victims of her mental illness."

"All this talk of you and your family, you seem to forget there was another innocent victim."

"That little waitress was hardly innocent."

Actually, she'd been talking about herself. "So you're like everyone else in this town and think Alice Jones got what she deserved."

"No one got what they deserved, but she was screwing around with a married man."

Now. Now she was truly good and angry. "So your mother was perfectly justified in shooting her in the face."

His head jerked back as if she'd slapped him. Obviously he hadn't seen the photos or read the report.

"And your father may have been a cheater, but did he deserve to be shot three times and bleed to death on a barroom floor while your mother watched?"

His voice rose for the first time. "You're full of shit. She wouldn't have watched my father die."

If he hadn't told her she was full of shit, she would have spared him, no matter her own anger. "Her bloody footprints were all over the bar. And she didn't get up and walk around after she shot herself."

His mouth clamped shut.

"Alice Jones had a child too. Did she deserve to lose her mother? Did she deserve to be made an orphan?" Maddie placed her hand in the center of his chest and pushed. "So don't tell me that your mother was just some sad housewife who'd been pushed too far. She had other options. Lots of other options that didn't involve murder." He took a step back out onto her porch. "And don't come here and think you can tell me what to do. I really don't give a damn if you like it or not. I'm going to write the book." She tried to shut the door, but his arm shot out and kept it open.

"You do that." With his free hand, he took his sunglasses from the top of his head and slid them in place, covering the anger in his blue eyes. "But you stay away from me," he said and dropped his hand from the door. "And you stay the hell away from my family."

Maddie slammed the door and pushed her hair from her face. Damn. That hadn't gone well. He'd been angry. She'd gotten angry. Heck, she was still angry.

She heard him start his truck, and out of habit, she locked her front door. She didn't need him or his family in order to write the book, but realistically, it'd be nice if she had their cooperation. Especially since she needed to get into the lives of Loch and Rose.

"Well, that sucked," she said and walked into the living room. She would have to write the book without their input. Her mother's photograph sat on the coffee table. She'd been so young and filled with so many dreams. Maddie picked up the photo and touched the glass above her mother's lips. It had been sitting on the table the whole time while Mick had been there, and he hadn't noticed.

She'd planned to tell him that she was more than just an author interested in writing a book. That his mother had left her an orphan too. Now he wanted nothing to do with her, and who she really was just didn't seem to matter anymore.

Mick pulled his truck to a stop in front of the Shore View Diner where Meg worked five days a week waiting tables and pulling in tips. He was still so angry he felt like hitting something or someone. Like picking Maddie Dupree up by her shoulders and shaking her until she agreed to pack up and go away. Like forgetting she'd ever heard of the Hennessys and their messed-up lives. But she'd made it really clear she wasn't going anywhere, and now he had to tell Meg before she heard it from someone else.

He turned off the truck and leaned his head back. His mother had watched his father die? He hadn't known that. Wished he didn't know it now. How could he possibly reconcile the woman who'd killed two people with the mother who'd made him peanut butter and strawberry jelly sandwiches, cut the crusts off, and sliced the bread at an angle just as he'd liked it? The loving mother who bathed him and washed his hair and tucked him in at night, with the woman who'd left foot-prints in her husband's blood all over his bar? How could that even be the same woman?

He rubbed his face with his hands and slid his fingers beneath his sunglasses to rub his eyes. He was so damn tired. After Jewel had given him Maddie's business card, he'd gone to his office in Hennessy's and locked himself in. He'd searched the Internet for information about Maddie, and there'd been a lot. She'd published five books, and he'd discovered head shots of her and photos of her at book signings. There was no mistaking that the Maddie Dupree whom he'd been plan-ning to get to know better was the woman who wrote about psychotic killers. The Madeline Dupree who was in town to write about the night his mother had killed his father. He opened the door to his truck and stepped outside. And there wasn't a damn thing he could do to stop her.

From as far back as he could remember, the Shore View Diner had smelled the same. Like grease and eggs and tobacco. The diner was one of the last places in America where a person could have a cup of coffee and a Camel or Lucky Strike, depending on his or her poison. As a result, it was always filled with smokers. Mick had tried to talk Meg into working someplace where she wasn't likely to get lung cancer from secondhand smoke, but she insisted that the tips were too good to work anyplace else.

It was around two in the afternoon and the diner was half empty when Mick entered. Meg stood behind the front counter, filling Lloyd Brunner's cup of coffee and laughing at something he'd said. Her black hair was pulled back into a ponytail, and she wore a bright pink blouse beneath a white apron. She looked up and waved at him.

"Hey, there. Are you hungry?" she asked.

"No." He took a seat at the counter and pushed his Revos to the top of his head. "I was hoping you could get off early."

"Why?" Her smile fell and she set the coffee carafe on the counter. "Has something happened? Is it Travis?"

"Travis is fine. I just wanted to talk to you about something."

She looked into his eyes as if she could read his mind. "I'll be right back," she said and walked into the kitchen. When she returned, she had her purse.

Mick rose and followed her outside. As soon as the door to the diner swung shut behind them, she asked, "What is it?"

"There's a woman in town. She's a true crime writer."

Meg squinted against the bright sun as they walked across the gravel lot to his truck. "What's her name?"

"Madeline Dupree."

Her jaw dropped. "Madeline Dupree? She wrote *In Her Place*, the story of Patrick Wayne Dobbs. The serial killer who killed women and then wore their clothes under his business suit. That book scared me so much I couldn't sleep for a week." Meg shook her head. "What is she doing in Truly?"

He slid his sunglasses down to cover his eyes. "Apparently, she's going to write about what happened with Mom and Dad."

Meg stopped. "What?"

"You heard me."

"Why?"

"God, I don't know." He raised a hand, then dropped it to his side. "If she writes about serial killers, I don't know what she finds so damn interesting about Mom and Dad."

Meg folded her arms across the front of her apron and they continued to walk. "What does she know about what happened?"

"I don't know, Meg." They stopped by his truck

and he leaned a hip into the front fender. "She knows Mom shot that waitress in the head." His sister didn't bat an eye. "Did you know that?"

Meg shrugged and bit her thumbnail. "Yeah. I heard the sheriff tell Grandma Loraine."

He looked into his sister's eyes and wondered what else she knew that he didn't. He wondered if she knew that their mother hadn't killed herself right away. He supposed it didn't matter. She was taking the news better than he'd expected. "Are you going to be okay?"

She nodded. "Is there anything we can do to stop her?"

"I doubt it."

She leaned back into the driver's-side door and sighed. "Maybe you can go talk to her."

"I did. She's going to write it, and she doesn't care what we have to say about it."

"Shit."

"Yeah."

"Everyone is going to start talking about it again."

"Yep."

"She'll say bad stuff about Mom."

"Probably about all three of them. But what can she say? The only people who know what really happened that night are dead."

Meg glanced away.

"Do you know something that happened that night?"

She dropped her hand. "Just that Mom had been pushed too far and she killed Dad and that waitress."

He wasn't so sure he believed her, but what difference did it make twenty-nine years later? Meg hadn't been there. She'd been home with him when the sheriff had arrived at their house that night.

He looked up at the clear blue sky. "I'd forgotten that the waitress had a little girl."

"Yeah, I can't remember her name, though." Meg returned her gaze to Mick. "Not that I care. Her mother was a whore."

"That wasn't the girl's fault, Meg. She was left without a mother."

"She was probably better off. Alice Jones was cheating with our father and didn't care who knew. She flaunted their relationship in front of the whole town, so don't expect me to feel sorry for some nameless, faceless orphan girl."

Mick didn't know if there'd been any flaunting, and if there had been, he figured their dad had to take the majority of the blame, since he'd been the married one.

"Are you going to be okay with this?"

"No, but what can I do about it?" She adjusted her purse on her shoulder. "I'll survive, just like I did before."

"I told her to stay away from you and Travis, so I don't think she'll be bothering you with questions."

Meg raised a brow. "Is she going to be bothering you with questions?"

There was more than one way a woman could bother a man. *And don't come here and think you can tell me what to do. I really don't give a damn if you like it or not. I'm going to write the book.* She'd been mad and obstinate and sexy as hell. Her big brown eyes had gotten kind of squinted at the corners just before she'd slammed the door in his face. "No," he answered. "She won't be bothering me with questions."

Meg waited until Mick's truck pulled out of the parking lot before she let out a breath and raised her hands to the sides of her face. She pressed her fingers into her temples and closed her eyes against the pressure building in her head. Madeline Dupree was in town to write a book about her parents. There had to be something someone could do to stop her. A person shouldn't be allowed to just . . . just ruin lives. There should be a law against snooping around and . . . digging into someone's past.

Meg opened her eyes and stared down at her white Reeboks. It wouldn't be long before everyone in town knew about it. Before they started talking and gossiping and looking at her as if she were liable to go off at any time. Even her brother sometimes looked at her as if she were crazy. Mick thought he was so good at forgetting the past, but there were some things even he'd never been able to forget. Tears clouded her vision and dropped on the gravel by the instep of her shoe. Mick also mistook emotion for mental illness. Not that she really blamed him. Growing up with their parents had been an emotional tug-of-war ending in their death.

A second truck pulled into the parking lot and Meg raised her gaze as Steve Castle opened the door of his Tacoma and got out. Steve was Mick's buddy and manager of Hennessy's. Meg didn't know much about him, other than he'd flown helicopters in the army with Mick, and there'd been some sort of accident in which Steve had lost his right leg beneath the knee.

"Hey, there, Meg," he called out, his deep voice booming across the lot as he moved toward her.

"Hey." Meg hurriedly wiped beneath her eyes, then dropped her hands to her sides. Steve was a big guy and shaved his head completely bald. He was tall and broad-chested and so . . . so manly that Meg felt a little intimidated by his size.

"Having a rough day?"

She could feel her cheeks get hot as she looked up into his deep blue eyes. "Sorry. I know men don't like to see women cry."

"Tears don't bother me. I've seen tough Marines cry like little girls." He folded his arms across the dogs playing poker on the front of his T-shirt. "Now, what's got you so upset, sweetheart?"

Meg usually didn't share her feelings with people she didn't know, but there was something about Steve. While his size intimidated her, he also made her feel safe at the same time. Or perhaps it was just because he'd called her "sweetheart," but she opened her mouth and confided, "Mick was just here, and he told me that there's a writer in town and she's going to write about the night our mother killed our father."

"Yeah. I heard about that."

"Already? How did you find out?"

"The Finley boys were in Hennessy's last night talking about it."

She raised a hand and chewed on her thumbnail.

"Then I think it's safe to assume the whole town knows, and everybody is going to be talking about it and speculating."

"Nothing to do about that."

She dropped her hand to her side and shook her head. "I know."

"But maybe you can talk to her."

"Mick tried that. She's going to write the book no matter what we think about it." She looked down at her shoes. "Mick told her to stay away from me and Travis."

"Why avoid her? Why don't you tell her your side of things?"

She looked up into his eyes and the sunlight bouncing off his shiny head. "I don't know if she'd care about my side."

"Maybe, but you won't know that unless you talk to the woman." He unfolded his arms and rested one big hand on her shoulder. "If there is one thing I know, it's that you have to confront something head-on. You can get through any-thing if you know what you're facing."

Which she was sure was true and very good advice, but she couldn't think past the weight of his hand on her shoulder. The solid feel and the warmth of his touch spread to her stomach. She hadn't felt warmth from a man since her ex-husband. The men in town talked to her and flirted with her, but they never seemed to want more than a coffee refill.

Steve slid his palm down her arm and grasped her hand. "I've wondered something since I moved to town."

"What's that?"

He tilted his head to one side and studied her. "Why you don't have a boyfriend."

"I think the men in this town are half afraid of me."

His brows lowered over his eyes and then he burst out laughing. A deep booming laugh that lit his face.

"It's not funny," she said, but at that moment, surrounded by Steve Castle's laughter, it was kind of funny. And standing so close, with her hand in his, was kind of . . . nice.

Chapter 8

The fishing at upper Payette Lake had been so good, Sheriff Potter hadn't returned until the following Tuesday, but once he'd been given Maddie's card he'd called her immediately and set up a meeting for the next day at his house. If there was one thing in Maddie's line of work that she could always count on, it was cops. Whether an LAPD detective or a small-town sheriff, cops loved to talk about old cases.

"I'll never forget that night," the retired sheriff said as he looked at the old crime scene photos through a pair of reading glasses. Unlike the stereotypical retired sheriff who'd gone to fat, Bill Potter was still quite thin and had a full head of white hair. "That scene was a mess."

Maddie scooted the small tape recorder closer

to the baby-blue La-Z-Boy recliner where Sheriff Potter sat. The inside of the Potters' home was a fusion of floral prints and wildlife art that clashed on so many different levels that Maddie feared her eyes would cross before the day was through.

"I'd known Loch and Rose since they were kids," Bill Potter continued. "I'm a few years older, but in a town this size, especially back in the seventies, everyone knows everyone. Rose was one of the most beautiful women I'd ever seen, and it was a shock to see what she'd done to those two people and then to herself."

"How many homicide cases had you investigated before the Hennessy case?" she asked.

"One, but it was nothing like the Hennessy case. Old Man Jenner got shot in a dispute over a dog. Mostly we get accidental shootings, and those are usually around hunting season."

"The first officer on the scene was a . . ." Maddie paused to look at the report. "Officer Grey Tipton."

"Yep. He left the department a few months after that and moved away," the sheriff said. "And I hear he died a few years ago."

Which was just one of the many hurdles she was always coming up against in this town. Either people weren't willing to talk about what happened or they were dead. At least she had Officer Tipton's report and notes. "Yes, he died in an ATV accident in 1981. Did the shooting have anything to do with him leaving the department?"

Sheriff Potter shuffled the photos. "It had everything to do with it. Grey had been really good friends with Loch, and seeing him shot like that haunted him so bad he couldn't sleep." He held up the photo of Rose lying beside her dead husband. "It was the first time any of us had seen anything like that. I'd responded to plenty of automobile accidents that were bloody as hell, but they weren't personal."

Since there would be no trial to write about, Maddie had to get as much personal information as possible. And since the Hennessys weren't talking, she had to rely on other sources.

"Grey had such a hard time with it. He had to quit. Just goes to show you that you don't know how you'll deal with a situation until you're knee-deep in blood."

For the next hour, they talked about the crime scene. The photos and reports answered the who, what, where, and when, but the why was still fuzzy. Maddie changed the tape in the little recorder, then asked, "You knew both Loch and Rose. What do you think happened that night?"

In every case like this, there was always a catalyst. A stressor was introduced that pushed the perpetrator over the edge. "From what I've heard and read, Alice Jones wasn't Loch's one and only affair."

"No. She wasn't. That marriage had been like a roller coaster for years." The sheriff shook his head and removed his glasses. "Before they moved into that farmhouse right outside of town, they used to live down by the lake on Pine Nut. Every few months I'd get a call from one of their neighbors and I'd have to drive over there."

"What did you find once you arrived?"

"Screaming and yelling, mostly. A few times Loch'd have his clothes torn or a red mark on his face." Bill chuckled. "One time I got there and the front window was busted out and a skillet was lying in the yard."

"Was anyone ever arrested?"

"Nah. Then the next time you'd see the two of them, they'd be all lovey-dovey and happy as pie."

And when they weren't lovey-dovey, they pulled other people into their messed-up marriage. "But once they moved into the farmhouse, the calls to your office stopped?"

"Yeah. No more neighbors around, you know."

"Where is the farmhouse now?"

"Burned down. . . ." He paused in thought and deep grooves wrinkled his forehead. "Must have been about twenty years ago. One night, someone went over there, doused it with kerosene, and lit it up good."

"Was anyone hurt?"

"No one lived there at the time." He frowned and shook his head. "Never did find out who started it. Always had my suspicions, though."

"Who?"

"Only a couple of people wanted that house gone bad enough to do such a good job. Kids just playin' around with matches don't torch a place like that."

"Mick?"

"And his sister, although I could never prove it. Didn't actually want to prove it, if truth be told. Growing up, Mick was always in trouble. A constant pain in the ass, but I always felt bad for him. He had a real hard life."

"Lots of children lose their parents and don't turn to arson."

The sheriff leaned forward. "Lots of kids don't live the life Rose Hennessy left behind for her kids."

That was true, but Maddie knew a bit about that life. She flipped a page in her notebook and said, "Alice Jones lived in the Roundup Trailer Court. Do you know a woman by the name of Trina who may have lived in the same trailer court in 1978?"

"Hmm, that doesn't sound familiar." He thought a moment, then leaned forward. "You might talk to Harriet Landers. She lived in that trailer court for years. When the land was sold to a developer, she had to be practically hog tied and carried away."

"Where does Harriet live now?"

"Levana," he called to his wife. When she appeared from the back of the house he asked, "Where is Harriet Landers living these days?"

"I believe she lives at the Samaritan Villa." Levana looked at Maddie and added, "That's a retirement center off of Whitetail and Fifth. She's a little hard of hearing these days."

What?" Harriet Landers yelled from her wheelchair. "Speak up, for pity's sake."

Maddie sat in an old iron chair in the small garden at the Samaritan Villa. Looking at the old woman, it was hard to gauge her age. Maddie would guess somewhere between one foot in the grave and fossilized. "My name is Maddie Dupree! I wonder if I might be—"

"You're that writer," Harriet interrupted. "I heard you're here to write a book about them Hennessys."

Wow, news traveled fast even on the nursing home circuit. "Yes. I was told that you once lived at the Roundup Trailer Court."

"For about fifty years." She'd lost almost all of her white hair and most of her teeth and she wore a pink housecoat with white lace and snaps. But there didn't seem to be anything wrong with her mind. "I don't know what I could talk to you about."

"How about living at the Roundup?"

"Humpf." She raised a knobby and gnarled hand and swiped at a bee in front of her face. "Not a lot to say that anyone wants to hear. Folks think that people who live in trailer houses are poor trailer trash, but I always liked my trailer. Always liked having the option of packing up the house and moving the whole damn thing if I wanted." She shrugged a bony shoulder. "Guess I never did, though."

"People can be very cruel and dismissive," Maddie said. "When I was little, we lived in a trailer, and I thought it was the best." Which was true, mostly because the trailer had been such an improvement over the other places she and her mother had lived. "We certainly weren't trash."

Harriet's sunken blue eyes gave Maddie the once-over. "You lived in a trailer?"

"Yes, ma'am." Maddie held up the tape recorder. "Do you mind if I record our conversation?"

"What for?"

"So that I don't misquote you."

Harriet put her skinny elbows on the arms of her wheelchair and leaned forward. "Go ahead." She pointed at the recorder. "What do you want to know?"

"Do you recall the summer that Alice Jones lived at the Roundup?"

"Sure, although I lived down the road from her and not next door. But I'd see her sometimes as I was driving past. She was a real pretty thing and had a little girl. That little girl used to swing all day and half the night on the swing set in her front yard."

Yes, that part Maddie knew. She remembered swinging so high, she thought her toes touched the sky. "Did you ever talk to Alice Jones? Have friendly conversations?"

A frown pulled at the wrinkles in her forehead. "Not that I can recall. That was a long time ago and my memory isn't so good these days."

"I understand. My memory isn't always in the best of shape either." She looked down at her notes as if to remind herself of what to ask next. "Do you recall a woman by the name of Trina who may have lived at the Roundup at that time?"

"That would probably be Trina Olsen. Betty Olsen's middle girl. She had flaming red hair and freckles."

Maddie wrote down the last name and circled it. Do you know if Trina still lives in Truly?"

"No. Betty's dead, though. Died of liver cancer."

"I'm sorry."

"Why, did you know her?"

"Ah . . . no." She put the cap back on her pen. "Is there anything else you can remember from around the time Alice Jones lived at the Roundup?"

"I remember lots of things." She shifted a little in her chair, then said, "I remember Galvin Hennessy, that's for sure."

"Loch's father?" Maddie asked, just to clarify. What could Galvin have to do with Maddie's mother?

"Yep. He was a handsome devil, just like all the Hennessy men." She shook her head and sighed. "But a girl would have to be an idiot to marry a Hennessy."

Maddie skimmed her notes looking for Galvin's name. She thumbed past a Founders Day flyer she'd been handed at the front desk, but as far as she could recall, he'd never been mentioned in any of the police reports.

"I dated that man off and on until the day he dropped dead in the backseat of my Ford Rambler."

Maddie's head came up. "Pardon me?"

Harriet laughed, a crackling, rattling sound that left her in a fit of coughing. Maddie became so concerned, she set her notes on the grass and rose to thump Harriet on the back. When Harriet got herself under control, Maddie asked, "Are you okay?" Gee, Harriet was old, but Maddie didn't want to be the reason she keeled over.

"I wish you could have seen your face. I didn't think it was possible to shock anyone in this town anymore. Not at my age." Harriet chuckled.

"So?" Maddie sat back down. "Did Galvin have anything to do with what happened at Hennessy's Bar?"

"No. He was dead before all that happened. Loraine never forgave me for Galvin dying in the back of my car, but shoot, you can't throw a rock in this town without hitting some woman who hasn't slept with a Hennessy."

"Why?" Maddie asked. Lots of men had looks and charm. "What makes the Hennessy men so irresistible to the women of Truly?"

"They're beautiful to look at, but mostly on account of what they got in their pants."

"You mean they've got . . ." Maddie paused and held up a hand as if she couldn't think of the word. She could, of course. Her favorite word, heft, came to mind, but for some reason she just couldn't say it in front of an old woman.

"They're blessed," Harriet provided. Then, over the next hour, she proceeded to give Maddie the details of her long and illustrious affair with Galvin Hennessy. Apparently, Harriet was one of *those* girls. No matter that she was well into her nineties and no more than a raisin with eyes, Harriet Landers was one of *those* girls who loved to talk about their sex lives with a perfect stranger.

And Maddie, lucky girl, got it all on tape.

Wednesday night at Hennessy's was Hump Night. In an effort to help the citizens get past the hump in the week, Hennessy's offered half-price well drinks and dollar drafts until seven. After seven, a few people left, but most stayed and paid full price for their booze. Galvin Hennessy had been the brains behind Hennessy's Hump Night, and the custom had been carried through the following generations.

There were those who'd feared the demise of Hump Night when Mick had taken over the place. After all, he'd done away with panty-tossing at Mort's, but after two years of cheap well drinks and dollar beers, Truly could breathe easier knowing that some traditions were still sacred.

Mick stood at the far end of the bar, weight resting on one booted foot and pool cue in hand as Steve Castle bent over the table and took a shot. Steve was slightly taller than Mick and wore a baby-blue ATTENTION LADIES: I LOVED THE NOTEBOOK T-shirt stretched across his barrel chest. Mick had known Steve since flight training. Back then, Steve had had a full head of blond hair. These days he was as bald as the billiard he sent down on the table.

When Mick had gotten out of the army, Steve had stayed in until his Black Hawk had been shot down over Fallujah by an SA-7 shoulder-fired missile. In the crash that had killed five soldiers and wounded seven, Steve had lost his leg. After months of rehabilitation and a new prosthesis, he'd gone home to Northern California to find his marriage in ruins. He'd gone through a real rough time and a bad divorce, and when Mick had asked him to move to Truly and manage Hennessy's, he'd climbed into his truck and arrived in days.

Mick had never expected him to last in the small town, but that was a year and a half ago, and Steve had just bought a house near the lake.

Steve was the closest thing Mick had to a brother. The two shared the same experiences and visceral memories. They'd shared a life that civilians did not understand, and their time in the military was something they never talked about in public.

The six ball landed in the corner pocket and Steve lined up the two ball. "Meg was in here yesterday looking for you," he said. "I guess the whole town is buzzing like a wasp nest because that writer talked to Sheriff Potter and Harriet Landers."

"Meg called me about it last night." Steve was the only person Mick had ever spoken to about Meg's unpredictable emotional outbursts and mood swings. "She isn't as upset about this whole book business as I thought she'd be." At least she hadn't freaked out, which was what Mick had expected from the woman who'd been known to lose it over the sight of a wedding ring.

"Maybe she's stronger than you give her credit for."

Maybe, but Mick doubted it.

Steve shot, but the two hit the corner of the pocket and bounced back. "I meant to do that."

"Uh-huh." Mick chalked his cue and hit the remaining ten ball into a side pocket.

"I better get back behind the bar," Steve said as he placed his cue in the rack. "Are you going to be here until close?"

"No." Mick put his cue next to Steve's and looked out over the bar. On weeknights, both Hennessy's and Mort's closed at midnight. "I want to see how the new bartender is doing at Mort's."

"How's he working out so far?"

"A hell of a lot better than the last one. I should have known better than to hire Ronnie Van Damme in the first place. Most of the Van Dammes are worthless." Mick had had to fire Ronnie two weeks ago for always coming in late and standing around jerking his gherkin when he had been there. "The new guy used to manage a bar in Boise, so I'm hoping he works out." Eventually Mick's goal was to find a manager for Mort's so he could work less and make more money. He didn't trust government pensions or Social Security to provide for him for the rest of his life and he'd made his own investments.

"Let me know if you need help," Steve said as he walked away, his limp barely noticeable. Mick hadn't been in Iraq when Steve's bird had been shot down, but he'd had a few close calls and been forced to make an emergency landing in Afghanistan when a rocket-propelled grenade hit his Apache. The landing hadn't been pretty, but he'd survived.

He'd loved flying and it was one of the things he missed most about his former life. But he didn't miss the sand and dust and the politics of army life. He'd take getting fired at over the tedium of sitting around waiting for orders, only to gear up and have the mission scrubbed at the last moment.

These days he lived in a small town where nothing much happened, but he was never bored. Especially lately.

Mick looked out at the empty dance floor at the other end of the bar. On the weekends, he usually hired a band and the floor was packed. Tonight a few people stood around talking, others sat at tables and at the bar. By nine on Hump Nights the bar usually cleared out except for a few stragglers. Growing up, his dad had brought him and Meg to the bar occasionally and let them pour root beer into mugs. He taught them how to pour the perfect head. Looking back, that hadn't been the best thing to teach your kids, but he and Meg had loved it.

Your father may have been a cheater, Maddie had said, *but did he deserve to be shot three times and bleed to death on a barroom floor while your mother watched?*

He'd thought more about his father in the past two days than he had in the past five years. If Maddie was right, his mother watched his father die, and he just couldn't get that image out of his head.

He sat on the edge of the pool table and crossed one booted foot over the other as he watched Steve grab a Heineken from the refrigerator and twist off the top. Mick knew that the waitress, Alice Jones, had been killed behind the bar, while his mother and father had both died in front of the bar. He'd never seen photos or read the reports, but throughout the years he'd certainly heard enough talk about the night his mother had killed his father and Alice that he thought he'd heard it all. Now he guessed he hadn't.

Over the past thirty-five years, he'd been in this bar thousands of time. Meg had a photograph of him at the age of three sitting on a barstool with his father. Generations of Hennessys had worked their asses off in the bar, and after his parents' deaths, the place had been completely renovated and any trace of what had happened that night had long since been removed. When he walked through the back door, he never thought about what his mother had done to his father and Alice Jones.

Until now.

So your mother was perfectly justified in shooting her in the face, Maddie had said. For some reason, he couldn't get Maddie Dupree and her damn crime book out of his mind. The last thing in the world he wanted to occupy his thoughts was the deaths of his parents. His past was best left buried, and the last person he wanted stuck in his head was the woman responsible for digging it all up again. She was a one-woman backhoe, uncovering things that were best left covered. But short of tying her up and shoving her in a closet, there wasn't anything he could do to stop her. Although tying her up did have a certain appeal that had nothing to do with stopping her from writing.

My God, you're like a tornado. Sucking up everything around you, she'd said, and it didn't seem to matter that she was the last person in the world that he should want. The memory of her lips beneath his, and the sight of her looking thoroughly kissed and gasping for breath, were trapped in the center of his brain.

Mick rose from the table and moved past the dance floor toward the bar. Reuben Sawyer sat on his regular stool, looking old and pickled. Reuben had lost his wife thirty years ago, and for the last three decades, he'd sat on the same stool almost every night drowning his sorrows. Mick didn't believe in soul mates and didn't understand that kind of sorrow. As far as he was concerned, if you're that lonely for a woman, do something about it that doesn't involve a bottle of Jack Daniel's.

Several people called out to Mick as he passed, but he didn't stop. He didn't feel like shooting the shit. Not tonight. As he moved down the hall toward the back door, an old high school girlfriend stopped him.

"Hey, Mick," Pam Puckett said as she stepped out of the ladies' room.

He supposed pushing past her would have been rude. "Hey, Pam." He stopped and she took it as an invitation to wrap her arms around his neck and give him a friendly hug that lingered a few seconds beyond friendly.

"How're you doing?" she asked next to his ear.

"Good." Since high school, Pam had been married and divorced three times. Mick could have predicted divorce in her future. He pulled back and looked into her face. "How about yourself?"

"Not bad." She dropped onto her heels, but kept

one hand on his chest. "I haven't seen you in here for a while."

"I've been spending a lot of time at the other bar." Pam was still attractive, and he knew that all he had to do was take her by the hand and he could take her home. He kept his palm on her waist, waiting to feel the first pull of interest behind his fly. "Are you still working in the sheriff's office?"

"Yeah. Still dispatching calls. I threaten to quit every other day." Her palm slid up and down his chest.

He had three hours before closing. It wasn't like he had to haul ass to Mort's. He'd been with Pam before and they both knew that it was just sex. Just two adults getting together and having a good time. "You here by yourself?" he asked.

Her hand slid to his waist and she hooked a finger through his belt loop. He should have felt a spark of interest, but he didn't. "With a few girl-friends."

Tell me, Mick, do all the women you sleep with know about each other? Sex was probably just what he needed to get Maddie out of his head. It had been a month since he'd gotten laid, and all he had to do was take Pam's hand and pull her behind him out the back door. "You know I don't ever plan on getting married. Right?"

Her brows lowered. "I think everyone knows that, Mick."

"So I've never lied to you about that."

"No."

Once he got Pam naked, he'd let her take his mind off other things. Pam didn't like sex long and drawn out. She liked it quick and as many times as a man could get it up, and Mick was in the mood to accommodate her. He brushed his thumb up her ribs and felt a little spark of interest.

"I heard about that writer talking to everyone in town," she said and snuffed out his spark.

He really wished she hadn't said that. "See ya around." He dropped his hand and took a step back toward the door.

"You're leaving?" What she meant was: *You're leaving without me?*

"Gotta work."

It was still light out when he stepped from the bar and drove toward Mort's. He shoved his glasses on the bridge of his nose as a dull ache settled between his eyes. Maddie Dupree was messing with his past, talking to the town about his family, and affecting his sex life. With each passing moment, he felt the growing appeal of tying her up and stashing her someplace.

His stomach growled as he pulled his truck to a

stop behind Mort's, and instead of walking into the back of his bar, he walked a few doors down to the Willow Creek Brewpub and Restaurant. It was a little after nine and he hadn't eaten since lunch. Small wonder that he had a headache.

The place was practically empty, and the scent of pub wings made him even hungrier as he made his way from the back. He walked to the hostess stand and placed his order to go with a young waitress. The restaurant made the best pastrami on marbled rye and kettle chips in three states. If Mick'd had the time, he would have ordered a summer ale. The brewpub made a damn good summer ale.

The inside of the restaurant was decorated with beer posters from around the world, and sitting in a booth beneath a Thirsty Dog Wheat poster was the one woman he'd been fantasizing about tying up and tossing in a closet.

A big salad and an open folder sat on the table in front of Maddie Dupree. She'd pulled her hair back from her face and painted her lips a deep red. Her brown eyes looked up as he sat on the bench seat across from her. "You've been busy," he said.

"Hello, Mick." She waved a fork toward him. "Have a seat."

Her orange sweater was left unbuttoned up the front and she wore it over a white T-shirt. A tight white T-shirt. "I hear you've been talking to Bill Potter."

"News travels fast." She speared some lettuce and cheese and opened her mouth. Her red lips closed over the tines of the fork and she slowly pulled it back out of her mouth.

Mick pointed to the open folder. "Is that my rap sheet?"

She watched him as she chewed. "No," she said after she swallowed. "The sheriff mentioned that you were a pain in the ass, but he didn't mention a rap sheet." She closed the folder and put it on the seat beside her. "What did he arrest you for? Vandalism? Urinating in public? Window-peeking?"

Smart-ass. "Fighting, mostly."

"He mentioned a fire. You wouldn't know about that, would you?" She took a bite of her salad and washed it down with iced tea.

He smiled. "I don't know anything about any fires."

"Of course not." She set her fork on her plate, then sat back and folded her arms beneath her large breasts. Her T-shirt was so thin he could clearly see the white outline of her bra.

"Did you have a nice chat with Harriet Landers?"

She bit the side of her lip to keep from laughing. "It was interesting."

Mick sank down on the seat and lowered his brows. The toe of his boot brushed her foot and she tilted her head to one side. Like smooth shiny silk, her hair fell across one shoulder as she looked at him. For several moments she stared into his eyes before she sat up straight and pulled her feet back.

"Harriet screwed my grandfather to death in the back of her car," he said. "That's hardly a crime."

She pushed her plate aside and folded her arms on the table. "That's true, but it's juicy stuff."

"And you're going to write about it."

"I hadn't thought to mention your grandfather's . . . ill-timed departure." She turned her head a little to one side and looked at him out of the corners of her big brown eyes. "But I do need to fill pages with family background."

"Uh-huh."

"Or I could fill pages with photos."

He sat up, placed his elbows on the table, and leaned forward. "You want me to give you photos? Nice happy family Polaroids? Maybe at Christmas or Thanksgiving or the summer we all went to Yellowstone?"

She took a drink of her tea, then set it back down. "That would be great."

"Forget it. I can't be blackmailed."

"It's not blackmail. More like both of us getting what we want. And what I really want is to take pictures of the inside of Hennessy's."

He leaned even farther across the table and said, "How does it feel to want?" A waitress set his plastic sack of food on the table and he said without removing his gaze from Maddie, "Stay out of my bar."

She leaned toward him until his face was just a few inches from hers. "Or?"

She was gutsy as hell, and he almost liked that about her. Almost. He stood and reached into his back pocket for his wallet. He tossed a twenty on the table. "I'll throw you out on your ass."

Chapter 9

"Y ou're crazy."

"It'll be fine." Maddie looked over her shoulder at Adele and opened the door to Mort's.

"Didn't he say he was going to throw you out on your ass?"

"Technically, we were talk about Hennessy's."

They stepped inside and the door closed behind them. Adele leaned close to Maddie and asked above the noise and the music pouring from the jukebox, "Do you think he's going to care about technicalities?"

Maddie figured that was pretty much a rhetorical question and her gaze scanned the crowd inside the dimly lit bar, looking for the owner. It was eight-thirty on a Friday night and Mort's was once again packed. She'd had no intention of setting foot inside the cowboy bar again until Mick had told her not to. She had to let him know that he didn't intimidate her. He had to know she wasn't afraid of him. She wasn't afraid of anything.

She recognized Darla from the last time she'd been in Mort's and her neighbor Tanya from the Allegrezzas' party. She didn't see Mick and breathed a little easier. She wasn't afraid. She just wanted to get more than three feet inside the bar before he laid eyes on her.

Earlier, she'd curled her hair on big rollers that gave it lots of volume and loose curls. She wore more makeup than usual and a white cotton jersey halter dress and sandals with two-inch heels. If she was going to get escorted out, she wanted to look good on the way. She carried her red angora cardigan because she knew that as soon as the clock struck nine she would freeze without it.

The juke pumped out a song about redneck women as Adele and Maddie wove their way through the crowd toward an empty table in the corner. Adele, with her long curls, tight jeans, and SAVE A HORSE, RIDE A COWBOY shirt, drew her share of attention.

"Do you see him?" Adele asked as they slid into chairs facing the bar with their backs to the wall.

They'd gone over the plan. It was simple. Nothing risky: just walk into Mort's, have a few drinks, and walk out. Easy, cheesy, lemon squeezy, but now Adele was kind of acting spooked, casting her big-eyed gaze about as if she expected a SWAT team to swoop in, whip out their AK-47s, and force them spread-eagled on the floor.

"No. I don't see him yet." Maddie placed her purse on the table by her elbow and looked out at the bar. Light from the jukebox and bar poured over the crowd but hardly penetrated the corner. It was the perfect spot to see without being seen.

Adele leaned her head close to Maddie and asked, "What does he look like?"

She held up one hand and signaled the waitress. "Tall. Dark hair and very blue eyes," she answered. *Charming when he wants something, and his kiss could make a woman lose her mind.* Maddie thought about the day he'd brought her the Mouse Motel, about his kiss and his hands on her waist, and her stomach got a little tight. "If the women in the bar start flipping their hair and reaching for a breath mint, you'll know he's here."

A waitress with an atrocious perm, butt-tight Wranglers, and a Mort's T-shirt took their drink order.

"He's that prime?" Adele asked as the waitress walked away.

Maddie nodded. Prime was a fairly accurate description. He was certainly drool-worthy, and there had been a time or two when she'd been tempted to bite into him. Like when she'd looked up from her salad at the Willow Creek Brewpub and Restaurant and he'd been sitting across from her. One moment she'd been minding her own business, reading her latest notes from Sheriff Potter, then, poof, there was Mick looking extremely hot and incredibly pissed off. Normally, she wouldn't consider an angry man the least bit hot, but Mick wasn't a normal man. As he'd sat across from her, working himself up, warning her to stay out of his bar, his eyes had turned a deep, fascinating blue. And she'd found herself wondering what he'd do if she climbed across the table and planted her mouth on his. If she kissed his neck and bit him just below his ear.

"I talked to Clare today," Adele said and pulled Maddie's attention away from the contemplation of Mick. The two friends talked about the upcoming wedding until the waitress returned with Adele's Bitch on Wheels and Maddie's extra-dry vodka martini. The waitress might have bad hair, but she was damn fine at her job.

"What is up with some of these women's hair?" Adele asked as the waitress walked away.

Maddie's gaze scanned the crowd and she figured the ratio of bad hair vs. good hair was about fifty-fifty. "I've been trying to figure that out myself." Maddie raised her glass to her lips. "Half of them have good hair and the other half are an overprocessed mess." Over the rim of her glass, she continued her surveillance. There was still no sign of Mick.

"Did I tell you about the guy I dated last weekend?" Adele asked.

"No." Maddie put on her sweater and prepared for a dating disaster story.

"Well, he picked me up in a souped-up Pinto."

"Pinto? Aren't those the cars from the seventies that explode?"

"Yeah. It was bright orange, like a moving target, and he drove like he thought he was Jeff Gordon." Adele pushed several springy curls behind her ears. "He even wore those fingerless racing gloves."

"You have got to be shitting me. Where did you meet this guy?"

"At the raceway."

Maddie didn't ask what Adele had been doing at the raceway. She didn't want to know. "Tell me you didn't have sex with him."

"No. I figure a guy who drove that fast had to do other things fast too." Adele sighed. "I think I've been cursed with bad dates."

Maddie didn't believe in curses, but she couldn't disagree. Adele had the worst luck with men of any woman she'd ever known. And Maddie had had a lot of bad luck herself.

An hour and three more bad date stories later, there was still no sign of Mick. Maddie and Adele ordered another drink and she began to wonder if he just might not show up at all.

"Hello, ladies."

Maddie glanced up from her martini at the two guys standing in front of her. They were both tall and blond and very tan. The man who'd spoken had an Australian accent.

"Hello," Adele said and took a sip of her Bitch on Wheels. Adele might have a lot of bad dates, but that was only because she attracted a lot of men. With her golden curls and big aquamarine eyes, Adele seemed to draw men in like bees to a barbeque. Obviously Adele's mojo worked on all nationalities. Behind her glass, Maddie glanced at Adele and laughed.

"Would you like to sit down?" Adele asked.

They didn't have to be asked twice and slid into the two empty chairs. "M'names Ryan," the guy closest to Maddie introduced himself, flattening his vowels like he was Crocodile Dundee.

She set down her drink. "Maddie."

"That's Tom. He's m'mate." He pointed to his friend. "D'ya live in Truly?"

"Just moved here." Good Lord, she half expected him to say "G'day" and "Crickey." It was too dark to see the color of his eyes, but he was cute. "How about you?"

He scooted his chair closer so she could hear him better. "We're just here for the summer fightin' fires."

Foreign and cute. "Are you a smoke jumper?"

He nodded and went on to explain that the fire season in Australia was the exact opposite of the season in the U.S. As a result, a lot of Australian smoke jumpers worked in the American West during the summer. The longer he talked, the more fascinated Maddie became, not only by what he said but by the sound of his voice as he said it. And the longer he talked, the more Maddie began to wonder if this wasn't the perfect man for her to fall off the wagon with. He would be in Truly for a short time and then he'd leave. He wasn't wearing a wedding ring, but she knew that didn't mean anything. She leaned in a little closer and asked, "Are you married?" just to make sure. But before he could answer, two hands grasped the backs her arms and lifted her to her feet. She was turned slowly around until her gaze landed on a broad chest in a black Mort's T-shirt. Through the dark surrounding them, she recognized the chest even before she raised her gaze up a thick neck, strong chin, and compressed lips. She didn't have to see his eyes clearly to know they burned an angry blue.

Mick leaned close and said next to her ear, "What are you doing here?"

He smelled like soap and skin. "Apparently I'm talking to you."

One of his hands slid to hers and grasped her like a hot vice. "Let's go."

She grabbed her purse from the table and looked over her shoulder at Ryan, then Adele. "I'll be right back," she hollered.

"You sound sure about that," said the man hauling her through the crowd toward the back of Mort's. "Excuse us," she said as she bumped into Darla. He kept a tight grip on her hand as he just kind of moved through the crowd like a linebacker. She was forced to issue a "Pardon me" and another "Excuse us" over the music pouring from the juke. They walked past the end of the bar, down a short hall, and he pulled her behind him into a small room.

He closed the door and dropped her hand. "I told you to stay out of my bar."

In one quick glance, Maddie's gaze took in an oak desk, a coatrack, a big metal safe, and a leather sofa. "You were talking about Hennessy's at the time."

"No. I wasn't." His gaze narrowed and she could practically feel anger rolling off him in waves. "Because I'm a nice guy, I'm going to give you the option of grabbing your friend and walking out the front door."

Once again, she didn't fear his anger. Instead, she almost liked the way it turned his eyes kind of fierce, and she leaned back against the door. "Or?"

"I'll toss you out on your ass."

She tilted her head to the side. "Then I should probably warn you that, if you touch me again, I have a Taser and I'll shoot fifty thousand volts in *your* ass."

He blinked. "You pack a Taser?"

"Among other things."

Again he blinked, kind of slow, like he couldn't believe he'd heard her right. "What things?"

"Pepper spray. Brass knuckles. A hundred-and-twenty-five-decibel screecher alarm. Handcuffs and a Kubaton."

"Is it even legal to pack a Taser?"

"It's legal in forty-eight states. This is Idaho. What do you think?"

"You're crazy."

She smiled. "So I've been told."

He stared at her for several moments before he asked, "Do you make it a habit of running around pissing people off?"

She occasionally did make people mad, but she never made a habit of it. "No."

"Then it's just me."

"I don't mean to make you mad, Mick."

One dark brow rose up his tan forehead.

"Well, I didn't mean to make you mad before tonight. But I kind of have a little problem with being told what I can and can't do."

"No shit." He folded his arms across his wide chest. "Why do you need all that stuff?"

"I interview people who aren't very nice." She shrugged. "They're usually in belly chains and leg irons and cuffed to a table when I talk to them, though. Or we talk through Plexiglas. Of course, prisons never let me take in my safety devices, but I always get them back when I leave. I feel safer when I'm packing."

He took a step back and his gaze raked her up and down. "You look normal. But you're not."

Maddie didn't know whether to take that as a compliment or not. He probably didn't mean it as a compliment, though.

He rocked back on his heels and looked down at her. "Were you planning on zapping the blond guy coming on to you in the corner?"

"Ryan? No, but if he plays his cards right, I might cuff him."

"He's a tool."

If she didn't know better, she'd think he was jealous. "Do you know him?"

"I don't have to know him to know he's a tool."

Which made no sense at all. "How can you say someone's a tool if you don't know him?"

Instead of answering, he said, "You were practically tongue-kissing him."

"That's ridiculous. I haven't made out with a stranger in a bar since college."

"Maybe you're tired of being 'kind of sexually abstinent.'"

That was an understatement. She was really tired of it, but when she thought of having hot, down-and-dirty, animal sex, she thought of Mick. Ryan was cute, but ultimately he was a stranger in a bar, and she no longer made out or picked up strangers in bars. "Don't worry about my celibacy."

His gaze slid to her mouth and lower, down her

chin and throat, and got hung up on her breasts. It was past nine, so of course she was cold. "Honey, your body isn't made for celibacy." Her hard nipples made two sharp points in the front of her dress. "It's made for sex." He raised his gaze to hers. "Lots of rough, sweaty sex that lasts all night long and into the next morning."

Normally she might have been tempted to Mace a guy for saying that, but when Mick said it, she felt hot little tugs in her stomach and her body urged her to raise her hand to volunteer for sweaty sex duty. "Celibacy is a state of mind."

"Which explains why you've gone insane."

"Now who's the tool?" She adjusted her purse to keep it from falling off her shoulder, but her fingers barely touched the bag before Mick pinned her wrists to the door beside her head.

She looked up into his face an inch above hers. "What are you doing?"

"I'm not going to just stand here and let you shoot my ass with fifty thousand volts."

She tried not to smile and failed. "I was adjusting my bag on my shoulder."

"Call me paranoid, but I don't believe you."

"You really thought I was going to zap you?" Zapping him had been the furthest thing from her mind.

"You weren't?"

She chuckled. "No. You're too pretty to get shot with fifty thousand volts."

"I'm not pretty." He let out a breath and it touched the side of her face and neck. "You smell like strawberries."

"It's my lotion."

"You smelled like strawberries that day in Handy Man Hardware." He buried his nose in her hair and she was so shocked, she felt like *she'd* been zapped. "You always smell so good. It's been driving me crazy." He pressed the length of his body into hers. "When I saw you across the bar, I wanted to do this." He lowered his face to the side of her throat.

"I thought you wanted to toss me out on my ass." How had it suddenly gotten so hot? A few minutes ago, she'd been cold. Now she felt hot little tingles rushing across her skin.

"I'll get to that. Later." He let go of her hands, but his hips held hers against the door. He'd definitely dressed left. He was long and hard and a dull ache settled between her thighs. Harriet had been right. The Hennessy men were blessed. "First I wanted to smell you right here." He pushed her sweater away and kissed her bare shoulder. "Where you're soft and taste good."

"I like soft skin." She took a shallow breath and closed her eyes. She wanted him to taste a little lower. "I'm kind of a hedonist that way."

"How can you be a hedonist and celibate?" he asked against her neck.

"It's not easy." And becoming more difficult by the second. If she wasn't careful, her hedonist side would rule her celibate side, and she would go down in a blaze of orgasmic glory. Which didn't sound so horrible. Just not with him. She lifted her hand to the side of his face and brushed her thumb across the slight stubble of his cheek. "Especially when you're around."

He chuckled. A low masculine sound that came from the center of his chest. He raised his face and his gaze had gone all half-mast with lust and his lashes looked very long. Desire shone bright in his eyes and his hands moved to her waist.

"You're the last man on the planet I can have." She raised her mouth to his and he lifted his weight. "And the one I want most."

"Ain't life a bitch," he whispered against her lips.

She nodded and rose to the balls of her feet. Her hand slid to the back of his head and she pressed her mouth to his. His hands on her waist tightened, and for several agonizing heartbeats, he remained perfectly still, his warm palms glued to her waist, his mouth against hers. Then a deep groan sounded low in his throat, and he slid one hand to the small of her back and the other between her shoulders on the outside of her sweater. He brought her against his chest and he kissed her. Soft, sweet. His lips created a delicious suction and he drew her tongue into his mouth, his cheeks sucking lightly.

Maddie's purse fell to the floor and she moved her free hand up the hard muscles of his arm and shoulder. Heat radiated from him and warmed her breasts where she was pressed against his chest. Maddie had never been a passive lover, and while he sweetly made love to her mouth, her fingers combed through his hair and her free palm roamed the hard contours of his chest and back. If he wasn't Mick Hennessy, she would have pulled his shirt from his Levi's and felt his bare skin.

Mick slid his mouth to the side of her throat. "You're the last woman I should want," he said between short gasps. "The only woman I can't stop thinking about." His hands moved to cup her behind and her hips cradled his erection. "What is it about you that drives me so crazy?" Pressed against her lower belly, he was enormous and so hard the pressure against her pelvis almost hurt.

Almost. She rocked against him as he pushed her sweater down her arms. He tossed the red angora somewhere behind him, but she didn't need it. She was too hot. Her fingers curled in the front of his shirt and her mouth moved to his neck. He tasted good beneath her tongue. Like warm flesh and aroused man, and she sucked his skin. She grasped handfuls of shirt and swayed against his stiff penis. It had been four years since she'd felt anything so delectable, and she'd missed it. She'd missed the touch of a man's hands, his hot mouth, and the sounds of arousal deep in his throat.

His fingers found the bow at the back of her neck and he tugged until her halter came untied in his hands. He pulled down the white straps as his lips once again sought hers. This time there was nothing soft or sweet in his kiss. It was all carnal and feeding, with hungry mouths and tongues, and she ate it up. She could have stopped him. She didn't want him to stop. Not yet. Not when she wanted more. The top of her dress slid to her waist and Mick's hands cupped her breast through the white strapless bustier. Underwires and metal corseting kept her double-Ds front and center, and his thumbs brushed her nipples through the stiff cotton. She pressed her belly against him, touching the aching places, and he groaned into her mouth. She was so hot, dizzy. Her skin tingled, her breasts felt heavy and her nipples painfully tight. It had been so long since she'd felt such delicious pleasure, and she slid her hand down his chest, over the waistband of his jeans, and pressed her palm against his turgid erection.

"Touch me," he groaned into her mouth. And she did. While his fingers brushed her nipples through her corset, she slid her hand up and down the length of him, from the bottom of his zipper up the long rock-hard length to the swollen tip. The man had heft, and the wet ache between her thighs urged her to take one of his hands and slide it between her legs, to cup her crotch, and touch her through her panties and . . . She dropped her hands. "Stop!"

He raised his head. "In a minute."

In a minute she'd be in the throes of orgasm. "No." She took a step back and his hands fell to his sides. "You know we can't do this. We can't ever have sex." She kept her gaze on his as she tied her dress behind her neck. "Not together."

He shook his head and his eyes looked a little wild. "I've been rethinking that."

"There's nothing to rethink." He was Mick

Hennessy and she was Maddie Jones. "Believe me, you're the last man on earth I can have sex with, and I'm the last woman you should have sex with."

"Right now I can't remember why."

She should tell him. All of it. Who she really was and who he was to her. "Because . . ." She licked her lips and swallowed, her throat suddenly dry. Sexual tension pulled between them, an almost irresistible hot pulsing force. His neck was red from where she'd marked him, and he looked at her through blue eyes all shiny with lust. The last thing she wanted was to see all that fiery need replaced with disgust. Not now. Later. "Because I'm writing a book about your parents and Alice Jones, and making love to you won't change that. It will only make it worse."

He took a few steps back and sat on the edge of his desk. He took a deep breath and ran his fingers through the sides of his hair. "I forgot about that." His hands fell to his sides. "For a few minutes, I forgot you're in town to dig up the past and make my life hell."

Maddie bent down and picked up her purse. "I'm sorry." And she was, but being sorry didn't change anything. She almost wished it did.

"Not sorry enough to stop."

"No," she said and reached for the door handle behind her. "Not that sorry."

"How long, Maddie?"

"What do you mean?"

He took a deep breath and let it out. "How long are you going to be in town messing with my life?"

Good question. "I don't know. Next spring, maybe."

He looked down at his feet. "Shit."

She slid her purse on her shoulder and looked across at him, sitting there with his dark hair sticking out from being finger-combed. She resisted the urge to smooth his hair.

He lifted his gaze. "Obviously, we can't be within ten feet of each other without tearing at each other's clothes. And since telling you to stay out of my bars is like waving a red flag in the face of a bull, I'm going to ask you to stay the hell out of my bars."

Her chest did some sort of constrict-and-expand thing, which was not only impossible, but alarming. "You won't see me in here again," she assured him and opened the door. She stepped out into the bar, with its loud country music and beer smells, and wove her way toward Adele. When she'd first entered Mort's she'd wondered if Mick would throw her out on her ass as he'd threatened.

Now she wondered if it wouldn't have been better if he had.

Mick shut the door to his office and leaned back against it. He closed his eyes and pressed a palm against his aching erection. If Maddie hadn't stopped him, he would have slid his hand up her thigh. He would have pulled off her panties and had sex with her right there, against the door. He would like to think he'd have had the presence of mind to lock the door first, but he wouldn't bet on it.

He dropped his hand and circled his desk. Her red sweater was thrown on the floor and he picked it up before sitting in his chair to stare at the safe across the office from him. Earlier, looking across his bar and seeing Maddie sitting at a table, sipping a martini as if he hadn't told her to stay out of his bars, had shocked the hell right out of him. Shocked him like that Taser she carried in her purse. On the heels of all that shock came a big dose of anger and an urge to smell the side of her neck.

Seeing her chatting it up with the Aussie, he'd felt something else too. Something a little uncomfortable. Something that felt a bit like he wanted to rip the man's head off. Which was absolutely ridiculous. Mick didn't have anything against the Aussie, and he certainly didn't have any sort of relationship with Maddie Dupree. He didn't feel anything for her. Well, except anger. And raging lust. A burning desire to bury his nose in the side of her neck while he buried himself between her soft thighs. Again and again.

There was something about Maddie. Something other than her beautiful body and pretty face. Something beyond the scent of her skin and her smart mouth. Something that drew his gaze across a crowded bar to a table in a dark corner. Something that recognized her dark outline as if he knew her. Some indefinable thing that made him kiss her and touch her and hold her tight against his chest as if that's where she belonged, when in reality, she didn't belong anywhere near him. A fact he tended to forget when she *was* near him.

He brought the sweater to his face. It smelled like her. Sweet, like strawberries, and he tossed it onto his desk.

A few weeks ago, his life had been fairly good. He had a plan for the future that didn't include thinking about his past. A past that he'd done a pretty good job of forgetting.

Until now. Until Maddie had driven her black Mercedes into town and run his life off the road.

Chapter 10

It took Maddie a little over a week to track down her mother's friend and neighbor from the Roundup Trailer Court. Shortly after her mother's death, Trina Olsen-Hays sold her trailer and moved to Ontario, Oregon. She'd married a fireman in the mid-'80s, had three grown children, and two grandchildren. Now, sitting across from her at a local café, Maddie had a slight recollection of the plump woman with red poufy hair, freckles, and painted-on eyebrows. She remembered staring at those brows and being somewhat frightened. Seeing Trina also brought back the fuzzy memory of a pink polka-dot quilt. She didn't know why or what it meant. Just that she'd felt warm and secure wrapped up in it.

"Alice was a real nice girl," Trina said over coffee and pecan pie. "Young."

Maddie glanced at the tape recorder sitting on the table between them, then returned her gaze to Trina. "She was twenty-four."

"We used to share a bottle of wine and talk about the future. I wanted to see the world. Alice just wanted to get married." Trina shook her head and took a bite of pie. "Maybe because she had a little girl. I don't know, but she just wanted to find a man, get married, and have more kids."

Maddie hadn't known that her mother thought about having other children, but she supposed it made sense. If her mother had lived, she'd no doubt have a brother or sister or both. Not for the first time, she was struck by how different her life would have been if not for Rose Hennessy. Maddie loved her life. She loved the woman she'd become. She wouldn't change it for anything, but sometimes she did wonder about how differently she might have turned out.

"Did you know either Loch or Rose Hennessy?" As she looked across the table at Trina, she wondered if her mother would have time-warp hair or if she would have kept up with changing styles.

"They were older than me, but I knew them both. Rose was . . . unpredictable." Trina took a drink of her coffee. "And Loch was a natural-born charmer. It was really no wonder Alice fell in love with him. I mean, everyone did. Even though most of us knew better."

"Do you know how Loch felt about Alice?"

"Only that she thought he was going to leave his wife and family for her." Trina shrugged one shoulder. "But every woman he ever got involved with thought that too. Only Loch never did. Sure, he had affairs, but he never left Rose."

"Then what do you think made the affair between Loch and Alice different? What set Rose over the edge and made her load a gun and drive to Hennessy's that night?"

Trina shook her head. "I always figured she'd finally had enough."

Maybe.

"Or it could have been that Alice was so much younger and prettier than the others. Who knows? What I remember most was how quickly Alice fell in love with Loch. You wouldn't believe how fast it was before she was madly in love."

After reading her mother's diaries, Maddie actually could believe it.

Trina took another bite of pie and her gaze dropped to Maddie's mouth as she chewed. Her painted brows lowered and she looked up into

Maddie's eyes. "I recognize your mouth. You're Alice's little girl, aren't you?"

Maddie nodded. It was almost a relief to have it out.

Trina smiled. "Well, how about that? I've always wondered what happened to you after your aunt took you away."

"She was my great-aunt and I moved to Boise with her. She died last spring. That's when I came across my mother's diaries and your name."

Trina reached across the table and patted Maddie's hand. The touch felt cool and a bit awkward. "Alice would be very proud of you."

Maddie liked to think so, but she would never know for sure.

"So, are you married? Have any kids?"

"No."

Trina patted her hand one last time, then reached for her fork. "You're still young. There's time."

Maddie changed the subject. "I have a faint memory of a polka-dot quilt. Do you recall anything about that?"

"Hmm." She took a bite and looked up at the ceiling in thought. "Yes." She returned her gaze to Maddie and smiled. "Alice made it for you, and she used to roll you all up in it like—"

"A burrito," Maddie finished as a recollection of

her mother whispered across her memory. *You're my polka-dot burrito.* If Maddie were an emotional woman, the little pinch to her heart would have brought tears to her eyes. But Maddie had never been an emotional person, and she could count on one hand the number of times she'd cried as an adult. She didn't consider herself a cold person, but she'd learned early on that tears never changed a thing.

She interviewed Trina for another forty-five minutes before packing up her notes and tape recorder and heading for Boise. She had another bridesmaid dress fitting that afternoon, and she met her friends at Nan's Bridal before grabbing a late lunch with them and heading home to Truly.

She stopped at the Value Rite to pick up some toilet paper and a six-pack of Diet Coke. The drugstore had a display of wind chimes and hummingbird feeders and she chose a simple chime made of green tubes. She'd never had a hummingbird feeder, and she reached for one and read the instructions. It was silly, really. More than likely she wouldn't be living in Truly next summer. No use in making the house homey. She placed the feeder in the cart next to her Coke. She could always take it with her when she sold the place. She'd bought the house as an investment. She was one woman. One woman did not need two homes, but she supposed there was no hurry to sell.

Carleen Dawson stood in the dog food aisle shelving collars and leashes and talking to a woman with long black hair. Maddie smiled as she wheeled her cart past and Carleen stopped in midsentence.

"That's her," she heard Carleen say. She kept on walking until she felt a hand on her arm.

"Just one minute."

She turned and looked into a pair of green eyes. The tiny hairs on the back of her neck tingled as if she should know her. The woman wore some kind of uniform as if she worked in a restaurant or diner. "Yes?"

The woman dropped her hand. "I'm Meg Hennessy and you're writing about my parents."

Meg. That's how she knew her. From photos of Rose. If Mick was the image of Loch, Meg looked a lot like her mother. The tingles on the back of her neck spread down her spine as if she were looking into the eyes of a killer. Her mother's killer, but of course Meg was as innocent as she was herself. "That's right."

"I've read your books before. You write about serial killers. The real sensational stuff. My mother wasn't a serial killer."

Maddie didn't want to do this here. Not in the middle of a drugstore with Carleen looking on. "Perhaps you'd like to talk about this somewhere else."

Meg shook her head and her dark hair swung about her shoulders. "My mother was a good person."

That was open for debate, but not in the middle of Value Rite. "I'm writing a fair account of what happened." And she was. She'd written some hard truths about her mother that she could have easily glossed over.

"I hope so. I know Mick doesn't want to talk to you about this. I understand how he feels, but you're obviously going to write this book with or without our input." She dug around in her purse and pulled out a pen and a silver gum wrapper. "I don't get why you think my parents' deaths are worthy of a novel, but you do," she said as she wrote on the white side of the gum wrapper. "But call me if you have questions."

Maddie wasn't easily shocked, but when Meg handed her the wrapper, she was so stunned that she didn't know what to say. She glanced at the telephone number and folded the paper in half.

"You've probably talked to that waitress's relatives." Meg shoved her pen back inside her purse and her black hair fell across her pale cheek. "I'm sure they told you lies about my family."

"Alice only has one living relative. Her daughter."

Meg looked up and pushed her hair behind one ear. "I don't know what she could tell you. Nobody around here even remembers her. She probably turned out just like her home-wrecking mother."

Maddie's grasp tightened on the handle of her shopping cart, but she managed a pleasant smile. "She's as much like her mother as I imagine you are like yours."

"I'm nothing like my mother." Meg stood up straighter and her voice got a bit more strident. "My mother killed her cheating husband. I divorced mine."

"Too bad your mother didn't consider divorce a better option."

"Sometimes a person is pushed too far."

Bullshit. Maddie had heard that excuse from every sociopath she'd ever interviewed. The old "she pushed me too far so I stabbed her a hundred and fifty times" excuse. She slid the gum wrapper into her pants pocket and asked, "What was it about your father's affair with Alice Jones that pushed your mother too far?"

Maddie expected the same response she'd gotten every time she asked that question. A shrug of the shoulders. Instead Meg got busy digging in her purse once more. She pulled out a set of keys and folded her arms across her chest.

"I don't know." She shook her head.

She's lying. Maddie looked into Meg's green eyes and Meg turned her gaze to bags of Purina ONE and Beggin' Strips. She knew something. Something she didn't want to talk about.

"Only three people know what really happened that night. My dad, my mom, and that waitress. They're all dead." Meg stuck one finger through the ring and closed her fingers around the keys. "But if you want to know the truth about my mom and dad's life, call me and I'll clear things up for you," she said and turned to walk away.

"Thank you. I will," Maddie answered even though she wasn't a bit fooled by Meg's eagerness to help, and she doubted that she'd get the entire truth about Rose and Loch's life. She'd get Meg's version, which Maddie was sure would be shaded and glossed over.

She pushed her cart to the checkout line and put her items on the counter. Mick had mentioned that his sister could be difficult. Did she suffer the same mental instability as Rose? Maddie had felt Meg's hostility and resentment toward Maddie's mother and even herself. Meg had refused to even say Alice's name, but she knew something about that night. Maddie was sure of it. Whatever it was, Maddie would find out. She'd extracted secrets from people a hell of a lot smarter and with more to lose than Meg Hennessy.

When Maddie walked into the house after being gone all day, the carcass of a dead mouse greeted her. Last week, Ernie's Pest Control had finally made it out and laid bait. As a result, Maddie kept finding dead mice all over the place. She set her Value Rite bags on the kitchen counter, then tore off some paper towels. She grabbed the mouse by its tail and carried it outside to the garbage cans.

"What're you doing?"

Maddie looked over her shoulder, into the deep shadows created by towering ponderosas, and her gaze landed on two boys dressed up like mini-commandos.

She held up the mouse. "Throwing this in the trash."

Travis Hennessy scratched his cheek with the barrel of a green Nerf gun. "Did its head pop off?"

"Sorry. No."

"Bummer."

She dropped the carcass into the garbage.

"My mom and dad are going to Boise," Pete informed her. " 'Cause my aunt had her babies."

Maddie turned and looked at Pete. "Really? That's great news."

"Yeah, and Pete is spending the night at my house."

"My dad's taking us to Travis's in three shakes. He says my uncle Nick needs a drink." Pete loaded his plastic camouflaged rifle with an orange rubber dart. "The babies' names are Isabel and Lilly."

"Do you know if—"

Louie called for the boys and interrupted Maddie. "See ya," they said in unison, then turned on the heels of their sneakers and took off through the trees.

" 'Bye." She replaced the garbage can lid and walked back into the house. She washed her hands and disinfected the floor where she'd found the carcass. It was after seven and she threw a chicken breast on her George Foreman Grill. She made a salad and drank two glasses of wine with her meal. She'd had a long day, and after she ate and put the dishes in the dishwasher, she changed out of her clothes and into a pair of blue Victoria's Secret lounging pants with the word PINK printed across her butt. She zipped up a blue hooded sweatshirt and pulled her hair back in a ponytail.

A yellow legal pad sat on her desk, and she grabbed it before turning on a few lamps and relaxing on her sofa. As she reached for the remote, she thought about Meg and their conversation in the middle of Value Rite. If Meg had lied about knowing what had set her mother off, she'd lie about other things too. Things that Maddie might not be able to prove or disprove.

Cold Case Files on A&E flashed on the television screen and Maddie tossed the remote on the sofa beside her. She put her feet up on the coffee table and jotted down her impressions of Meg. Then she wrote a list of questions she intended to ask and got as far as "What do you recall about the night your parents died?" when the doorbell rang.

It was nine-thirty, and she looked through the peephole at the only man who'd ever been in her house or stood on her porch. It had been over a week since she'd kissed Mick inside his office at Mort's. Eight days since he'd untied her dress and made her ache for him. Tonight he wasn't wearing his happy face, but her body didn't seem to mind.

A sharp tug pulled deep in the pit of her belly as she opened the door.

"I just talked to Meg," he said as he stood there with his hands on his hips, all male belligerence and seething testosterone.

"Hello, Mick."

"I thought I made it clear that you stay away from my sister."

"And I thought I made it clear that I don't take orders from you." Maddie folded her arms beneath her breasts and simply looked at him. The first pale shadows of night painted him in a faint gray light and made his eyes appear a startling blue. Too bad he was so bossy.

They stared at each other for several prolonged moments before he dropped his hands to his sides and said, "Are we going to stand here all night staring at each other? Or are you going to invite me in?"

"Maybe." She'd invite him in eventually, but she wasn't going to be all happiness and sunshine about it. "Are you going to be rude?"

"I'm never rude."

She lifted a brow.

"I'll try to be nice."

Which was kind of half-assed, Maddie thought. "Are you going to *try* and keep your tongue out of my mouth?"

"That depends. Are you going to keep your hands off my dick?"

"Jerk." She turned and walked into the living room, leaving him to let himself in.

The yellow legal pad sat face up on the coffee table and she turned it over as he came into the room.

"I know Meg told you to call her."

Maddie reached for the remote and turned off _Cold Case._ "Yes, she did."

"You can't."

She straightened. It was so typical of him to think he could tell her what to do. He stood in her house, tall and imposing, as if he were king of _her_ castle. "I thought you might have learned by now that I don't follow your orders."

"This isn't a game, Maddie." He wore a black Mort's polo shirt tucked into a pair of Levi's resting low on his hips. "You don't know Meg. You don't know how she gets."

"Then why don't you tell me?"

"Right," he scoffed. "So you can write about her in your book?"

"I told you that I'm not writing about you or your sister." She sat on the arm of the sofa and put one foot on the coffee table. "Frankly, Mick, you're just not that interesting." Lord, that was such a lie she was surprised her nose didn't grow.

He looked down at her. "Uh-huh."

She placed a hand on her chest. "I stayed away from Meg just like you wanted me to, but she approached me. I didn't approach her."

"I know that."

"She's a grown woman. Older than you, and she can certainly decide whether or not to talk to me."

He moved to the French doors and looked out at the deck and the lake beyond. Light from the lamp near the sofa touched his shoulder and the side of his face. "She might be older, but she's not always predictable." He was silent a few moments, then he turned his head and looked at her over his shoulder. His voice changed: gone was the demanding tone when he asked, "How do you know my mother's footprints were all over the bar that night? Is it in a police report?"

Maddie slowly rose. "Yes."

She barely heard his next question. "What else?"

"There are photographs of her footprints."

"Jesus." He shook his head. "I meant, what else was in the report?"

"The usual. Everything from time of arrival to positions of the bodies."

"How long did my father live?"

"About ten minutes."

He rested his weight on one foot and folded his arms across his big chest. He was silent for several more seconds before he said, "She could have called an ambulance and maybe saved his life."

"She could have."

Across the short distance, he looked at her. This time a wealth of emotion burned in his blue eyes. "Ten minutes is a long time for a wife to watch her husband suffer and bleed to death."

She took a few steps toward him. "Yes."

"Who called the police?"

"Your mother did. Right before she shot herself."

"So she made sure my father and the waitress were dead before she called."

Maddie stopped. "The waitress had a name."

"I know." A sad smile curved one corner of his lips. "Growing up, my grandmother always called her 'the waitress.' It's just a habit."

"You didn't know any of this?"

He shook his head. "My grandmother didn't talk about things that were unpleasant. Believe me, my mother murdering my father and Alice Jones were at the top of the list of things we didn't talk about." He turned his gaze outside. "And you have photographs."

"Yes."

"Here?"

She thought about her answer and decided to tell the truth. "Yes."

"What else?"

"Besides the police reports and crime scene photos, I have interviews, newspaper accounts, diagrams, and the coroner's report."

Mick opened the French doors and stepped outside. Soaring ponderosa pines cast black shadows across the deck, chasing away the muted grays of dusk. A slight breeze scented the night with pine and lifted strands of Mick's hair where it touched his forehead. "I went to the library when I was about ten, thinking I'd get a look at old newspaper reports, but the librarian was a friend of my grandmother's. So I left."

"Have you seen any accounts of that night?"

"No."

"Would you like to see them?"

He shook his head. "No. I don't have a lot of memories of my parents, and reading about what happened that night would ruin those that I do have."

She didn't have a lot of memories of her mother either. Recently, with the help of the diaries, a few had come back. "Maybe not."

He laughed without humor. "Until you blew

into town, I didn't know that my mother watched my father die. I didn't know she hated him that much."

"She probably didn't hate him. Both love and hate are very powerful emotions. People kill the people they love all the time. I don't understand it, but I know that it happens."

"That isn't love. It's something else." He walked to the dark edge of the deck and his hands gripped the wood railing. Across the lake, the moon began to rise over the mountains and reflected a perfect mirror image into the smooth water. "Until you came to town, everything was buried in the past where it belonged. Then you started digging and prying and it's all anybody around here can talk about now. Just like when I was growing up."

She moved toward him and leaned her butt into the rail. She folded her arms beneath her breasts and looked up into the darkening outline of his face. She was so close, his hand rested next to her behind on the railing. "Other than in your own house, I take it the subject of your mother and father used to come up a lot."

"You could say that."

"Is that why you fought all the time?"

He looked into her eyes and laughed without sound. "Maybe I just liked fighting."

"Or maybe you didn't like people saying un-kind things about your family."

"You think you know me. You think you have me all figured out."

She shrugged one shoulder. Yeah, she knew him. In some regards, she imagined they'd lived mirror lives. "I think it must have been hell to live in a town where everyone knows that your mother killed your father and his young lover. Children can be very cruel. That's not just a cliché, it's true. Believe me, I know. Kids are mean."

The breeze blew a few long strands of hair across Maddie's cheek and Mick raised a hand and brushed them from her face. "What did they do? Not pick you for kickball?"

"I didn't get picked for anything. I was a little pudgy."

He pushed her hair behind her ear. "A little?"

"A lot."

"How much did you weigh?"

"I don't know, but in the sixth grade I got a re-ally awesome pair of black boots. My calves were too big and I couldn't zip them up all the way. So I folded them down, deluding myself that every-one would think they were supposed to be worn that way. They weren't fooled and I never wore the boots again. That was the year they started calling me Cincinnati Maddie. At first I was just so happy they weren't calling me Fattie Maddie anymore. Then I found out why they called me that and I wasn't so happy." Through the dusky space that separated them, he raised an inquiring dark brow and she explained, "They said I was so fat because I ate Cincinnati."

"The little bastards." He dropped his hand. "No wonder you're so ornery."

Was she ornery? Maybe. "What's your excuse?"

She felt his gaze touch her face for several moments before he answered, "I'm not as ornery as you."

"Right," she scoffed.

"Well, I wasn't until you moved to town."

"Long before I moved to town you were giving Sheriff Potter hell."

"Growing up in this town was sometimes hell."

"I can imagine."

"No, you can't." He took a deep breath and let it out. "People have wondered my whole life if I was going to lose it like my mom and kill someone. Or if I'd grow up and be like my dad. That's a hard thing for a kid to live with."

"Do you ever worry about that?"

He shook his head. "No. I never do. My mother's problem, one of them, was that she never should have put up with a guy who repeatedly cheated on her. And my old man's problem was he never should have married at all."

"So your solution is to avoid marriage?"

"That's right." He sat beside her on the railing and took her hand into his. "Kind of like you solved your fat problem by avoiding carbs."

"It's different. I'm a hedonist and I have to avoid more than just carbs." At the moment, her hedonist nature felt the warmth of his palm spread up her arm and across her chest.

"You're avoiding sex too."

"Yes, and if I fall off either of those wagons, it could get ugly."

"How ugly?"

He was suddenly too close and she stood. "I'd binge."

"On sex?"

She tried to pull her hand away, but he tightened his grasp. "Or carbs."

He grabbed the bottom of her sweatshirt with his free hand. "On sex?"

"Yeah."

Through the darkness that separated them, he flashed a white seductive smile. "How ugly will you get?" Slowly, he drew her toward him until she stood between his thighs.

The warmth of his hand, the touch of his thighs, and his wicked smile conspired to pull her in, suck out her will to resist, and shove her headfirst off the wagon. Her breasts felt heavy, her skin tight, and the relentless ache that Mick had created the first time he had kissed her hit her now, sharp, painful, and overwhelming.

"You don't want to know."

"Yeah," he said. "I think I do."

Chapter 11

I thought you were going to keep your tongue out of my mouth."

Mick glanced up into Maddie's face bathed in moonlight, and he reached for the zipper on the front of her sweatshirt. "I guess I'll just have to put my tongue somewhere other than your mouth." He pulled the zipper down, and the sweatshirt parted to give him a glimpse of her deep cleavage. She wasn't wearing anything beneath, and his testicles tightened as the pale swells of her naked breasts were revealed a few inches from his face.

"Someone will see us," she said and grabbed his wrist.

"The Allegrezzas are in Boise." He pulled until the zipper parted at her waist.

"What about the neighbors on the other side?" she asked, but she didn't stop him from pushing the edges of the sweatshirt aside. Her breasts were firm and pale white in the moonlight, her puckered nipples an erotic outline in the darkness.

"No one is out, but even if they were, it's too dark to see anything." He slid his hands around her waist to the small of her back and brought her closer. "No one can see me do this." He bent forward to kiss her belly. "Or this." He kissed her cleavage.

"Mick."

"Yeah?"

She combed her fingers through the sides of his hair; her nails scrapping his scalp sent a tingling pleasure down his spine. She took short choppy breaths and said, "We probably shouldn't do this."

"Do you want me to stop?"

"No."

"Good. I've found a place to put my tongue." He opened his mouth and rolled her puckered nipple beneath his tongue. She smelled like sugar cookies tonight and she tasted a bit like sugar cookies too.

"Mmm," she moaned and pulled him closer. "That feels good, Mick. It's been so long." She was a talker, but then, he could have guessed that about her. "Don't stop."

Mick had no intention of stopping, not when he was doing exactly what he'd wanted to do to her since the day he saw her at the hardware store. He slid one hand from around her back to cup her breast. "You're a beautiful woman." He pulled back far enough to look up into her face, at her parted lips and the desire shining in her dark eyes. "I want to put my tongue all over you. Starting here." He sucked her into his mouth and drew lightly. Her flesh puckered even more and he loved the feel and the taste of her. His palm cupping her breast moved down her smooth flat stomach and slid beneath her loose pants. Since that night he'd kissed her at Mort's, he'd had wild fantasies of what he'd do to her if he got her alone again. He slipped his hand between her thighs and cupped her through her thin panties. She was incredibly hot, and wet, and lust twisted and tightened painfully in his groin. He wanted her. He wanted her as he hadn't wanted a woman in a very long time. He'd tried to stay away from her, but at the first excuse to see her, here he was with his mouth on her breast and his hand in her pants, and he wasn't going anywhere this time until he satisfied the lust pounding through his body.

She wanted him and he was beyond ready to give her what she wanted. He wasn't going anywhere until both of them were too exhausted to move.

"Yes, Mick," she said just above a whisper, "touch me there." Her sweatshirt fell to her feet and he pulled back to look up past her breasts and into her face. He slid his fingers beneath her panties and stood.

"Right here?" He parted her slick flesh and touched her there. She was incredibly wet, and he wanted to put more than his fingers there.

"Yes." Her breathing was rapid and her hands clung to his shoulders.

"I love knowing I get you this wet," he said just above her mouth. "I want to use my tongue on you." He brushed his fingers across her small feminine bump. "Here." She nodded. "You don't mind, do you?" She shook her head, then nodded, and then combined the two.

"Mick," she whispered as her grasp on his shoulders tightened. "If you don't stop . . ." She sucked in a breath. "Oh, my God, don't stop," she moaned as a powerful orgasm buckled her knees. He wrapped an arm around her waist to keep her from falling as his fingers touched and stroked and felt her pleasure in his hand. He kissed the side of her throat and ached to be inside her, feeling her tight walls gripping him with each pulsation.

When it was through, she said, "I didn't mean for that to happen."

He pulled his hand from her pants and pressed his erection into her. "Let's make it happen again. Only next time, I'm going to join you." He brushed his wet fingers across the tip of her breast and lowered his mouth to her lips and fed her his need and greed and uncontrolled lust.

She pulled back from the kiss and gasped. "You have condoms? Right?"

"Yes."

Bare from the waist up, she took his hand and led him into the house. "How many do you have on you?"

How many? How many? "Two. How many do you have?"

"None. I've been celibate." She closed the door behind them, then turned to face him. "We're going to have to make those two condoms last all night."

"What do you have planned?"

She pushed him against the closed door, pulled his shirt over his head, and tossed it aside. "Something you should not have started." She took control and her impatience got him so hard, he thought he might burst the buttons on his Levi's. "But something you *are* going to finish." Her breasts brushed his chest as she kissed his neck and her hands worked his fly. "I'm going to use you for your body." She sucked the side of his neck and shoved his pants and boxer briefs to his knees. "You don't mind. Do you?"

"God, no." His dick poked her belly and she took him into her warm hand. She cupped his balls and stroked him up and down, pressing her thumb into the corded vein of his shaft.

"You're a beautiful man, Mick Hennessy." She brushed her thumb over the head. "Hard."

No shit.

"Big."

Mick sucked in a breath. "You can handle it."

"I know I can." She bit the hollow of his throat, then slowly sank to her knees, kissing his belly and abdomen on the way down. "Can you?"

Oh, God. She was going to use her gorgeous mouth on him. His "Yes" came out on a rush of pent-up breath.

"You don't mind if I use my tongue on *you*?" She knelt before him and looked up, a little smirk on her red lips. "Do you?"

"Christ, no."

Her gaze locked with his as she ran her velvet

tongue up his thick shaft, and he locked his knees to keep from falling on her. "Do you like my tongue here?"

"Yes." God, was she going to talk the whole time?

She licked the cleft in the head of his cock. "Like it here?"

She was driving him insane, but he had a feeling she knew that. "Yes."

She smiled. "Then you'll love this." She parted her lips and she took him into her warm, wet mouth, drawing him to the back of her throat. "Holy shit," he whispered and placed his hands in her hair. Most women were hesitant to take a man into their mouths. Obviously she wasn't one of them. She sucked him into a sexual vortex that left him oblivious to anything but her. Anything but her warm hands, hot liquid mouth, and soft tongue giving him raw carnal pleasure. The glass door was cool against his back and his eyes slid shut. He expected her to stop at some point. Women always stopped, but she didn't. She stayed with him as he came, an intense, powerful climax that squeezed the breath from him and hit him like a freight train. She stayed with him until the last flush of orgasm stopped and he was able to breathe. Most women thought they knew how to pleasure a man with their mouths. Some were better than others, but he'd never experienced anything like the intense pleasure Maddie had just given him.

"Thank you," he said, his voice rough and his breathing rapid.

"You're welcome." She stood in front of him and touched a finger to the corner of her mouth. "So, you liked that?"

He reached for her. "You know I did."

She wrapped her arms around his shoulders and her nipples brushed his chest. "Now that we both got the first one out of the way, I hope you weren't planning on going to work, because I have plans for you here."

No, he didn't have to go to Mort's. The new manager he'd hired was doing a good job. He kissed the side of her throat and raised a hand to her breast. In the pit of his belly, the lust that had been thoroughly sucked out of him a moment ago caught fire once again.

He had plans of his own.

$\mathcal{S}$he should not have fallen off the wagon. Having sex with Mick was wrong of her on so many levels, but the time to stop things before they got out of control had passed an hour ago. She should have stopped him before he put his mouth on her breast and slid his hand into her pants. But of course she hadn't. Once she'd felt his moist mouth and skilled fingers, she'd become selfish and greedy. She'd wanted to feel his hands all over her body. To feel him touch her in places she hadn't been touched in a long time. To look into his eyes and see how much he wanted her.

Within the spill of lamplight pouring across the gold and red quilt, Mick kissed the small of Maddie's bare back and continued up her spine. "You always smell so good." His hands and knees were planted on her bed on both sides of her body and his erection brushed the inside of her bare thigh as he leaned down to kiss the back of her shoulder.

No, she should not have fallen off the wagon with Mick, but she wasn't sorry. Not yet. Not when he made her feel things. Wonderful things she hadn't even known she missed. Tomorrow she would be sorry when she thought about all the ways she'd just complicated her life and his, but tonight she was going to be completely selfish and enjoy the naked man in her bed.

Maddie turned onto her back and looked up into Mick's lusty blue eyes surrounded by thick black lashes. "You feel good," she said and ran her hands up his arms and across the hard muscles of his shoulders. "You make me feel good too."

He bent down, lightly bit the ball of her shoulder, and his penis touched her between her legs. "Tell me all the ways you're going to use my body."

She turned her head and said next to his ear, "It's a surprise."

"Should I be afraid?"

"Only if you can't get it up."

He pressed his erection into her. "That's not going to be a problem." And it wasn't. He kissed and teased and tortured her with his hands and mouth, bringing her to the point of climax, then backing off. Just when she thought she might have to pin him to the bed and jump on him, he reached for the condom on the nightstand. Maddie took it and put it on him while she kissed his belly. Then he pinned *her* to the bed and knelt between her thighs. He wrapped his hand around the thick shaft of his penis and brought the broad head to her slick opening. He pressed into her, hot and enormous, and she gasped from the sheer pleasure of his entry.

"Are you okay?"

"Yes. I love this part," she said.

He pulled out and plunged a little deeper. "This part?"

She licked her lips and nodded. She wrapped one leg around his waist and forced him even deeper. His nostrils flared slightly as he pulled out, then buried himself to the hilt, thrusting into her and shoving them up the bed.

She cried out, whether in pain or in intense pleasure, she wasn't quite sure. She only knew that she didn't want it to end.

"Sorry." He spread kisses across her cheek. "I thought you were ready."

"I am," she moaned. "Do it again." And he did. Again and again. Maddie hadn't had sex in a long time, but she didn't remember it feeling so good—if it had been this good, she was positive she would not have given it up for so long.

He groaned deep, deep within his chest and placed his hands on the sides of her face. "You feel tight around me." He kissed her lips and said just above her mouth, "And so good."

Heat flushed her skin, radiating outward from where they were joined, and she slid her fingers up his warm shoulders and into his hair. "Faster, Mick," she whispered. She loved the feeling of him touching her deep inside, the plump head of his penis rubbing her G-spot, then pushing into her cervix. She loved the press of his moist skin against her and the intensity of his blue eyes. Without missing a beat of his pumping hips, he ran a hand down her side and bottom to the back of her thigh.

"Put this leg around my back," he said just above a whisper. He pressed his forehead against hers and his breathing rasped against her temple. He plunged faster. Harder.

"Mick," she cried out as he thrust in and out, pushing her closer and closer toward climax. "Please don't stop."

"Not a chance."

Like a flash fire, heat spread from the apex of her thighs, across her body, and she was completely mindless of anything but Mick and the pleasure of his body. She called his name once, twice, maybe three times. She tried to tell him how good it felt, how much she loved and missed sex, but her words came out short and abbreviated as he relentlessly thrust his erection into her, and slammed her into a pleasure so intense she opened her mouth to scream. The sound died in her throat as wave after luscious wave rolled through, and her vaginal muscles pulsed and contracted, gripping him hard. On and on it went as he plunged into her, his labored breath hot against her cheek until finally he shoved into her one last time and a long tortured groan died in his throat.

"Oh . . . my . . . God," she said when she could catch her breath.

"Yeah." He raised up onto his elbows and looked into her face.

"I don't remember sex being that good."

"It usually isn't." He pushed a few strands of her hair off her forehead. "In fact, I don't think it's ever been that good."

"You're welcome."

He laughed, and his two dimples dented his cheeks. "Thank you." When she didn't reciprocate, he lifted one brow up his forehead.

She smiled and unwrapped her legs from around his waist. "Thank you."

He pulled out of her and moved off the bed. "You're welcome," he said over his shoulder as he walked into the bathroom.

Maddie rolled on her side and closed her eyes. She sighed and settled within a nice comfy bubble of afterglow. She didn't have a tense muscle in her body and couldn't recall ever being so relaxed. She heard the toilet flush, and she wrapped her arms around the pillow under her head. She should probably have sex more often, as a sort of stress reducer.

"Who's Carlos?"

Maddie opened her eyes and her afterglow bubble popped. "What?"

Mick sat on the bed and looked at her over his shoulder. "You called me Carlos."

She didn't remember that. "When?"

"When you were coming."

"What did I say?"

A little scowl turned down the corners of his mouth. " 'Yes. Yes. Carlos.' "

Heat rose up her neck to her cheeks. "I did?"

"Yeah. I've never been called another man's name." He thought a moment, then added, "I don't think I like it."

She sat up. "Sorry."

"Who's Carlos?"

He obviously wasn't going to let it drop and she was forced to confess, "Carlos isn't a man."

He blinked and stared at her for several moments. "Carlos is a woman?"

She laughed and pointed to the bedside dresser. "Open that top drawer."

He leaned forward and pulled the drawer open. His brows lowered, then slowly rose up his forehead. "Is that a . . . ?"

"Yes, that's Carlos."

He looked at her. "You named it?"

Maddie sat up. "I thought since we're intimately acquainted he should have a name."

"It's purple."

"And glows in the dark."

He chuckled and shut the drawer. "It's big."

"Not as big as you."

"Yeah, but I can't . . ." He scratched his cheek. "What does it do?"

"It can pulse, vibrate, throb, and get hot."

"All that and glows in the dark too?" He dropped his hand to the bed.

"You're better than Carlos." She moved to kneel behind him and slid her hands down his chest. "I'd much rather spend time with you."

He looked up into her face. "I don't glow in the dark."

"No, but your eyes get all sexy, and I love the way you kiss and touch my body." She pressed her breasts into his warm back. "You make me vibrate and you make me hot."

He turned and pushed her down on the bed. "You make me feel like the last time I was in this room. Like I can't get enough. Like I'm fifteen and can go at it all night."

A lock of dark hair fell over his forehead and she reached up and smoothed it back. "Is this room a lot different from the last time you were here with . . . what was her name?"

"Brandy Green." He glanced about the bedroom. At the mahogany dressers and bedside tables and lamps. "To tell you the truth, I don't remember what it looked like."

"Too long ago?"

He returned his gaze to her. "Too busy to notice." Laugh lines creased the corners of his eyes. "Brandy was a senior and I was a sophomore and I was just trying to impress the hell out of her."

"Did you?"

"Impress her?" He thought a moment, then shook his head. "I don't know."

"Well, you've impressed me."

"I know." He moved over the top of her onto his back, then pulled her across his chest.

"How do you know?"

"You're a moaner."

She pushed her hair over her shoulder. "I am?"

"Yeah. I like it." He brushed his hand up and down her arm. "It lets me know you're into what I'm doing to you."

She shrugged. "I like sex. I've liked sex since my first time when I was a sophomore at UCLA and lost my virginity to my first boyfriend, Frankie Peterson."

His hand stilled. "You waited until you were, what . . . twenty?"

"Well, I was Cincinnati Maddie, remember? But once I moved out of my aunt's house and went away to college, I dropped sixty pounds by virtue of being so poor I didn't have money to spend on food. In those days, I used to work out a lot too. So much so that I burned myself out, and now I refuse to work up a sweat on anything that is painful and boring." She ran her fingers up the thin line of hair on his belly.

"You don't need to work out." He slid his hand down her back to her behind. "You're perfect."

"I'm too soft."

"You're a woman. You're supposed to be soft."

"But I'm—"

He rolled her onto her back and looked down at her. "I look at you and there isn't anything I can tell myself that makes me not want to be with you." His gaze moved over her face. "I've tried to stay away. Tried to keep my hands off you. I can't." He looked into her eyes. "Maybe after tonight I can."

Maddie's breath got caught in her chest. She didn't want one night. She wanted several nights, but he was Mick Hennessy and she was Maddie Jones. She would have to tell him. Soon.

"We better make it good, then." She slid her hand to the back of his head and ran her fingers through his short hair. "And tomorrow you can go back to being mad at me, and I'll go back to being celibate. Everything will go back the way it was before tonight."

One corner of his mouth lifted. "You think?"

She nodded. "Neither of us is looking for love, nor even a commitment beyond this room. We both want the same thing, Mick." She brought his mouth down to hers and whispered against his lips, "No strings. Just a one-night stand." Since it was the last time she figured she'd have sex before she jumped back on the wagon, she made sure it was memorable.

She left him long enough to turn on the jetted tub and pour mango-scented bubble bath into the water. Then she took him by the hand and led him into the bathroom. They played within the foamy bubbles, and when it was time, she rode him like a seahorse. This time when she hit her peak, she made sure she called out his name.

Once it was over and Mick flushed the last condom, she fell asleep with her back pressed against his chest and his hand on her breast. He'd been talking to her about something, and she'd nestled her bottom against his groin and passed right out. She'd meant to put on a robe and walk him to the door, but it had been a long time since she'd let herself feel safe and secure and protected. It was an illusion, of course. It had always been an illusion.

No one except Maddie could keep her safe and secure and protected, but it had felt so good.

When she woke in the morning, she was alone. Just as she wanted. No strings. No commitment. No demands. He hadn't even said good-bye.

She rolled onto her side and looked at the morning shadows playing across her wall. She placed her hand in the indent on the pillow next to hers and curled her fingers into a fist. It was better this way.

Even if she never told him who she was, if she just left town and never set eyes on him again, he'd find out eventually. He'd find out when the book hit the stores.

Yes, it was better that he'd left without a good-bye. One night was bad enough; anything more would be impossible.

Chapter 12

The voice of Trina Olsen-Hays filled Maddie's office as she scribbled notes on index cards in an attempt to try and make some sort of order out of the taped conversation. Once she finished transcribing the pertinent information, she would shuffle and mix them with other cards she'd made in order to make a timeline she would then pin across her office wall. She'd learned after her first book that it was easier to move things around if they were written on cards as opposed to a straight line.

After an hour of writing notes, she turned off the tape and leaned back in her chair. She yawned and knitted her fingers together on the top of her head. It was Sunday and she figured the citizens of Truly were just getting out of church. Maddie hadn't been raised in any one religion. As with most everything else while she was growing up, when Maddie had attended church, it had been totally arbitrary and dependent on her aunt's fickle whims or one of her "programs." If Great-Aunt Martha saw a *60 Minutes* episode about religion, it reminded her that she might be falling down on the job in the God department, and she'd drop Maddie off at a random church and reassure herself on the way home that she was being a good guardian. After a few Sundays, Martha would forget about church and God and move on to something else.

If Maddie had to choose a religion, she'd probably choose Catholicism. For no other reason than the stained glass, rosary beads and Vatican City. Maddie had visited Vatican City several years ago, and it was definitely awe-inspiring. Even to a heathen like herself. But if she was Catholic, she'd have to go to church and confess the many sins she'd committed upon the body of Mick Hennessy. If she understood confession, she should feel repentant, but she didn't. She might get away with lying to a priest, but God would not be fooled.

Maddie stood and moved into the living room. She'd had a great time with Mick last night. They'd had sex. Good sex, and now it was over. She knew she should feel bad that she hadn't told him her mother was Alice Jones, but she didn't. Okay, maybe a little, but probably not as bad as she should feel. She might feel worse if she had any sort of relationship with Mick, but she didn't. Not even a friendship, and if she felt bad about anything it was that she and Mick could never be friends. She would have liked that. Not just for the sex, but because she liked him.

She moved to the French doors and looked out at the lake. She thought of Mick and his sister and his insistence that she not speak with Meg. Why? Meg was a grown woman. A single mother who supported herself and her son. What was Mick afraid would happen?

"Meow."

Maddie looked down at her feet. On the other side of the glass door sat a small kitten. It was pure white and had one blue eye and one green. Its head looked almost too big for its body, like maybe it was inbred or something. Maddie pointed at it and said, "Go home."

"Meow."

"I hate cats." Cats were nasty creatures. They shed all over your clothes, shredded the furniture with their claws, and slept all day.

"Meow."

"Forget it." She turned and walked through the house and into her bedroom. Her sheets, pillowcases, and duvet cover lay in a heap on the floor and she carried them to the laundry room off the kitchen. She needed to get all reminders of Mick out of her house. No indents in her pillows. No empty condom wrappers on the nightstand. Mick was like cheesecake, and she just couldn't have anything around to remind her how much she liked and missed cheesecake. Especially when it was so good she'd just gorged herself into a coma the night before.

She stuffed her sheets and pillowcases into the washing machine, loaded it up with soap, and turned it on. As she shut the lid, the doorbell rang, and her stomach kind of got light and heavy at the same time. There had only ever been one person who rang her doorbell. She tried to ignore the feeling in her stomach and the sudden spike in her heartbeat as she moved toward the front of the house. She looked down at her green Nike T-shirt and black shorts. They were old and comfy and not the sort of clothes to inspire lust, but neither had the sweatshirt and pants she'd had on last night, and Mick hadn't seemed to mind.

She looked through the peephole, but it wasn't Mick. Meg stood on her porch wearing dark sunglasses, and Maddie wondered how Meg knew where she lived. Maybe from Travis. She also wondered what Meg could possibly want on a Sunday afternoon. The obvious answer was she wanted to talk to Maddie about the book. But Meg looked so much like her mother that another answer came to mind; she'd come over for some kind of confrontation. Maddie wondered if she should break out her Taser, but she'd hate to shoot Meg with fifty thousand volts if she'd just come over to talk about what had happened twenty-nine years ago. That wouldn't be very nice, and would be counterproductive, since she wanted to hear what Meg had to say. She opened the door.

"Hi, Madeline. I hope I'm not disturbing you," Meg began. "I just dropped Pete off next door, and I was wondering if I could talk to you a moment or two."

"The Allegrezzas are back so soon?"

"Yes. They came home this morning."

A slight breeze played with the ends of Meg's dark hair, but she didn't appear agitated or crazy, and Maddie stepped back. "Come in."

"Thank you." Meg pushed her sunglasses to the top of her head and stepped inside. She wore a khaki skirt and a black short-sleeved blouse. She looked so much like her mother it was spooky, but

Maddie supposed it was no more fair to judge her by her mother's behavior than it was for people to judge Maddie by hers.

"How can I help you?" Maddie asked as the two moved into the living room.

"Was my brother here last night?"

Maddie's footsteps faltered a fraction before she continued across the living room. While she'd been wondering what brought Meg to her porch, it hadn't occurred to her that Meg was here to talk about last night's debauchery. Perhaps she'd need the Taser after all. "Yes."

Meg sighed. "I told him not to come here. I'm an adult and I can take care of myself. He's worried that if I talk to you about Mom and Dad, I'll get upset."

Maddie smiled with relief. "Please sit," she said and indicated the couch. "Would you like something to drink? I'm afraid I only have Diet Coke or water."

"No, thank you." Meg sat and Maddie took the chair. "I'm sorry that Mick felt he needed to come to your house and order you not to talk with me."

He'd done more than that. "Like you, I'm an adult, and I don't take orders from your brother." Except for when they'd been in the spa tub, and he'd looked at her through those gorgeous eyes of his and said, "Come over here and sit on my lap."

Meg set her purse on the coffee table. "Mick isn't a bad person. He's just protective. Growing up, he had it rough and doesn't like talking about our parents. If you'd met him under different circumstances, I'm sure you'd like him."

She liked him more than was wise under the current circumstances. She didn't even want to think about how much she might like sitting in his lap if he wasn't a Hennessy. "I'm sure that's true."

A frown wrinkled Meg's brow. "There's a rumor going around town that a movie is going to be made out of your book."

"Really?"

"Yeah. Carleen came into my work yesterday and told me that Angelina Jolie is going to play my mother, and Colin Farrell my dad."

Colin Farrell made a little sense because he was Irish. But Angelina Jolie? "I haven't been offered a movie deal." Hell, she hadn't even told her agent about the book. "So you can tell everyone that there isn't going to be a film crew arriving anytime soon."

"That's a relief," Meg said, then turned her attention toward the French doors. "Your cat wants in."

"It's not mine. I think it might be a stray." Maddie

shook her head and leaned back into her chair. "Do you want a kitten?"

"No. I'm not really a pet person. I've promised my son a dog if he behaves for a month." She chuckled. "I don't think I'll have to make good on that promise anytime soon."

When Meg laughed, she looked a bit like Mick. "I'm not really a pet person either," Maddie confessed and wondered if Meg had come over for a chat about pets or to talk about her parents. "They're a lot of bother."

"Oh, I wouldn't mind that. I'm not a pet person because they die."

As far as Maddie was concerned, that was the only good thing about cats.

"Growing up, we had a poodle named Princess. She was mostly Mick's dog."

Mick had a poodle? Not only could she not see Mick owning a poodle, she couldn't imagine him naming it Princess. "Did he name her?"

"Yes, and she died when he was about thirteen. The only time I've seen Mick cry was when he had to bury that dog. Even at our parents' funeral, he was a stoic little man." Meg shook her head. "I've had too many people die in my life. I don't want to get attached to a pet and have it die on me. Most people don't understand that, but it's how I feel."

"I understand." And she did. More than Meg would ever know. Or at least know for now.

"You're probably wondering why I stopped by instead of waiting for you to contact me."

"I assume you are anxious to talk about your mother and father and what happened on that night in August."

Meg nodded and pushed her hair behind her ears. "I don't know why you want to write about what happened, but you do. So I think you should hear it from my family, and Mick's not going to talk to you. That leaves me."

"Do you mind if I tape-record the conversation?"

Meg took such a long time to answer, Maddie thought she might refuse. "I guess that would be okay. As long as I get to stop if I feel uncomfortable."

"That's perfectly fine." Maddie rose from the chair and walked to her desk. She popped a new cassette into the tiny recorder, grabbed a folder and pen, then returned to the living room. "You don't have to say anything you don't feel like saying," she said, although it was her job to get Meg to spill it all. Maddie held the recorder in front of her mouth, gave Meg's name and the date, then set it on the edge of the coffee table.

Meg looked at the tape recorder and asked, "Where do I begin?"

"If you feel comfortable, why don't you talk about what you recall of your parents?" Maddie sat back in her chair and rested her hands lightly on her lap. Patient and nonthreatening. "You know, the good times." And after Meg talked about those, they would get to the bad.

"I'm sure you heard that my parents fought."

"Yes."

"They didn't fight all the time, it was just that when they did . . ." She paused and looked down at her skirt. "My grandmother used to say that they were passionate. That they fought and loved with more passion than other people."

"Do you believe that?"

A wrinkle furrowed her brow and she clasped her hands in her lap. "I just know that my dad was . . . bigger than life. He was always happy. Always singing little songs. Everyone loved him because he just had a way about him." She looked up and her green eyes met Maddie's. "My mother stayed at home with Mick and me."

"Was your mother happy?"

"She . . . she was sad sometimes, but that doesn't mean she was a bad mother," Meg said and pro- ceeded to talk about wonderful picnics and birthday parties. Big family gatherings and Rose reading bedtime stories that made the family sound like one big Hallmark card of happiness.

Bullshit. After about thirty minutes of listening to Meg cherry-pick her stories, Maddie asked, "What happened when your mother was sad?"

Meg sat back and folded her arms across her chest. "Well, it's no secret that things got broken. I'm sure Sheriff Potter told you about the time my mother set my father's clothes on fire."

Actually, the sheriff hadn't mentioned it. "Mmm."

"She had the fire under control. There was no need for the neighbors to call the fire department."

"Perhaps they were concerned because this area is a forest and it doesn't take much to start it on fire."

Meg shrugged. "It was May. So it wasn't likely. The fire season isn't until later."

Which didn't mean the fire wouldn't have caused serious damage, but Maddie figured it was pointless and counterproductive to argue, and time to move things along. "What do you recall of the night your parents died?"

Meg looked across the room at the empty television screen. "I remember that it had been hot that day and Mom took Mick and me to the public beach to swim. My dad usually went with us, but he didn't that day."

"Do you know why?"

"No. I suspect he was with the waitress."

Maddie didn't bother reminding her that the waitress had a name. "After you went to the public beach what happened?"

"We went home and had dinner. Dad wasn't home, but that wasn't unusual. I'm sure he was at work. I remember we had 'whatever night,' meaning we could have whatever we wanted for dinner. Mick had hot dogs and I had pizza. Later we ate ice cream and watched *Donny & Marie*. I remember what we watched because Mick was really mad that he had to watch Donny and Marie Osmond. But later he got to watch *The Incredible Hulk*, so he cheered up. My mom put us to bed, but sometime around midnight, I woke up because I heard her crying. I got out of bed and went into her room, and she was sitting on the side of her bed and she had all her clothes on."

"Why was she crying?" Maddie leaned forward.

Meg turned to Maddie and said, "Because my father was having another affair."

"Did she tell you that?"

"Of course not, but I was ten years old. I knew

about the affairs." Meg's gaze narrowed. "Daddy wouldn't have left us for her. I know he wouldn't have really done that."

"Alice thought he was going to."

"They all thought that." Meg laughed without humor. "Ask them. Ask Anna Van Damme, Joan Campbell, Katherine Howard, and Jewel Finley. They all thought he was going to leave my mother for them, but he never did. He never left her and he wouldn't have left her for the waitress either."

"Alice Jones." Maddie had almost felt sorry for Meg, rattling off the names of her father's lovers.

"Yes."

"Jewel Finley? Wasn't she friends with your mother?"

"Yeah," Meg scoffed. "Some friend."

"Did something happen that day out of the ordinary?"

"I don't think so."

Maddie put her forearms on her knees, leaned forward, and looked into Meg's eyes. "Usually when you see an otherwise sane woman kill her husband and then herself, there is something that has added stress to the relationship. Usually it's the belief that the person feeling the most stress feels powerless, like she's losing everything and therefore she has nothing else to lose. If it wasn't your father's infidelity, then it had to be something else."

"Maybe she just planned to frighten them with the gun. Maybe she wanted to scare them and things got carried away."

That was usually the excuse, but rarely the case. "Is that what you believe?"

"Yes. Maybe she found them naked together."

"They were both clothed. Alice was behind the bar and your father was in front of it. They were at least ten feet apart."

"Oh." She bit her thumbnail. "I still think she went there to scare Dad and things got out of control."

"You *think* that, but you don't know."

Meg dropped her hand and stood. "My mother loved my father. I just don't think she went there with the intention of killing anyone." She put her purse over her shoulder. "I've got to get home."

Maddie stood. "Well, thanks for your help," she said and walked Meg to the door. "I appreciate it."

"If I can clear anything up, give me a call."

"I will." After Meg left, Maddie moved into the living room and turned off the tape. She felt sorry for Meg. She truly did. Meg was a victim of the past just like she was, but Meg was older than both Mick and Maddie and recalled more of that horrible night. Meg also recalled more than she was willing to talk about too. More than she wanted Maddie to know, but that was okay—for now. Maddie had written the first chapter of the book but had stopped to work on the timeline. When she got the sequence of—

"Meow."

Maddie leaned her head back. "For the love of God." She moved to the door and look down at the kitten on the other side. "Go away."

"Meow."

She pulled the cord to her vertical blinds and turned them so that she could no longer see the annoying cat. She moved into the kitchen and made a low-carb dinner. She ate in front of the television with the sound turned way up. After dinner, she took a leisurely bath and scrubbed her skin with a vanilla body scrub. A white jar of Marshmallow Fluff body butter sat on the counter next to a towel. She'd received it in the mail at her house in Boise yesterday and had tossed it into her purse.

Lord, had it only been yesterday that she'd met with Trina, had a bridesmaid fitting, and had sex with Mick? She unplugged the bathtub drain and stood. She'd been a busy girl.

Maddie dried herself, then rubbed the creamy

lotion into her skin. She pulled on her striped pajama pants and PINK T-shirt, then moved to the living room and picked up the tape recorder from the coffee table where it still sat. A cell phone commercial blared from the televison and she hit the off button on the remote control. She wanted to replay Meg's recollections of the evening her mother had killed two people and then herself.

"Meow."

"Damn it!" She pulled the cord to the blinds and there, sitting like a white snowball in the darkening shadows of evening, sat her tormenter. She put her hands on her hips and glared at the kitten through the glass. "You have gotten on my last nerve."

"Meow."

How such a racket could come from such a tiny mouth was beyond Maddie. "Go away!" As if it understood, the kitten stood, walked around in a circle, then sat in the same exact spot.

"Meow."

"I've had it." Maddie went to the laundry room, shoved her arms into a jean jacket, then stomped across the floor to the French doors. She threw them open and scooped up the kitten. The kitten was so small its entire torso fit in one hand. "You probably have fleas or ringworm," she said.

"Meow."

She held the kitten out at arm's length. "The last thing I need is a big-headed *inbred* cat."

"Meow."

"Shh. I'm going to find you a good home." The dang kitten started to purr like they were going to be friends or something. As quietly as possible, she moved down the steps and tiptoed across the cold grass to the Allegrezzas' yard. A light in the kitchen burned and through the sliding glass door, she watched Louie make a sandwich. "You're going to love these people," she whispered.

"Meow."

"Really. They have a kid, and kids love kittens. Act cute and you're in." She set it on the deck, then ran like hell back to her house. As if she were escaping a demon, she closed the door, locked it, and shut the blinds. She sat on the couch and leaned her head back. Quiet. Thank God. She closed her eyes and told herself she'd just performed a very good deed. She could have chased it off by throwing something at it. Little Pete Allegrezza was a nice kid. He probably wanted a cat and would give it a good home. It obviously hadn't eaten in a while and Louie would no doubt hear it and feed it a hunk of lunch meat. Maddie was practically a friggin' saint.

"Meow."

"Are you shitting me?" She sat up and opened her eyes.

"Meow."

"Fine. I tried to be nice." She stormed into her bedroom and shoved her feet into a pair of black flip-flops. "Stupid cat." She returned to the living room, threw open the back door, and scooped up the kitten. She held it up in front of her face and glared into its spooky eyes. "You're too stupid to know I found you a good home."

"Meow."

This was karma. Bad karma. Definitely a payback for something she'd done. She grabbed her purse with her free hand and flipped on the outside lights by the laundry room door. Once she was outside, the transponder in her purse unlocked the car's door. "Don't you even think about scratching this leather," she said as she set the cat on the passenger seat. It was Sunday night and the animal shelter was closed. So dropping off the cat was not an option. If she drove to the other side of the lake and dumped it on a doorstep over there, the damn thing would not be able to find its way back.

She hit the start button on the gearshift. She wasn't totally heartless. She wouldn't dump it somewhere with a big pit bull chained in the yard. She didn't want that kind of karma.

She put the car into reverse and glanced over at the kitten sitting on her expensive leather seat and staring straight ahead. *"Hasta la vista,* baby."

"Meow."

M ick drove his Dodge into the parking lot of the D-Lite Grocery Store and parked in a slot a few rows from the front doors. Pulling in, he'd seen the black Mercedes parked beneath one of the lot's bright lights. Although he'd never personally seen the car, everyone in town knew Madeline Dupree drove a black Mercedes like Batman. Within the slightly tinted windows, Mick could just see the outline of her head and face. He walked to the car and knocked on the driver's-side window. Without a sound, the glass lowered inch by inch. The parking lot light shone into the window and suddenly he was staring into the dark brown eyes of the woman who'd wrung him out the night before.

"Nice car," he said.

"Thanks."

"Meow."

He looked down past her face to a white ball of

fur in her lap. "Why, Maddie, you have a pussycat on your—"

"Don't say it."

He laughed. "When did you get a cat?"

"It's not mine. I hate cats."

"Then why's it on your . . . lap?"

"It wouldn't go away." She turned and looked ahead; her hands gripped the steering wheel. "I tried to find it a home across the lake. I even had a house all picked out. A nice one with yellow shutters."

"What happened?"

She shook her head. "I don't know. I was sneaking up to the porch, ready to toss the cat up there and run, but the damn thing purred and rubbed its head on my chin." She looked up at him as a frown settled between her brows. "And here I am, thinking about all the cat food commercials on TV and wondering if I should buy Whiskas or Fancy Feast."

He chuckled. "What's its name?"

She closed her eyes and whispered, "Snowball."

His chuckle turned to laugher, and she opened her eyes and glared at him. "What?"

"Snowball?"

"It's white."

"Meow."

"It's so girly."

"This from a guy who named his poodle Princess."

His laugher died. "How do you know about Princess?"

Maddie opened her car door and he stepped back. "Your sister told me." She rolled up the window, grabbed the kitten with her free hand, and got out of the car. "And before you get all bossy, your sister showed up on my porch this afternoon and wanted to talk to me about your parents."

"What did she say?"

"A lot." She locked the door and shut it. "Mostly, though, I think she wanted *me* to think that growing up you were all happy as clams until Alice Jones moved to town."

"Do you believe her?"

"Of course not." She shoved the kitten inside her jean jacket and hung a big purse over one shoulder. The same big purse that carried her Taser. "Especially when she let it slip that your mother set a pile of your father's clothes on fire."

"Yeah. I remember that." It was certainly no secret. "I remember the grass in the front yard didn't grow back for a long time." He'd probably been five at the time. A year before his mother had completely lost it.

"And in case you've heard the rumor, no, there is not going to be a movie starring Colin Farrell and Angelina Jolie."

He'd heard the rumor and was relieved to hear it wasn't true. "Are you wearing your pajamas?"

The kitten poked its head out of her jacket as Maddie looked down. "I don't think anyone will notice."

"I noticed."

"Yeah, but I was wearing pajama pants like this last night." She looked up and a sexy little smile teased the corners of her lips. "For a little while anyway."

And she didn't think they were going to have sex again. Right. "Is that you?" he asked.

"Is what me?"

"I smell Rice Krispies treats." He took a step toward her and dipped his head. "Of course it's you."

"That's my Marshmallow Fluff body butter."

"Body butter?" Oh, God. Did she really think they wouldn't end up in bed together again? "I've thought about you all day." He put his hand on the side of her throat and pressed his forehead to hers. "Naked." Beneath his thumb, her pulse pounded through her veins almost as hard as his beat through his body.

"I'm back on the wagon."

"You're back to being sort of, kind of, celibate?"

"Yes."

"I can change your mind." He was trying to convince a woman to be with him, something he didn't normally do. Either they wanted to or they didn't.

"Not this time," she said, although she didn't sound particularly convinced.

But when it came to Maddie, nothing was normal. "You love the way I kiss and touch your body. Remember?"

"I, ahh . . ." she stammered.

Normally he didn't think and obsess about a woman all day. He didn't wonder what she was doing. If she was working or finding dead mice or how he was going to get her naked again. "You're already dressed for bed." He brushed his mouth across hers and her lips parted on a little gasp. Normally he didn't waste his time because there were others he didn't have to try and convince. "You know you want to."

"Meow."

She took a step back and his hand dropped to his side. "I have to buy cat food."

Mick lowered his gaze to the white furry head poking out of Maddie's jean jacket. That cat was pure evil.

"Good girl, Snowball," she said and patted her kitten's head. She looked up at him, then turned toward the front of the store. "Watch out for him. He's a very bad man."

Chapter 13

The little collar had pink sparkles and a tiny pink bell and when Maddie had walked to the road to check her mail at around three, she'd found it in her mailbox. No note. No card. Just the collar.

Mick was the only other person who knew about Snowball. She hadn't told any of her friends for fear they'd all die of shock. Maddie Jones—cat owner? Impossible. She'd spent most of her life hating cats, but here she stood, pink collar in hand and staring down at a white ball of fur curled up in her office chair.

She scooped the kitten up in both hands and brought it face level. "This is my chair," she said. "I made you a bed." She carried the kitten to the laundry room and set her on a folded towel inside an Amazon box. "Rule number one: I'm the boss. Number two: you can't get on my furniture and get it all hairy." She knelt down and placed the collar around Snowball's neck.

"Meow."

Maddie scowled.

"Meow."

"Fine. You look cute." She stood and pointed a finger in the kitten's direction. "Rule number three: I let you in and gave you some food. That's where it ends. I don't like cats." She turned on her heels and walked out of the laundry room. The tinkling of a bell followed her into the kitchen and she looked down at her feet. She sighed and pulled a local telephone book out of a drawer. She turned to the yellow pages, reached for her cell phone, and punched in the seven numbers.

"Mort's," a man answered, but it wasn't Mick.

"Is Mick available?"

"He usually doesn't show up until eight."

"Could you give him a message for me?"

"Let me grab a pen." There was a pause and then, "Okay."

"Mick, thanks for the pink collar. Snowball."

"Did you say 'Snowball'?"

"Yeah. Sign it 'Snowball.'"

"Got it."

"Thanks." Maddie disconnected and closed the phone book. At ten minutes after eight while Maddie glanced through a crime magazine, her phone rang.

"Hello."

"Your cat called me."

Just the sound of Mick's voice made her smile, which was a very bad sign. "What did she want?"

"To thank me for her collar."

Maddie glanced at Snowball lying in the red chair, licking her leg and in flagrant disregard of rule number two. "She has good manners."

"What are you doing tonight?"

"Teaching Snowball which fork to use."

He chuckled. "When is she going to bed?"

She flipped a page in the magazine and her gaze scanned an article about a man who'd killed three of his trophy wives. "Why?"

"I want to see you."

She wanted to see him too. Bad. And that was the problem. She didn't *want* to feel all happy inside just at the sound of his voice on her telephone. She didn't *want* to see him in a parking lot and remember the touch of his hands and mouth. The more she saw him, thought about him, wanted him, the more their lives became entangled. "You know I can't," she said and flipped a few more pages.

"Meet me at Hennessy's and please bring your camera."

Her hand stilled. "Are you offering to let me take photos inside your bar?"

"Yes."

She didn't usually take the photos for her books, but there wouldn't be a problem if she did.

"I want to see you."

"Are you bribing me?"

There was a pause on the line and then he asked, "Is that a problem?"

Was it? "Only if you think I'll have sex with you for a few photos."

"Honey," he said through what sounded like a sigh of exasperation, "I wish getting you naked was that easy, but no."

Just because she went to Hennessy's and took some photographs didn't mean anyone was going to end up naked. She'd lived without sex for four years. Clearly she did have some self-control.

"Why don't you come here around midnight? The place will be cleared out and you can take as many pictures as you want."

If she went, she'd be using the undeniable attraction between them to get what she wanted.

Just as he was using her desire to photograph the inside of the bar to get what he wanted. She wondered if her conscience should rise up and decline the tempting offer, but as had happened from time to time in her life when it came to her work and her scruples, her conscience was silent.

"I'll be there." After she hung up the phone, she took a deep breath and held it in. Entering that bar would not be the same as every other crime scene she'd walked and explored and stood within. This was personal.

She let out her pent-up breath. She'd viewed the crime scene photos and read the reports. Twenty-nine years after the fact would not be a problem. She'd sat across a mesh barrier from killers who told her exactly what they'd do to her body if they ever got the chance. Compared to that nightmare, walking into Hennessy's was going to be a piece of cake. No sweat.

Hennessy's was painted a nondescript gray and was bigger than it looked from the outside. Inside it had two pool tables and a dance floor on either side of the long bar. In the middle, three steps led down to the sunken floor surrounded by a white railing and fitted with ten round tables.

Hennessy's had never had the unruly-girls-gone-bad reputation of Mort's. It was more laid-back and was known for good drinks and music. And for a time, murder. Hennessy's had finally lived down the latter—until a certain true crime writer had blown into town.

Mick stood behind the bar and poured South Gin into a cocktail shaker. He glanced up at Maddie, at the light shining in her hair, picking out reddish brown strands in her ponytail. He returned his gaze to the tall clear bottle in his hand. "My great-grandfather built this bar in 1925."

Maddie set her camera on the bar and glanced about her. "During Prohibition?"

"Yeah." He pointed to the sunken middle. "That part was a restaurant dining room," he said. "He made and sold grain alcohol out of the back."

Maddie looked at him through those big brown eyes that turned all warm and sexy when he kissed her neck. At the moment her eyes were a little wide, like she was seeing ghosts. "Was he ever caught?" she asked but looked about once again, her mind clearly not on his masterful attempt at conversation. When he'd opened the back door and seen her standing there, she'd looked so tense, he'd had to check his first impulse to push her against the wall and kiss the breath out of her.

"Nah." Mick shook his head. They both knew she was there to take photographs, and Mick was surprised at how uptight she was about being inside the bar. He thought she'd be happy. He was giving her what she wanted, but she didn't look happy. She looked ready to break. "The town was too small and unimportant in those days, and Great-Grandfather was too well liked by everyone. When Prohibition ended, he gutted most of the place and turned it into a bar. Except for maintenance and a few necessary renovations, it's been like this since." He added a splash of vermouth, then put the lid on the cocktail shaker. "My grandfather turned the area over there into a dance floor and my father brought in the pool tables." He shook the premium gin and vermouth with one hand and reached below the bar with the other. "I've decided to leave it as is." He set first one and then another frosted martini glass on the bar. He added a few olives on toothpicks, and as he poured, his gaze lowered from the firm set of her jaw down her throat to her white blouse and the top button that look perilously close to popping open and giving him a great view of her cleavage. "I've put my money and energy into Mort's. Next week my buddy Steve and I have a meeting with a couple of investors to talk about starting a business giving helicopter tours in the area. Who knows if it will pan out? Owning bars is what I know, but I really want to branch out and have other interests. That way I don't feel as if I'm standing still." He pushed the martini glass toward her and wondered if she was even listening to him.

Her fingers touched the stem. "Why do you feel as if you're standing still?"

He guessed she had been listening. "I don't know. Maybe because as a kid I couldn't wait to get the hell out of here." He reached for the toothpick in his martini and bit an olive off the end. "But here I am."

"Your family is here. I don't have family—well, except for a few cousins I've met briefly. If I had a brother or sister, I'd want to live by them. At least I hope I would."

He recalled that her mother had died when she'd been young. "Where's your father?"

"I don't know. I never met him." She stirred her martini with the olives. "How do you know what I drink?"

He wondered if she'd purposely changed the subject. "I know all your secrets." She looked a bit alarmed and he laughed. "I remember what you were drinking the first night I saw you." He walked around the end of the bar and sat next to her. She turned to face him and he planted one of his feet between hers on the rungs of her stool. She wore a black skirt and his knee forced the material up her smooth thighs.

"Really?" She picked up the drink and gazed at him over the top of the glass. She drained half of her drink. Sucking down his best gin as if it were water, and if she wasn't careful, he'd have to drive her home. Which wasn't a bad idea. "I'm surprised you remember anything beyond Darla's tempting offer to show you her bare bottom," she said and licked her bottom lip.

"I remember you were being a smart-ass that night too." He took her hand and brushed his thumb across the backs of her knuckles. "I wondered what it would be like to kiss your smart mouth."

"Now you know."

"Yes." He moved his gaze across her face, her cheeks, and jaw and wet lips. He looked back up into her eyes. "Now that I know, I think about all the places I didn't get to kiss you the other night."

She set her glass on the bar. "Lord, you're good."

"I'm good at a lot of things."

"Especially at saying just the right thing to make a woman feel like you really mean it."

He dropped her hand. "You don't think I mean it?"

She grabbed her camera and spun around on her stool. Mick moved his foot and she stood. "I'm sure you do mean it." She turned her back on him and raised her camera. "Every time you say it and to every woman you say it to."

Mick picked up his glass and also stood. "You think I've said that to other women?"

She adjusted the focus and snapped a picture of the empty tables. The strobe flashed and she said, "Of course."

That stung, especially since it wasn't true. "Well, honey, you don't give yourself enough credit."

"I give myself a lot of credit." Another click and flash, then she said, "But I know how things are."

He took a drink and the cool gin warmed a path down his throat and settled next to a spot of irritation. "Tell me what you think you know."

"I know I'm not the only woman you spend time with." She lowered her camera and moved to one end of the bar.

"You're the only woman I'm seeing right now."

"Right now. You'll move on. I'm sure we're all interchangeable."

Mick walked away as the strobe flashed. "I didn't think you had a problem with that." He moved into the dark shadows and leaned a hip into the jukebox.

"I don't. I'm just saying that I'm sure we're all the same in the dark."

She was really starting to piss him off, but he had a feeling that was her point. He wondered why the hell he'd wanted to see her so damn bad. She believed the gossip about him, and he wondered why he cared. She didn't mind if he saw other women, and he wondered why that bothered him. Maybe he should. Maybe he should kick her ass out and call someone else. The problem was he didn't want to call someone else, and that ticked him off almost as much as her attitude.

She took several photos of the floor in front of the bar from different angles, then he said, "You're wrong about that. Not all pussy is the same in the dark."

She glanced over at him. He'd meant to offend her, but typical of Maddie, she didn't act like other women. Instead, she took a deep breath and let it out slowly. "Are you trying to make me mad?"

"It seems fair. You're trying to make me mad."

She thought a moment and then confessed, "You're right."

"Why?"

"Maybe because I don't want to think about what I'm doing." She moved to the end of the bar and looked at the no-skid mats on the floor. She snapped a few photos, then lowered her camera. Just above a whisper, barely loud enough for him to hear, she said, "This is harder than I thought it would be."

He straightened.

"It's the same bar and mirrors and lighting and old cash register." She set the camera down and grasped the end of the bar. "The only things that are different are the blood and the bodies."

Mick walked toward her and set his glass on the railing as he passed it.

There was a catch in her voice when she said, "She died here. How can you stand it?"

He placed his hands on her shoulders. "I don't think about it anymore."

She turned and looked up at him, her eyes wide and stricken. "How is that possible? Your mother killed your father right at the top of the stairs."

"It's just a place. Four walls and roof." He slid his hands down her arms and back up again. "It happened a long time ago. Like I said, I don't think about it."

"I do." She bit her lip and turned her head away to wipe at her eyes.

Mick had never met a writer before Maddie, but it did seem to him as if she were awfully emotional for a woman writing a book about people she didn't even know.

"This has just been so much harder than I thought it was going to be. I don't take my own photos for the books, and I thought I could do this."

Maybe she had to immerse herself in the details and feel them in order to write about them. Hell, what did he know? He didn't even read books that often.

She looked up at him. "I have to go." She grabbed her camera off the bar and walked around him. On her way out, she picked up her jacket and purse off one of the stools where she'd set them earlier.

This evening had turned to shit and he did not know why. He didn't know what he'd done or hadn't done. He'd thought she'd take a few photos. They'd have a drink, talk, and, yeah, hopefully get naked. He followed Maddie through the back and out into the alley.

"Are you going to be okay to drive?" he asked as he stepped from the back door.

She stood just inside the pool of light and fumbled to shove her arms into the sleeves of her jacket. She nodded, and her purse dropped to the ground by her foot. Instead of picking it up, she covered her face with her hands.

"Why don't I take you home?" He moved toward her, then bent down and picked up her purse. He'd been raised by females, but he did not understand Maddie Dupree. "You're too upset to drive."

She looked up at him through liquid eyes as a tear spilled over her bottom lashes. "Mick, I have to tell you something about me. Something I should have told you weeks ago."

He didn't like the sound of that. "You're married." He put her bag on the hood of her car and waited.

She shook her head. "I . . . I'm . . ." She let out a breath and brushed the tears from her cheeks. "I'm not . . . I'm afraid . . . I can't . . ." She wrapped her arms around his neck and glued her body to his. "I can't get the crime scene photos out of my head."

That was it? That's why she was so upset? He didn't know what to say. What to do. He felt helpless and he slid his hands around her sides and held her. The skin across his abdomen got tight, and he knew what he'd like to do. He figured it was a good thing she couldn't read his mind, but it was her fault, really. She shouldn't have pressed into him and clung to his neck.

"Mick?"

"Hmm?" Tonight she smelled like vanilla again and he ran his hands up and down her back. Holding her was almost as good as sex.

"How many condoms do you have on you?"

His hand stilled. He'd bought a box of Trojans yesterday. "I have twelve in the truck."

"That ought to be enough."

He pulled back to look into her face, her profile lit by the light at the back of Hennessy's. "I don't understand you, Maddie Dupree."

"Lately, I don't understand myself." She ran her fingers through his hair and brought his mouth down to hers. "And where you're concerned, I just can't seem to do the right thing."

Late the next morning, Maddie stood in her kitchen and raised a steaming cup of coffee to her lips. She wore her white bathrobe and her wet hair was slicked back from her shower. Last night she'd almost told Mick that Alice Jones was her mother. She should have told him, but each time she opened her mouth, she couldn't say the words. She hadn't been afraid to tell him, but for some reason, she just couldn't tell him. Maybe the timing was off. Another time would be better.

More than anything, she'd needed him to help

clear her head of the horrible images. She'd been to her mother's grave and she hadn't fallen apart. But standing in the exact spot where her mother had died, she'd felt like someone had reached inside her chest and ripped out her heart. Perhaps if she hadn't seen the photos of her mother's blood and her blond hair stained a dark brown. Perhaps her world wouldn't have flipped upside down and she wouldn't have gotten so emotional.

She hated getting emotional, especially in front of other people. Most specifically in front of Mick, but he'd been there and seen it and she'd needed someone to hold on to and focus on when everything seemed so unbalanced.

He'd followed her home and she'd taken his hand and led him into the bedroom. He'd kissed her in all those places he'd said he'd been thinking about. He set every nerve ending in her body on fire, and she knew she should feel bad about being with him again. It was wrong of her, but being with him felt too good to feel really bad.

"Meow."

Snowball wove a figure eight between her feet and she looked down at her cat. How had her life come to this? She had a cat in her house and a Hennessy in her bed.

She set her cup on the counter and moved to the pantry to grab a bag of kitten food. A dead mouse lay on the floor and Snowball sniffed its tail. She'd moved the poison the night she'd decided to keep Snowball, but that didn't mean the mouse hadn't eaten the bait. "Don't eat that or you'll get sick." She grabbed Snowball and carried her into the laundry room. Snowball purred and butted her head against Maddie's chin. "And I know for a fact you did not sleep in your bed. I found white fur on my office chair." She set the kitten in her Amazon box and poured food onto a little dish. "I do not want to walk around with white fur on my butt." Snowball jumped out of her box and attacked her food as if she hadn't eaten in a week. Last night as Mick had walked from the bathroom, a smug, satisfied smile tilting one corner of his lips, the kitten had stalked him across the carpet and attacked his leg.

"What the hell?" he'd yelped and danced around as Snowball had dashed back under the bed. "I can't believe I wasted money buying that damn thing a collar."

Maddie had laughed and patted the bed next to her. "Come here so I can make you feel better after the big bad cat attack."

He'd moved to the bed and pulled her up so she knelt before him. "I'm going to make you pay for laughing at me." And he had. All night long, and when she'd woken this morning, she was alone. Again. She would have liked to have woken and seen his face, his blue eyes looking at her, all sleepy and sated, but it was better this way. Better to keep a distance even though they'd shared a night as physically close as two people could possibly get.

While Snowball chowed, Maddie picked up the mouse with a paper towel and carried it to the garbage outside. She called a local veterinarian and made Snowball an appointment for the first week in August. Her low-carb granola bars had teeth marks on the outside of the box, but the bars looked okay. As she took a bite, her doorbell rang.

Through the peephole she gazed at Mick, standing on her porch, looking showered and shaved and relaxed in a pair of Levi's and an untucked striped shirt over a wife beater. She ignored the little tumble in her stomach and opened the door.

"How'd you sleep?" he asked as a knowing little smile brought out his dimples.

She opened the door wide and he stepped inside. "I think it was around three when I finally passed out."

"It was three-thirty." He walked past her and she shut the door behind him. "Where's your cat?" he asked as they moved into the living room.

"Eating breakfast. Are you scared of a little kitty?"

"Of that Tasmanian furball?" He made a rude scoffing sound and pulled a little stuffed mouse from the front pocket of his jeans. "I got her some catnip to mellow her out." He tossed it on the coffee table. "What are your plans?"

She planned to work. "Why?"

"I thought we could drive to Redfish Lake and get a bite to eat."

"Like in a date?"

"Sure." He reached for the terrycloth belt and pulled her toward him. "Why not?"

Because they weren't dating. They shouldn't even be having sex. Dating couldn't happen no matter how her stomach tumbled or her skin tingled.

"I'm hungry and I thought you might be hungry too." He dipped his head and kissed the side of her neck.

She moved her head to one side. She did have to eat, though. "Why Redfish Lake?"

"Because they have a good restaurant in the lodge there, and I want to spend the whole day with you." He kissed the side of her throat. "Say yes."

"I'll need to get dressed." She pulled her belt from his grasp and turned away. As she entered her bedroom she called out, "How far is Redfish Lake?"

"About an hour and a half," he answered from the doorway.

She hadn't expected him to follow her and she looked over at him as she grabbed a pair of under-wear from a drawer. He leaned against the door-frame, and his eyes watched her, moving with her hands as she pulled up a pair of pink silky pan-ties. His gaze felt very intimate. More intimate than when he kissed the insides of her thighs and his eyes turned that certain sexy blue. Intimate like they were a couple and it was normal for him to watch her dress. Like this relationship was more than it really was and more than it was ever going to be. As if there were a chance at tomor-rows and the day afters. She raised her brows up her forehead. "Do you mind?"

"You're not going to get all modest, are you? Not after last night." She continued to stare at him until he sighed and pushed away from the door-frame. "All right. I'll go get your cat stoned."

She watched him leave and tried not to think about tomorrow or the days after and things that could never be. She dressed quickly in a pink cotton sundress. She pulled her hair back in a claw and gazed in the mirror as she put on a little mascara and lip gloss.

In the harsh light of day, with her sexual desire sated and her emotions tightly under control, she knew she had to tell him she was Madeline Jones. He deserved to know.

The thought of telling him cramped her stomach and she wondered if he really had to be told at all. Last night she might not have been real tactful when she'd brought up other women. She'd obviously made him mad, but the fact was, Mick Hennessy was no more a one-woman man than his father had been. Or his grandfather. Even if he wasn't seeing anyone else right now, he would get tired of Maddie. He'd move on sooner or later, so why tell him today?

If anything, she should clear up her mortifying outburst last night. She wasn't a woman who got all weepy and cried on a man's neck. Perhaps she hadn't broken down like some women were apt to do, but for her, it was a loss of control that embarrassed her. Even twelve hours later.

A half hour into their drive to Redfish, she

decided to clear it up. "Sorry about last night," she said above the country music filling the cab of Mick's truck.

"You don't have anything to be sorry about. You got a little loud, but I like that about you." He grinned and glanced at her through the lenses of his blue mirrored sunglasses before returning his gaze to the road. "Sometimes I don't always understand everything you say, but you sound real sexy while you're saying it."

Somehow she suspected they weren't talking about the same thing. "I was talking about getting all emotional at Hennessy's."

"Oh." His thumb tapped against the steering wheel, keeping time to a song about a woman liking chrome. "Don't worry about it."

She wished she could take his advice, but it wasn't that easy for her. "There are just certain girls I've never wanted to be. One of them is the emotional girl who cries all the time."

"I don't think you're an emotional girl." Air from the vents touched the dark hair about his forehead. "What are the other girls?"

"What?"

"You said there are girls you never wanted to be." Without taking his eyes from the road, he turned off the CD player and spoke into the suddenly silent cab. "One is the emotional girl. What are the others?"

"Oh." She counted them off on her fingers. "I don't ever want to be the stupid girl. Nor the get-drunk-and-slutty girl. The stalker girl or the butt girl."

He looked over at her. "The butt girl?"

"Don't make me explain it to you."

He returned his gaze to the road and smiled. "Then you're not talking about a girl with a big butt."

"No."

"Oh, so I guess I don't ever . . ."

"Forget it."

He laughed. "Some women say they like it."

"Uh-huh. Some women say they like to be paddled, but I'll never know the pleasure of either."

Mick reached across the center console and took her hand. "What about being tied to a bed?"

She shrugged. "I kind of like that."

He brought her hand to his mouth and smiled against her skin. "I guess I know what we're doing after I get off work."

Maddie laughed and turned her attention to the scenery. To the pines and thick brush and the South Fork of the Payette River. Idaho might grow famous potatoes, but it also had spectacular wilderness areas.

At the lodge, they sat at a table that looked out at the blue-green water of Redfish Lake and at the snow-covered peaks of the Sawtooth Mountains. They ate lunch and talked about the people in Truly. She told him about her friends, and about Lucy's wedding last year and Clare's impending nuptials. They talked about everything from the weather to world events, sports to the latest West Nile virus outbreaks.

They talked about almost everything but the reason she moved to Truly. By tacit agreement they avoided talking about the book she was writing and about the night his mother had killed two people and then herself.

The day was relaxing and fun, and during those rare moments when Maddie looked into his eyes, her conscience reminded her that he would not be with her if he knew who she really was. She shoved it down and ignored it. She turned a deaf ear, and by the ride home, she'd buried her conscience so deep, it was just a faint whisper that was easily ignored.

Chapter 14

After he got off work that night, Mick showed up on Maddie's doorstep with silk neckties in one hand and another catnip mouse in the other. While he tied Maddie's wrists, Snowball batted the mouse around, then later flagrantly disregarded the rules and passed out in Maddie's office chair. Disregarding the rules was becoming a bad habit for Snowball. Just as Mick Hennessy was becoming a habit for Maddie. A habit she was eventually going to have to break, but there was a problem. Maddie liked spending time with him, in and out of bed, and that created another problem. She wasn't getting a lot of work done. She hadn't finished her notes or completed the timeline, and she really needed to do that before she sat down to write Chapter Two. She needed to remember why

she was in Truly and get to work. No more dropping everything to have a good time with Mick,
but when he called the next night and asked her to
meet him at Mort's after he closed for the night, she
didn't think twice. At twelve-thirty, she knocked
on the back door wearing a red trench coat, four-
inch pumps, and one of Mick's blue neckties nestled between her bare breasts.

"Like the tie," Mick said as he opened her coat.

"I thought I'd return it."

He put his hands on her bare waist and brought
her against his chest. "There's something about
you, Maddie," he said as he looked into her eyes.
"Something more than the way you make love.
Something that makes me think about you when
I'm pouring drinks or watching Travis strike out
in T-ball."

She put her arms around his neck and her nipples brushed the front of his polo shirt. Against
her pelvis, he was enormous and ready. This was
the part where she should tell him that she thought
about him too, but she couldn't. Not because it
wasn't true. It was true, but it was best to keep
things platonic until he moved on.

Instead of talking, she brought his mouth down
to hers and her hand slid to the front of his pants.
What had started as a one-night stand had turned

into more nights. He wanted to see more of her. She wanted to see more of him, but it wasn't love. She did not love Mick, but she liked him a whole lot. Especially when he laid her on his bar and, between the bottles of alcohol, she caught glimpses in the mirror of his long hard body moving, driving, pushing her toward a release that curled her toes inside her pumps.

It was sex. Just sex. Ironically, the kind of relationship she'd waited four years to find. Nothing more, and if she were to ever forget that fact, she had only to remind herself that while she knew his body intimately, she didn't even know his home phone number or where he lived. Mick might say that there was something about her, but whatever that something was, it wasn't enough to want her in his life.

The morning of Snowball's vet appointment, Maddie packed up her kitten and drove into town. August was the hottest month of summer, and the weatherman predicted that the valley would heat up to a scorching ninety-three degrees.

Maddie sat in an examination room and watched as veterinarian John Tannasee checked out her kitten. John was a tall man with hard muscles beneath his lab coat and a Tom Selleck moustache. His voice was so deep it sounded as if it came from his feet. He gently looked in Snowball's ears and then checked her bottom, determining that Snowball was indeed a girl. He took her temperature and gave her a clean bill of health.

"Her heterochromia doesn't appear to affect her vision." He scratched her between the ears and pointed out her other genetic defect. "And her malocculusion isn't so bad that it will affect her eating."

Maddie understood what he'd meant by heterochromia, but, "Malocculusion?"

"Your cat has an overbite."

Maddie had never heard of such a thing in a cat and didn't quite believe it until he tipped the kitten's head back and showed her Snowball's upper jaw was a bit longer than the bottom. For some strange reason, the kitten's oral affliction made Maddie kind of like Snowball.

"She's bucktoothed," Maddie said in astonishment. "She's a hillbilly." She made a follow-up appointment to get Snowball spayed so that she couldn't produce any more big-headed hillbilly cats, then she and Snowball drove to the grocery store.

"Behave," she warned her kitten as she pulled into the D-Lite Grocery Store's parking lot.

"Meow."

"Behave and maybe I'll get some Whisker Lickin's." She groaned as she got out of the car and locked the door. Had she just said Whisker Lickin's? She was embarrassed for herself. As she moved across the parking lot, she wondered if she was destined to become one of those women who doted on their cats and told boring cat stories to people who didn't give a flying crap.

Once inside the grocery store, she loaded up on chicken breasts, salad, and Diet Coke. She couldn't find Whisker Lickin's, so she tossed in Pounce Caribbean Catch. She wheeled her cart to the front of the store and register five. A clerk by the name of Francine scanned the Pounce while Maddie dug around in her purse.

"How old's your cat?"

Maddie looked up and into Francine's long face surrounded by eighties *Flashdance* hair.

"I'm not sure. She just showed up on my deck and wouldn't go away. I think she's inbred."

"Yep. That happens around here a lot."

Francine's eyes were slightly googly and Maddie wondered if she was talking about the cat or herself.

"I heard there's a second suspect in your book," Francine said as she scanned the chicken breasts.

"Pardon?"

"I heard you found a second suspect. That maybe Rose didn't shoot Loch and the waitress and then herself. That maybe someone else came in and killed all three of them."

"I don't know where you heard that, but let me assure you it isn't true. There is no other suspect. Rose shot Loch and Alice Jones, then turned the gun on herself."

"Oh." Francine looked a bit disappointed, but that could have been her uneven eyes. "Then I guess the sheriff isn't going to reopen the investigation and call that *Cold Case* show."

"No. There isn't a second suspect. No *Cold Case* show, no movie deal, and Colin Farrell isn't coming to town."

"I heard it was Brad Pitt." She scanned the last item and hit total.

"Good Lord." Maddie handed over the exact cash and grabbed her groceries. "Brad Pitt," she scoffed as she put the bags in the backseat.

When she got home, she fed Snowball brightly colored shaped fish and cooked herself lunch. She worked on the timeline for the book, writing down events as they unfolded minute by minute, moving them around, and tacking them to the wall behind her computer screen.

At ten that evening, Mick called and asked her to meet him at Mort's. Her first instinct was to say she would. It was Friday night and she wouldn't mind getting out, but something held her back. And that something had everything to do with the way her stomach got light at the sound of his voice.

"I'm not feeling well," she lied. She needed to put some time and distance between them. A little breathing room. A break from what she feared was becoming more than casual sex. At least for her.

In the background she could hear the muffled sound of the jukebox competing with several dozen raised voices. "Are you going to be okay?"

"Yeah, I'm just going to bed."

"I could come by later and check up on you. We don't have to do anything. I could just bring you soup or some aspirin."

She'd like that. "No, but thank you."

"I'll call you around noon tomorrow to check up on you," he said, but he didn't. Instead he showed up at her boat dock, wearing a white Cerveza Pacifico T-shirt, a pair of navy blue swim trunks that hung low on his hips, and driving a twenty-one-foot Regal.

"How're you feeling?" he asked as he stepped into her house through the French doors.

He removed his sunglasses and she gazed up into his handsome face. "About what?"

"You were sick last night."

"Oh." She'd forgotten. "It was nothing. I'm over it now."

"Good." He gathered her up against his chest and kissed her hairline. "Change into your swimsuit and come with me."

She didn't ask where they were going or how long she'd be gone. As long as she was with Mick, she didn't care. She pulled on her one-piece swimsuit and tied a blue wrap with red sea horses around her hips.

"Aren't you getting tired of me yet?" she asked him as they walked toward his yellow and white boat.

His brows lowered and he looked at her as if the thought hadn't entered his head. "No. Not yet."

Mick gave her a tour of the lake and some of the truly spectacular cabins that could not be seen from the road. He handed Maddie a Diet Coke from the cooler and pulled out a bottle of water for himself.

Set in the cloudless August sky, the relentless sun warmed Maddie's skin. At first it felt nice, but after an hour, trickles of sweat slid between her breasts and down the back of her neck. Maddie hated to sweat. It was one of the reasons she didn't exercise. That and she didn't believe in "no pain, no gain." She was a believer in "no pain is a good thing."

Mick dropped anchor in Angel Cove and shucked his white T-shirt. "Before the Allegrezza boys developed this area, we used to come here to swim every summer. My mom would bring us here and later Meg or I would drive." He stood in the middle of the boat and looked out at the sandy shoreline, now dotted with big homes and docks filled with boats and Jet Skis. "I remember lots of bikinis and baby oil. Sand in my shorts and my nose peeling like crazy." He kicked off his flip-flops and moved to the back. "Those were some good times."

Maddie dropped the wrap from her hips and followed him. They stood side by side on the swimming platform. "Sand in your shorts doesn't sound like a good time."

He laughed. "No, but Vicky Baley used to come up out of the water in a string bikini that kind of slid around, and she had this amazing rack that—"

Maddie shoved him and as he teetered, he grabbed her wrist and they both went into the lake. He surfaced with a loud, "Whaaaa, that's cold," while Maddie surfaced, trying to catch her breath. The icy water stole the air from her lungs and Maddie grabbed on to the ladder at the back of the boat.

Mick's quiet laughter skimmed along the rippled surface as he swam toward her.

She pushed her wet hair from her eyes. "What's so funny?"

"You, getting all jealous over Vicky Baley."

"I'm not jealous."

"Uh-huh." He grabbed the edge of the swimming platform and said, "Her rack isn't as good as yours."

"Gee, thanks."

Droplets of water fell from a strand of hair touching his forehead and ran down his cheek. "You have no reason to be jealous of anyone. Your body is beautiful."

"You don't have to say that. My breasts aren't—"

He placed a finger on her lips. "Don't do that. Don't dismiss what I feel as if I'm just saying something to get into your pants. I'm not. I've already been in your pants and you're amazing." He placed his free hand behind her head and gave her a kiss that was all hot mouths and cool lips, drips of water and smooth gliding tongues.

When he kissed her like that, she felt amazing.

"I missed you last night," he said as he pulled back. "I wish I didn't have to work late tonight, but I do."

She licked the taste of him from her lips and swallowed. "I understand."

"I know you do. I think that's why I like you so much." He smiled at her. A simple little curve of his mouth that felt anything but simple. It pinched her chest and stole her breath and she knew she was in trouble. Big bad trouble, with a way of saying things that made her feel like she was drowning in his beautiful eyes. She dunked herself under and came up with her head tilted back and her hair out of her face. "We both work inconvenient hours," she said and climbed up the ladder. She stood on the back of the boat and squeezed water from her hair. "But it works for us because we're nocturnal and can sleep late."

"And because you want me." He climbed out of the water.

She looked at him out of the corners of her eyes. At his hard chest muscles and the line of wet, dark hair trailing down his abdomen and belly and disappearing beneath the waistband of his swimming trunks. "True."

"And Lord knows I want you too." He pulled up

the anchor and put it in a side compartment. Then he moved to the captain's chair and looked over at her while she tied her sarong around her hips.

"What?"

He shook his head and started the motor, a deep throaty churning of the prop. The boat rocked from side to side and Maddie took the companion seat. For several more seconds, Mick gazed at her before he finally looked away and pushed the throttle forward.

Maddie held her hair with one hand as they shot across the lake. Conversation was impossible, but she wouldn't have known what to say. Mick's behavior was a little odd. She'd thought she knew how to read most of his expressions. She knew how he looked when he was angry, when he was teasing and charming, and she certainly knew how he looked when he wanted sex. He was oddly quiet, as if he were thinking about something, and didn't say much until they stood on her deck twenty minutes later.

"If I didn't have to go to work tonight, I'd stay here and play with you," he said.

"You can come back later."

He sat in an Adirondack chair facing her and pulled the sarong from her hips. It fluttered to her feet. "Or you could come over tonight when

I get off work." He placed his hands on the backs of her thighs and brought her between his knees.

"To Mort's?"

He shook his head and nibbled the side of her leg. "Throw some stuff in a bag and come over to my house. I know you like to fall asleep and have me gone in the morning, but I think we've moved beyond pretending this is nothing more than sex. Don't you?"

Did she? It couldn't be more. It could never be more. She closed her eyes and ran her fingers through his hair. "Yes."

He softly bit the outside of her thigh. "I should probably pick you up so you don't have to drive at night."

This was bad. Wrong, but it felt so good. So right. "I can drive."

"I know you can, but I'll pick you up."

From somewhere behind Maddie, a little voice asked, "What are you doing?"

Mick lifted his head and froze. "Travis." He dropped his hands and stood. "Hey, buddy. What's up?"

"Nothin'. What were you doing?"

Maddie turned to see Mick's nephew standing on the top stair of the deck.

"I was just helping Maddie with her swimming suit."

"With your mouth?"

Maddie laughed behind her hand.

"Well, ah . . ." Mick paused and looked at Maddie. It was the first time she'd ever seen him flustered. "Maddie had a thread," he continued and pointed vaguely at her thigh, "and I had to bite it off for her."

"Oh."

"What are you doing here?" Mick asked.

"Mom dropped me off to play with Pete."

Mick looked toward the neighbors' deck. "Is your mother still at the Allegrezzas'?"

Trevor shook his head. "She left." He looked from his uncle to Maddie. "You got more dead mice?"

"Not today. But I did get a cat and she'll be old enough in a few months to kill them for me."

"You have a cat?"

"Yeah. Her name is Snowball. She has different colored eyes and an overbite."

Mick looked at her. "Seriously."

"I'll show you two boys."

"What's an overbite?" Travis asked as the three of them moved into the house.

*   *   *

Mick was home half an hour before his sister knocked on the door. She didn't wait for him to answer.

"Travis told me he saw you kissing Maddie Dupree's butt," she said as she walked into the kitchen, where she found Mick fixing a sandwich before work.

He looked up. "Hello, Meg."

"Is it true?"

"I wasn't kissing her butt." He'd been biting her thigh.

"Why were you there? Travis saw your boat at her dock. What is going on between the two of you?"

"I like her." He sliced the ham sandwich and put it on a paper plate. "It's not a big deal."

"She's writing a book about Mom and Dad." She grabbed his wrist to get his attention. "She's going to make us all look bad."

"She says she's not interested in making anyone look bad."

"Bull. She's digging up dirt to make money off our pain and suffering."

He looked into his sister's deep green eyes. "Unlike you, Meg, I don't dwell on the past."

"No." She let go of his wrist. "You just choose to not think about it as if it didn't happen."

He picked up half the sandwich and took a bite. "I know what happened, but I don't live it every day like you do."

"I don't live it every day."

He swallowed and took a drink from a bottle of Sam Adams. "Maybe not every day, but every time I think you've finally moved on, something happens and it's like you're ten again." He took another bite. "I'm going to live my life in the present, Meg."

"You don't think I want you to live your life? I do. I want you to find someone, you know I do, but not her."

"You talked to her." He was getting bored with the conversation. He liked Maddie. He liked everything about her, and he was going to keep seeing her.

"Only because I wanted her to hear that our mother wasn't a crazy woman."

He took another drink and set the bottle on the counter. "Mom was crazy."

"No." She shook her head and grabbed his shoulder to turn him toward her. "Don't say that."

"Why else would she kill two people and then herself? Why else would she leave her two children orphaned?"

"She didn't mean to."

"You say that, but if she'd just wanted to scare them, why did she load the .38?"

Meg dropped her hand. "I don't know."

He set his sandwich back on the plate and crossed his arms over his chest. "Do you ever wonder if she gave us a thought?"

"She did."

"Then why, Meg? Why was killing Dad and then herself more important than her children?"

Meg looked away. "She loved us, Mick. You don't remember the good things. Just the bad. She loved us and she loved Dad too."

He wasn't the one with the faulty memory. He remembered the good and the bad. "I never said she didn't. Just not enough, I guess. You can stick up for her for another twenty-nine years, but I'll never understand why she felt her only option was to kill Dad and then herself."

She glanced at her feet and said just above a whisper, "I never wanted you to know, but . . ." She returned her gaze to his. "Dad was leaving us."

"What?"

"Dad was leaving us for that waitress." She swallowed hard, as if the word were stuck in her throat. "I heard Mom talking about it on the telephone to one of her friends." She laughed bitterly. "Presumably one of her friends who hadn't slept with Dad."

His father had planned to leave his mother. He knew he should feel something, anger and outrage, maybe, but he didn't.

"She'd put up with so much from him," Meg continued. "The humiliation of the whole town knowing about all the sordid affairs. Year after year." Meg shook her head. "He was leaving her for a twenty-four-year-old cocktail waitress and she couldn't take it. She couldn't let him do that to her."

He looked at his sister, with her pretty eyes and black hair. The same sister who'd protected him as he'd protected her. Or as much as they'd been able. "And you've known about this for all these years and you didn't tell me?"

"You wouldn't have understood."

"What's not to understand? I understand that she killed him rather than let him divorce her. I understand that she was sick."

"She wasn't sick! She was pushed too far. She loved him."

"That isn't love, Meg." He grabbed his plate and beer and walked out of the kitchen.

"Like you would know."

That stopped him, and he turned back and looked at her from the small dining room.

"Have you ever been in love, Mick? Have you

ever loved someone so much that the thought of losing her ties your stomach up in knots?"

He thought of Maddie. Of her smile and her dry humor and the buckedtoothed kitten that she'd taken into her house even though she professed to hate cats. "I'm not sure, but I am sure of one thing. If I ever did love a woman like that, I wouldn't hurt her, and I sure as hell wouldn't hurt any children I had with her. I might not know a lot about love, but I do know that."

"Mick." Meg moved toward him with her hands palms up. "I'm sorry. I shouldn't have said that."

He set his plate on the table. "Just forget it."

"I want the best for you. I want you to get married and have a family because I know you'd be a good husband and father. I know you would because I know how much you love me and Travis." She wrapped her arms around his waist and rested her cheek on his shoulder. "But even if you don't ever find someone, you'll always have me."

Mick drew breath into his lungs even as he felt as if he were suffocating.

Chapter 15

M addie sat on her sofa, Snowball curled up in her lap, and stared into the blank screen of her television. Her stomach ached and her chest was so tight it hurt to breathe. She was going to be sick. She thought about calling her friends and getting their advice, but she couldn't. She was the strong, fearless one of the group, but at the moment she didn't feel so strong or fearless. Far from it.

For the first time in a very long time, Maddie Jones was afraid. There was no denying it. She couldn't call it apprehension and move on. It was too real. Too deep, and too terrifying. Worse than sitting across from a serial killer.

She'd always assumed that falling in love would be like getting slammed into a brick wall. That you'd just be going along as usual and you'd get knocked on your ass and think, *Gee, I guess I'm in love.* But it hadn't happened that way. It had just kind of snuck up on her before she'd realized it. It had happened one smile and one touch at a time. One look. One kiss. One pink cat collar. One pinch to the heart and one breathless anticipation after another until she was in so deep there was no denying it. No turning back before it was too late. No more lying about what she felt.

Maddie slid her hand down Snowball's small back and didn't care that the cat's fur clung to her black shirt and the lap of her skirt. She'd always thought that she couldn't lie to herself about anything. Apparently she'd gotten better at it.

She'd fallen in love with Mick Hennessy and the minute he found out who she really was, she would lose him. And she didn't have a clue what she was going to do about it.

Her doorbell rang and she looked at the clock sitting on a shelf above the television. It was eight-thirty. Mick was at work and she didn't expect to see him until sometime around one.

She set Snowball on the floor and moved to the door. The kitten chased after her and she scooped her up rather than step on her. She looked through the peephole and got that little heated flush she now recognized. Evidently Mick had skipped work.

He stood on her porch wearing jeans and his Mort's polo. She opened the door and stared at him standing there with the first shadows of night bathing him in a light gray and making his eyes a vibrant blue. As he stared at her across the short distance, elation and despair collided in her heart and twisted her stomach.

"I needed to see you," he said and stepped across the threshold. He wrapped one arm around Maddie's waist and placed his free hand on the back of her head. His mouth swooped down and he kissed her. A long drugging kiss that made her want to attach herself to him and never let go.

He pulled back and looked into her face. "I was at work pulling beer and listening to the same old stories, and all I could think about was you and the night we had sex on the bar. I can't get you out of my head. Put your cat down, Maddie."

She bent down to set Snowball on the floor and he shut the door behind him. "I didn't want to be there. I wanted to be here."

She straightened and looked into his face. She'd never felt love like this in her life. Not really, not the stomach-lifting and skin-tingling kind of love. Not the kind that made her want to hold his hand forever. To leech herself into his body so she didn't know where he stopped and she began. "I'm glad you came back." But she had to tell him she was Maddie Jones. Now.

He pushed her hair behind her ear. "I can breathe here with you."

At least one of them could. She rubbed her cheek into his hand, and before she told him who she was, before she lost him forever, she wrapped her arms around his neck and kissed him one last time. She poured her heart and soul into it, her ache and joy, showing him without words what she felt inside. She kissed his mouth and jaw and the side of his throat. She ran her hands over him, touching and memorizing the feel of him beneath her hands.

Mick slid his warm palms to her behind and then the backs of her thighs. He lifted until she wrapped her legs around his waist. A deep groan vibrated through his chest as he returned her hungry kisses, and he carried her into the bedroom.

She would tell him. She would. In a minute. Her legs slid from his waist and he pulled her shirt over her head. She just wanted a few more minutes, but the more she poured her heart in each kiss, the more he wanted from her. The more he sucked the breath from her lungs and made her light-headed. He slid his hands all over her,

her shoulders and arms, her back and behind, until she was left wearing nothing but her bra, unhooked and open in the back.

Mick took a step back from the kiss and gasped. He looked at her through eyes so far gone, there was no thought to stopping him when he slowly pulled her bra straps and the blue satin cups slid down the slopes of her breasts, shimmered across her nipples, then fell down her arms to the floor.

"We've only known each other for a short time." He lightly brushed the tips of his fingers across the tips of her breasts and her breathing became shallow. "Why does it feel longer?" He moved behind her and Maddie looked down at his big hands on her breasts, touching her, squeezing her puckered nipples. Her back arched and she raised her arms. Her hands cupped the sides of his face as she brought his mouth down to hers. She gave him a hot, greedy kiss as she tilted her hips and pressed her naked behind into his erection. He groaned deep within his chest as he played with her breasts. He still wore his jeans and his shirt, and the feeling of worn denim and soft cotton against her skin was erotic as hell. His mouth left hers and trailed hot little kisses down the side of her throat, and he slid one hand down her stomach. He placed one of his feet between hers, then he slipped his hand between her parted thighs, and he touched her. Her insides melted, pooling deep and low in her pelvis, and she let herself savor the touch of the only man she'd ever loved. She'd always wondered if there was a difference between sex and making love. And now she knew. Sex started with physical desire. Making love started in a person's heart.

She didn't know what would happen after this, after she told him who she was, but perhaps it wouldn't matter. She turned and looked up at him as her hands drifted down his stomach to the end of his polo shirt. She pulled the stretchy cotton from the waistband of his pants and Mick raised his arms. She yanked it over his head and tossed it aside. Maddie lowered her gaze from his passion-filled eyes to his strong chest. The tips of her breasts touched him a few inches below his flat brown nipples. A trail of fine hair ran down his chest, between her cleavage, to his waistband.

His voice was husky with lust when he said, "Why did I ever think I would get enough of you?"

Maddie pulled at his button fly and slipped her hands inside his jeans and cupped him through his boxer briefs. "I'll never get enough of you, Mick. Whatever happens, I'll always want you."

She closed her eyes and kissed the side of his throat. "Always," she whispered.

His breath whooshed from his lungs as she slipped her hand inside his underwear and wrapped her palm around his hot shaft. He grabbed his wallet out of his pants and tossed it on the bed.

"I'll never get enough of the way you feel in my hand," she whispered. "Hard and smooth at the same time. I will never forget what it feels like to touch you like this."

"Who says you have to forget?" He walked her to the side of the bed and pushed her shoulders until she sat.

Who? He would. She laid down and watched him quickly undress until he stood completely naked in front of her, a tall, beautiful man who made her heart and soul ache. She raised a hand to him and pulled him on top of her. The voluptuous head of his hot penis touched between her legs. "I've loved being together," she whispered as she sucked his earlobe and rubbed against his warm body. She delivered little nibbling bites to his neck and shoulder.

Mick pushed her onto her back. "We have a lot more time to be together." He kissed her chin and throat. "A lot more." He sucked her nipple into his warm mouth while his other hand slid down her stomach to touch her with his fingers. As she watched him kiss her breast, raw emotion pumped through her veins. This was Mick, the man who could make her feel beautiful and desired. The man she loved and would probably lose.

Mick raised his head and the cool night air brushed across her breasts where his mouth had left her wet and shining. He reached into his wallet and pulled out a condom, but Maddie took it from his hands and stretched the thin latex down the length of him. She could feel his pulse in her hand, strong and steady. She pushed him onto his back and straddled his hips. His lids lowered over his eyes and the breath left his body as he watched her lower herself and take him inside her.

"You look good up there," he said, his voice low, rough. His hands grasped her waist. "Feel good too." He slid his hands up her sides to her breasts.

Maddie rocked her pelvis as she raised a little and slid back down. The head of his penis stroked her inside and she moaned deep in her throat. Up and down she moved, tilting her hips as she rode him. Tingling heat flowed outward from where his body touched hers. "Mick. Oh, God." He moved with her, matching her with powerful thrusts, until the sensations swamped her completely and her head fell back as a hot liquid orgasm washed through her, starting at her pelvis and spreading to her fingers and toes. "Mick. I love you," she said as new emotions wrapped around her pounding heart, squeezing her chest in its fiery grasp.

Just as the climax ended, Mick wrapped an arm around her back and bottom, and turned with her so that she lay on the bed looking up at him. He was still buried deep inside her and she automatically wrapped her legs around his waist as she knew he liked. She brought his mouth down to her and gave him wet wild kisses as he withdrew and thrust deep inside her again. She clung to him as he drove into her over and over. His chest heaved and he placed his hands on the bed beside her face. With each stroke, he pushed her toward a second climax, and she cried out as her body milked him hard for a second time.

Mick's eyes drifted shut, and his breath hissed between his teeth. "Holy shit," he swore, then groaned his satisfaction. He dove into her one last time, then collapsed on top of her.

His weight pushed down on her, heavy and welcome. His face rested on the pillow next to hers and he kissed her shoulder.

"Maddie?" he asked, breathless.

"Yeah?" She slid her hands across his back.

He raised onto his elbows and looked into her face, his breathing still heavy. "I don't know what was different this time, but that was the hottest sex I've ever had."

She knew what was different. She loved him. Her face got hot and she shoved at his shoulders. She loved him and she'd told him so too.

He rolled off her and lay on his back.

"I need some water," she said as she crawled off the bed and stood. Her ears were ringing from embarrassment and she moved to her closet and grabbed her robe.

"Where's your cat?" he asked.

"Probably on my office chair." She looked down at her shaking hands as she tied the terrycloth around her waist.

"If she attacks me, I'm getting her some G13."

Maddie had no idea what he was talking about. "Okay," she called from the closet.

"I have more condoms in my pants pocket," he said, all chipper as he walked to the bathroom. "But you're going to have to give me some time to get up to speed again."

While Mick used the bathroom, Maddie walked to the kitchen. She opened the refrigerator and pulled out a bottle of Diet Coke. She placed it against her burning cheeks and closed her eyes. Maybe he hadn't heard her. He'd told her on the way to Redfish that sometimes he didn't understand everything she said during sex. Perhaps she hadn't spoken as clearly as she'd thought.

She unscrewed the cap and took a long drink. She hoped like hell it had been one of those times, which only took care of one problem. The bigger problem loomed ahead, black and devastating and unavoidable.

Mick walked from the bedroom and made his way into the kitchen. He wore his Levi's low on his hips and his hair was tousled from her fingers. "Are you embarrassed about something?" he asked as he moved behind Maddie and wrapped his arms around her.

"Why?"

He took the bottle from her hands and raised it to his lips. "You practically ran out of the bedroom and your cheeks are red." He took a long drink, then handed it back to her.

She looked down at her feet. "Why would I be embarrassed?"

"Because you shouted, 'I love you,' in the throes of passion."

"Oh, God." She covered the side of her face with her free hand.

He turned her, placed his fingers beneath her chin, and brought her gaze to his. "It's okay, Maddie."

"No, it's not. I didn't mean to fall in love with you." She shook her head and insisted, "I don't *want* to be in love with you." Her chest felt raw and tears stung the backs of her eyes, and she didn't think it was possible to be in any worse pain. "My life sucks."

"Why?" He softly kissed her lips and said, "I'm in love with you too. I didn't think I would ever feel for a woman what I feel for you. These past few days, I've been wondering how you felt."

She took a few steps back and his hands fell to his sides. This should be the best, most euphoric time of her life. This wasn't fair, but as she'd discovered as a five-year-old child, life was not fair. She opened her mouth and forced the truth past the horrible clog in her throat. "Madeline Dupree is my pen name."

His brows rose up his forehead. "Madeline is not your real name?"

She nodded. "Madeline is my name. Dupree is not."

He tilted his head to one side. "What is your name?"

"Maddie Jones."

He looked at her, his eyes clear. He shrugged one bare shoulder and said, "Okay."

She didn't for one second believe he meant "okay" like he was okay with who she was. He wasn't connecting the dots. She licked her dry lips. "My mother was Alice Jones."

A slight frown creased his brow and then he jerked back like someone had shot him. His gaze moved across her face as if trying to see something he'd never noticed before. "Tell me you're making a joke, Maddie."

She shook her head. "It's true. Alice Jones isn't some face in a newspaper article that caught my attention. She was my mother." She reached a hand toward him, but he took a step back and her hand fell to her side. She hadn't thought she could be in more pain; she'd been wrong.

His eyes stared into hers. Gone was the man who'd just told her that he loved her. She'd seen Mick angry, but she'd never seen him so coldly furious. "Let me see if I'm getting this right. My father fucked your mother and I've been fucking you? Is that what you're telling me?"

"I don't see it that way."

"There's no other way to see it." He turned on his heels and moved from the kitchen.

Maddie followed him through the living room and into her bedroom. "Mick—"

"Have you gotten some sort of sick pleasure out of all this?" he interrupted her as he picked up his shirt and shoved his arms through the sleeves. "When you came to town, was it your intention from the beginning to totally screw with my head? Is this some sort of twisted revenge for what my mother did to yours?"

She shook her head and refused to give in to the tears that threatened to fill her eyes. She would not cry in front of Mick. "I didn't want to get involved with you. Ever. But you kept pushing. I wanted to tell you."

"Bullshit." He pulled the shirt over his head and down his chest. "If you'd wanted to tell me, you'd have found a way. You had no problem sharing every other detail of your life. I know you grew up fat and lost your virginity at twenty. I know you wear different scented lotion every day, and that you keep a vibrator named Carlos next to your bed." He bent forward and picked up his socks and shoes. "For Christ's sake, I even know you're not a butt girl." He pointed one of his shoes at her and continued, "And I'm supposed to believe that you couldn't work the truth into any conversation at some point before tonight!"

"I know that it's no consolation, but I never wanted to hurt you."

"I'm not hurt." He sat on the edge of the bed and shoved his feet into a pair of white socks. "I'm disgusted."

She felt her anger rise up and she was amazed she could feel anything beyond the deep mortal pain in her chest. She reminded herself that he had a right to be furious. He had a right to know early on whom he was getting involved with instead of after the fact. "That's harsh."

"Baby, you don't know harsh." He glanced up at her, then looked down as he put on his black boots and tied the laces. "I spent an hour tonight trying to defend you to my sister. She tried to tell me not to get involved with you, but I was thinking with my cock." He paused to let his gaze rake her up and down. "And now I have to go tell her about you. I have to tell her you're the daughter of the waitress who ruined her life and watch her come apart."

He might have more right to be angry than she did, but hearing him call her mother "the waitress" and worrying more about his sister than her scraped her raw emotions and pushed her over the top. "You. You. You. I am so sick of hearing about you and your sister. What about me?" She pointed to herself. "Your mother killed my mother. At the age of five, I moved in with a great-aunt who never wanted children. Who showed more love and affection for her cats than she ever did for me. Your mother did that to *me*. I've never been given so much as a second thought by you or your family. So I don't want to hear about you and your poor sister."

"If your mother hadn't been sleeping around—"

"If your father hadn't been sleeping around with about every woman in town and your mother hadn't been a vindictive bitch with a healthy dose of psychosis, then we'd all be happy as clams, wouldn't we? But your father was sleeping with my mother and your mother loaded a pistol and killed them both. That's our reality. When I moved to Truly, I expected to hate you and your sister for what your family has done to me. You look so much like your father that I expected to loathe you on sight, but I didn't. And as I got to know you, I realized that you are nothing like Loch."

"I used to believe that until tonight. If you are anything in the sack like your mother, then I get why my dad was ready to walk out the door and leave us for her. You Jones women drop your clothes and the Hennessy men get stupid."

"Wait!" Maddie interrupted him and held up

one hand. "Your dad was going to leave? For my mother?" Her mother had been right about Loch.

"Yeah. I just found out. Guess you have something to put in your book." He smiled, but it wasn't pleasant. "I'm just like my dad, and you're just like your mother."

"I am nothing like my mother, and you are nothing like your father. When I look at you, I just see you. That's how I fell in love with you."

"It doesn't matter what you see, because when I look at you, I don't know who you are." He stood. "You aren't the woman I thought you were. When I look at you now, I feel sick that I fucked the waitress's daughter."

Maddie's hands clenched into fists. "Her name was Alice and she was my mother."

"I don't really give a shit."

"I know you don't." She stormed out of the room and into her office, only to return a few moments later with a file and photograph. "This was her." She held up the old framed picture. "Look at her. She was twenty-four and beautiful and had her whole life ahead of her. She was flighty and immature and made horrible choices in her young life. Especially when it came to men." She pulled the crime scene photo from the files. "But she didn't deserve this."

"Jesus." Mick turned his head away.

Maddie dropped everything onto the dresser. "Your family did this to her and to me. The least you could do is say her goddamn name when you talk about her!"

Mick looked at her, his brows lowered over his beautiful eyes. "I've spent most of my life not talking or thinking about her. I'm going to spend the rest of it not thinking about you." He reached for his wallet on her bed, then walked out of the room.

Above the sound of her beating heart, Maddie heard the front door slam and she flinched. That had gone worse than she'd imagined. She'd thought he'd be angry, but disgusted? That had hit like a punch to the stomach.

She walked to the front door and, through the peephole, watched his truck pull out of her driveway. She locked the deadbolt and leaned her back against the solid door. The tears she'd refused to shed filled her eyes. A sound she almost didn't recognize as coming from her broke past the emotion in her chest. Like a puppet whose strings had been cut, she slid down until her butt hit the floor.

"Meow."

Snowball climbed into her lap and scaled the front of her robe. Her tiny pink tongue licked the tears from Maddie's numb cheek.

How was it possible to hurt so much but feel absolutely hollow inside?

Chapter 16

Meg raised her fingers to her temples and pushed, like she had as a kid. "She shouldn't be allowed to get away with this." The ends of her pink robe flapped about her ankles as she paced her small kitchen. It was nine A.M. and luckily her day off work. Travis had spent the night with Pete and was blissfully unaware of the turmoil brewing within his home.

"She shouldn't be allowed to live here," Meg ranted. "Our lives were fine until she showed up. She's just like her mother. Moving to town and messing up our lives."

After Mick had left Maddie's house, he'd gone back to work and tried to ignore the anger and chaos in his soul. After the bar closed, he stayed and worked on business. He looked over his bank records and wrote out payroll checks. He checked inventory and made notes on what he needed to order, and after the clock struck eight, he drove to his sister's.

"Someone should do something."

Mick set his coffee on the old oak table where he'd eaten dinner as a kid and sat in a chair. "Tell me you're not going to do anything."

She stopped and looked over at him. "Like what? What can I do?"

"Promise you won't go anywhere near her."

"What is it you think I'm going to do?"

He simply looked at her, and she seemed to deflate before his eyes.

"I'm not like Mom. I'm not going to hurt anyone."

No, just herself. "Promise," he insisted.

"Fine. If it will make you feel better. I promise that I'm not going to burn her house down." She laughed quietly and sat in the chair next to him.

"That's not funny, Meg."

"Maybe not, but no one got hurt that night, Mick."

Only because he'd shown up in time to pull her out of their farmhouse the night she'd torched it. She'd always insisted that she hadn't been trying to kill herself. To this day, he wasn't sure he believed her.

"I'm not crazy, you know."

"I know," he said automatically.

She shook her head. "No, you don't. Sometimes you look at me and I think you see Mom."

That was so close to the truth that he didn't even bother denying it. "I just think that sometimes your emotions are over the top."

"To you they are, but there is a big difference between being an emotional person who rants and raves as opposed to a person who takes a gun and kills herself or anyone else."

He thought calling her outbursts "being an emotional person" an understatement, but he didn't want to argue. He stood and walked to the sink. "I'm tired and going home," he said and poured his coffee down the drain.

"Get some sleep," his sister ordered.

He grabbed his keys off the kitchen table and Meg rose to hug him good-bye.

"Thanks for coming by and telling me everything."

He hadn't told Meg everything. He hadn't mentioned that he'd had sex with Maddie, nor that he'd fallen for her. "Tell Travis I'll come by tomorrow morning and take him fishing."

"He'll like that." She rose and walked him to the door. "You've been so busy with work lately that you boys haven't had much time together."

He'd been busy, but mostly busy chasing after Maddie Dupree. No. Maddie Jones.

"Take a shower," she called after him as he made his way to his truck. "You look like crap."

Which he figured was perfect, since he felt like crap. He jumped in his truck and ten minutes later he stood in his bedroom, wondering how his life had gone to complete hell.

He pulled his shirt over his head and caught a scent of Maddie. Last night she'd smelled like coconut and lime and this morning was the first time since he'd met her that he didn't want to bury his face in her neck. No, he wanted to wring her neck.

He tossed the shirt in the laundry basket in his closet and took off his shoes. Standing in her kitchen last night, realizing who she was, had hit him like a blow to the side of the head. If that hadn't been good enough for her, she'd held up the bloody photo of her mother, which finished him off with a round-house kick to the gut. She'd beat the hell out of him and he'd gone down for the count.

He took off his shoes and undressed. He was a fool. For the first time in his life, he'd truly fallen hard for a woman. So hard it ate at his chest like acid. Only she wasn't who she'd led him to believe she was. She was Maddie Jones. Daughter of his father's last girlfriend. It didn't matter that she didn't see Loch when she looked at him or that she looked nothing like her mother. It really didn't matter that she'd lied to him, or at least not as much as *knowing* who she really was mattered. He'd spent most of his life fighting to free himself from the past, only to fall for a woman deeply tangled up in it.

Mick walked into the bathroom and turned on the shower. Evidently he was more like Loch than he'd ever thought, and that just pissed him off. From almost the beginning, he'd known there was something about Maddie. Something that drew him in. He hadn't known what it was and couldn't have even guessed. Now he understood, and it sat in his gut like hot lead. He understood that it was the same single-minded attraction his father must have felt for her mother. The same fascination that made him want to see her smile, watch her laugh, and listen to her whisper his name as he gave her pleasure. The same sort of calm his father must have felt when he was near her mother. As if everything else dropped away and his vision cleared, and he saw what he wanted even before he knew he'd wanted anything.

He stepped into the shower and let the warm

water run over his head. For his father to have been planning to leave his mother for Alice Jones, Loch must have been in love with her. Mick understood that too. He was in love with Maddie Jones. He hated to admit it now. He was ashamed and embarrassed, but when she'd opened her door last night and he'd seen her standing there holding her cat, his heart had felt like the sun was warming him up from the inside. And he'd known. Known what it felt like for a man to love a woman. Known it in every cell in his body. Every beat of his heart. Then he'd carried her to her bed, and he'd known what it felt like to make love to a woman, and he'd been amazed.

Then she'd ripped his heart from his chest.

Mick tipped his head back and closed his eyes. He'd seen and done things in his life that he regretted. Experienced heart-wrenching pain at the deaths of fellow soldiers. But the things he'd done and experienced were not as bad as the regret and pain he felt over loving Maddie.

There was only one thing to do. He'd told her that he hadn't thought about her mother and that he wasn't going to think about her, and that was exactly what he planned to do. He was going to forget about Maddie Jones.

*   *   *

Meg opened her front door and looked into Steve Castle's calm blue eyes. She'd taken a shower and he'd arrived just as she'd finished drying her hair. "I didn't know who else to call."

"I'm glad you called me."

He stepped inside and followed her into the kitchen. He wore a pair of jeans and T-shirt with a cornucopia and the words EVERYBODY HATES VEGETARIANS across his chest. Over a fresh pot of coffee, she told him what she'd learned from Mick.

"The whole town is going to find out, and I don't know what to do."

Steve wrapped his big hand around the mug and raised it to his mouth. "Doesn't sound like there is anything you can do except hold your head up," he said, then took a drink.

"How can I?" The last time she'd talked with Steve about Maddie Dupree Jones, he'd given good advice and made her feel better. "This is just going to keep everyone talking about what my mother did and all my father's affairs."

"Probably, but that isn't your fault."

She stood and moved to the coffeepot. "I know, but that won't keep people from talking about me." She reached for the coffee, then refilled Steve's mug and hers.

"No. It won't, but while they're talking, you just keep telling yourself that you didn't do anything wrong."

She returned the coffeepot and leaned a hip against the counter. "I can tell myself that, but it won't make me feel better."

Steve placed a hand on the kitchen table and stood. "It will if you believe it."

"You don't understand. It's so humiliating."

"Oh, I understand about humiliation. When I returned from Iraq, my wife was pregnant and everyone knew the baby wasn't mine." He moved toward her, his limp barely noticeable. "Not only did I have to deal with the loss of my leg and my wife, but I had to deal with her being unfaithful with an army buddy."

"Oh, my God, I'm sorry, Steve."

"Don't be. My life was hell for a while, but it's good now. Sometimes you have to go taste the shit to appreciate the sugar."

Meg wondered if that was some sort of army saying.

He reached for her hand. "But you can't appreciate the sugar until you let go of all the bad shit." He brushed his thumb across the inside of her wrist and the hair on her arms tingled. "What your parents did didn't have anything to do with you. You were a kid. Just like my wife screwing my buddy didn't have anything to do with me. Not really. If she was unhappy because I was gone, there were other, more honorable ways to handle it. If your mama had been unhappy because your daddy was having affairs, there were other ways to handle that too. What my wife did wasn't my fault. Just like what your mama did wasn't your fault. I don't know about you, Meg, but I don't plan on paying the rest of my life for other people's dumb-ass mistakes."

"I don't want to."

He squeezed her hand and somehow she felt it in her heart. "Then don't." He pulled her toward him and placed his free hand on the side of her neck. "One thing I know for sure is that you can't control what other people say and do."

"You sound like Mick. He thinks I can't get over the past because I dwell on it." She turned her face into his palm.

"Maybe you need something in your life to take your mind off the past."

When she'd been married to Travis's daddy, she hadn't let it bother her as much as it did these days.

"Maybe you need someone."

"I have Travis."

"Besides your son." He lowered his face and spoke against her lips. "You're a beautiful woman, Meg. You should have a man in your life."

She opened her mouth to speak, but she couldn't remember what to say. It had been a very long time since a man had told her she was beautiful. A long time since she'd kissed anyone but her son. She pressed her mouth against Steve's and he kissed her. A warm gentle kiss that seemed to go on forever within the sunlight spilling into the kitchen. And when it was over, he cupped her face in his rough hands and said, "I've wanted to do that for a long time."

Meg licked her bottom lip and smiled. He made her feel beautiful and wanted. Like more than just a waitress, a mom, and a woman who'd just hit forty. "How old are you, Steve?"

"Thirty-four."

"I'm six years older than you."

"Is that a problem?"

She shook her head. "No, but it might be a problem for you."

"Age is not a problem." He slid his hands to her back and pulled her against his chest. "I just have to figure out a way to tell Mick that I want his sister."

Meg smiled and wrapped her arms around his neck. She knew there were a lot of things Mick kept to himself. Most recently his relationship with Maddie Jones. "Let him figure it out on his own."

Chapter 17

Maddie lay curled up in bed. She didn't have the energy to get up. She was drained and empty except for the ball of regret sitting in her stomach. She regretted not telling Mick sooner. If she'd told him who she really was the first night she'd walked into Mort's, he never would have shown up at her door with mousetraps and catnip. He never would have touched her and kissed her, and she never would have fallen in love with him.

Snowball climbed onto the bed and picked her way across the quilt toward Maddie's face.

"What are you doing?" she asked her kitten, her voice raw from the emotion she'd expended all night. "You know I don't like cat hair. This is completely against the rules."

Snowball crawled beneath the covers, then stuck her head back out just beneath Maddie's chin. Her soft fur tickled Maddie's throat. "Meow."

"You're right. Who gives a shit about the rules?" She stroked the cat's fur as her eyes filled with tears. She'd cried so much the night before, she was surprised she had any water left in her body, that she wasn't all dehydrated and wrinkled like a raisin.

Maddie rolled to her back and looked up at the shadows spread across her ceiling. She could have lived her entire life quite happy if she'd never fallen in love. She'd be happy to never know the high dopamine rush or the heart-wrenching anguish and despair of having loved and lost. Lord Tennyson was wrong. It was not better to have loved and lost than to have never loved at all. Maddie would have much preferred to have never loved at all than to love Mick only to lose him.

I'm not hurt, he'd said. *I'm disgusted*. She could take his anger and even the hate she'd seen in his eyes. But disgust? That hurt to the core. The man she loved, the man who'd not only touched her heart but her body, was disgusted by her. Knowing how he felt made her want to curl up in a ball and cover her head until it didn't hurt anymore.

Around noon her back began to ache, so she grabbed her kitten and a quilt off her bed. She and Snowball lay on the couch and watched mindless television all day and into the evening. She even watched *Kate & Leopold*, a movie she'd always hated because she'd never understood why any sane woman would jump off a bridge for a man.

However, this time her dislike of the movie didn't keep her from crying into a Kleenex. After *Kate & Leopold*, she watched *Meerkat Manor* and *Project Runway* reruns. When she wasn't crying over Leopold, the poor Meerkats, or the abomination of Jeffrey's rocker pants, she was thinking about Mick. What he'd said, his face when he'd said it, and what he'd told her about his father leaving his mother for Alice. Alice had been right about Loch's feelings. Who would have thought it? Not Maddie, or rather she had *thought* of it, but given Alice's history with men, especially married men, and Loch's history with women, Maddie had dismissed the possibility.

Rose's reasoning for what she'd done was a classic case of loss of control and the feeling of loss of self. The typical "if I can't have you, no one can" that had been analyzed and studied and found throughout history.

It had been so simple, and right in front of her the whole time. Knowing the truth made writing the book easier, but on a personal level, it really didn't change anything. Her mother had still made a bad choice that ended in her death. Three people died and three children were left devastated. Motive didn't really matter a whole lot.

At around midnight she fell asleep and woke the next morning feeling as bad as ever. Maddie had never been a whiner or a crier. Most likely because she'd learned at an early age that whining and crying and feeling sorry for yourself didn't get you anywhere. Even though she still felt like emotional roadkill, she took a shower and moved into her office. Lying around and feeling bad wasn't going to get her work done. That was the thing about writing her books, she was the only one who could do it.

Her timeline was pinned to the wall and everything was ready. She sat down and began to write:

At three p.m. on July ninth, Alice Jones put on her white blouse and black skirt and sprayed Charlie on her wrists. It was the first day of her new job at Hennessy's, and she wanted to make a good impression. Hennessy's had been built in 1925 during Prohibition and the family had prospered by selling grain alcohol out of the back. . . .

At around noon, Maddie got up to fix lunch, feed Snowball, and grab a Diet Coke. She wrote until midnight, when she fell into bed, and woke the next morning with Snowball under the covers and curled beneath her chin.

"This is a bad habit," she told her cat. Snowball purred, a steady rattling of love, and Maddie couldn't quite bring herself to kick the kitten out of bed.

During the next several weeks, Snowball developed other bad habits as well. She insisted on lying in Maddie's lap while she wrote or walking on the desk and batting off paper clips, pens, and blocks of sticky notes.

Maddie kept herself busy, writing ten hours a day, taking occasional breaks out on her back deck to feel the sun on her face, before getting back to work until she fell into bed exhausted. During those moments when she wasn't thinking about work, her mind always turned to Mick. She wondered what he was doing and who he was seeing. He'd said that he wasn't going to think about her, and she believed him. If not thinking about the past was easy for him, not thinking about her would be even easier.

On those occasions when her mind wasn't filled with work, she recalled their conversations, their lunch at Redfish, and the nights he'd spent in her bed.

She wished she could hate Mick. Or even dislike him. It would be so much easier if she could. She'd tried to recall all the mean and nasty things he'd said the night she'd told him who she was, but she couldn't hate Mick. She loved him and was fairly sure she'd love him forever.

On the anniversary of her mother's death, she wondered if Mick was alone, remembering that night that had changed their lives. If he felt as alone and sad as she did. As the clock struck a minute after midnight, her heart sank as she realized she'd been holding on to a tiny shred of hope that he might show up on her porch. He didn't, and she was forced to accept all over again that the man she loved didn't love her.

The last day of August, she dressed in a pair of khaki shorts and a black cotton tank and took Snowball for her vet appointment. Leaving her kitten in the big hands of Dr. Tannasee was more traumatic than Maddie was willing to admit. She ignored the little burst of panic as she walked out of the examining room without the crazy-eyed, bucktoothed, rule-breaking ball of white fur, and she was forced to face an inconceivable fact. Somehow, Maddie had become a cat person.

When she returned home, the house seemed intolerably still and empty, and she forced herself to work for a few hours before moving out onto the deck to take a break in the fresh air and sunshine. She sat in an Adirondack chair and tilted her face to the sun. Next door, the Allegrezzas stood on their deck, laughing and talking and barbequing something.

"Maddie, come over and see the twins," Lisa called out to her. She stood and took a quick inventory, but she didn't spot a Hennessy. Her black flip-flops slapped the bottoms of her feet as she walked the short distance to the neighbors'.

Wrapped like burritos and lying in the same baby carriage shaded by a big ponderosa, Isabel and Lilly Allegrezza slept, oblivious to the fuss around them. The girls had dark glossy hair like their father and the most delicate faces Maddie had ever seen.

"Don't they look like little porcelain dolls?" Lisa asked.

Maddie nodded. "They're so tiny."

"They both weigh a little more than five pounds now," Delaney said. "They were early, but they're perfectly healthy. If there was the slightest concern, Nick would have them at home in a germ-free bubble." She looked over at her husband manning the grill with Louie. She lowered her voice and added, "He's bought every gadget imaginable. The baby book calls that nesting."

Lisa laughed. "Who would have thought he'd be a nester?"

"Are you talking about me?" Nick asked his wife.

Delaney looked over at the grill and smiled. "Just saying how much I love you."

"Uh-huh."

"When are you going back to work?" Lisa asked her sister-in-law.

"I'll open the salon again next month."

Maddie looked at Delaney and her smooth blond hair, cut straight across at her shoulders. "A hair salon?"

"Yeah. I own the salon on Main." Delaney looked at Maddie's hair and added, "If you need a trim before next month, let me know and I'll bring over my shears. Whatever you do, don't go to Helen's

Hair Hut. She'll fry your hair and make you look like a bad eighties rock video. If you want your hair done right, come to me."

Which explained why half the town had badly fried hair.

The back door opened and Pete and Travis walked out, each with a hot dog bun in his hand. They waited patiently as Louie slid a hot dog in each bun and Nick provided a stream of ketchup. Seeing Travis reminded Maddie of his uncle. She wondered where Mick was, and if he was likely to show up. If he did, would he be alone or have a woman on his arm who expected more from Mick than he would give? He'd said he loved her, but she didn't believe him. As she'd learned all too painfully, love didn't go away just because you didn't want to think about it.

"Hey, Travis, how are you?" she asked as he moved toward her.

"Good. How's your cat?"

"She's at the vet's today, so it's fairly quiet around my house."

"Oh." He looked up at her and squinted against the glare of the sun. "I'm going to get a dog."

"Oh." She remembered what Meg had said about getting Travis a pet. "When?"

"Someday." He took a bite of his hot dog and

said, "I went fishing with my uncle Mick on his boat. We got skunked." He swallowed, then added, "We drove by on the water and saw you. We didn't wave, though."

Of course not. She said her good-byes and went home. The house was still much too quiet, and she drove to Value Rite Drug to do a little nesting of her own. It was time Snowball got a proper pet carrier, and she planned to look for a better bed for the kitten. Obviously the Amazon box wasn't a hit.

What Maddie hadn't planned was to run smack-dab in the middle of the Founders Day celebration. She vaguely recalled seeing something about it somewhere, but she'd forgotten all about it. The trip to Value Rite Drug, which normally took about ten minutes, took half an hour. The parking lot was packed with cars from the Founders Day Arts and Crafts Fair held in the park across the street.

Maddie had to circle the parking lot like a vulture until she finally found a slot. Normally she wouldn't have bothered, but she figured it would probably take her another half hour to get home anyway.

Once inside the store, she found a little cat bed but no carrier. She tossed it into her cart along with a catnip toy, and a cat DVD filled with footage of birds, fish, and mice. She was a bit embarrassed to find herself buying a DVD for a cat, but she figured Snowball might stay off the furniture if she was mesmerized by watching fish.

While at the store, she stocked up on toilet paper, laundry soap, and her most secret indulgence, the *Weekly News of the Universe*. She loved the stories of fifty-pound grasshoppers and about women who were having Big Foot's baby, but her favorites were always the Elvis sightings. She dropped the black-and-white magazine into her cart and headed for the checkout lanes.

Carleen Dawson was working register five when Maddie set her items on the counter.

"I heard you're Alice's daughter. Or is that just a rumor like Brad Pitt comin' to town?"

"No, that's true. Alice Jones was my mother." Maddie dug around in her purse and pulled out her wallet.

"I worked with Alice at Hennessy's."

"Yes, I know," she said and braced herself for what Carleen might say next.

"She was a nice girl. I liked her."

Surprise curved Maddie's lips into a smile. "Thank you."

Carleen rung up everything and put it all,

except the bed, into a bag. "She shouldn't have been fooling around with a married man, but she didn't deserve what Rose did to her."

Maddie swiped her card and entered her PIN number. "I obviously agree." She paid for her items and walked out of Value Rite feeling a lot better than when she'd walked in. She put everything in the trunk of her car and decided that since she was there, she'd check out the arts and crafts fair. She put her big black sunglasses on the bridge of her nose as she crossed the street and entered the park. She'd never been into arts and crafts, mostly because she didn't really decorate.

At the Pronto Pup stand, she splurged on a corn dog with extra mustard. She saw Meg and Travis with a tall bald man wearing a SPARROW IS MY CO-PIRATE T-shirt. She noticed right away that Mick wasn't with them, and she waited for them to pass before she moved to the PAWS booth and looked at pet collars, pet clothes, and feeders. The pink princess cat ottoman was over the top, but she did find a carrier in the shape of a bowling bag. It was red with black mesh hearts and lined in black fur. It also came with a matching wristlet for pet treats. She ordered Snowball a three-story kitty condo and an electronic litter box, to be delivered the following week. The carrier she took with her so that she could bring Snowball home in it the next day.

She hung the carrier on her shoulder and threw her corn dog stick away as she left the booth. As she hooked a right by the Mr. Pottery stand, she practically ran headfirst into Mick Hennessy's chest. She looked up past the blue T-shirt covering his wide chest, past the throat she'd kissed so often, the stubborn set of his chin and angry press of his mouth, and up into his eyes covered by sunglasses. Her heart pounded and pinched, and heat flushed her body. Her first instinct was to run away from the anger rolling off him in waves. Instead she managed a very pleasant, "Hello, Mick."

He frowned. "Maddie."

Her gaze skimmed across his face, feeding images of him to the lonely places inside her, images of his black hair touching his brow and of the bruise on his cheek.

"What happened to your face?"

He shook his head. "Doesn't matter."

Panty-tossing Darla stood beside him and asked, "Are you going to introduce me to your friend?"

Until that moment, Maddie had not realized they were together. Darla's big hair was as fried as ever, and she wore one of her sparkly tank tops and painfully tight jeans.

"Darla, this is Madeline Dupree, but her real name is Maddie Jones."

"The writer?"

"Yes." Maddie adjusted the cat carrier on her shoulder. What was Mick doing with Darla? Surely he could do better.

"J.W. told me that he heard you were trying to get the Hennessys and your mother exhumed."

"Christ," Mick swore.

Maddie glanced at Mick, then returned her gaze to Darla. "That's not true. I would never do something like that."

Mick pulled a wad of cash out of his front pocket and handed it to the other woman. "Why don't you head over to the beer garden and I'll meet you there in a minute?"

Darla took the money and asked, "Is Budweiser all right?"

"Fine."

As soon as Darla walked away, Mick said, "How much longer are you going to be in town?"

Maddie shrugged and watched Darla's big behind disappear into the crowd. "Can't really say." She looked back up into the face of the man who made her broken heart pound in her throat. "Please tell me you aren't dating Darla."

"Jealous?"

No, she was angry. Angry that he didn't love her. Angry that she would always love him. Angry that a part of her wanted to throw herself on his chest like some desperate high school girl and beg him to love her. "Are you shitting me? Jealous of a low-exception dumb-ass? If you want to make me jealous, start dating someone with half a brain and a modicum of class."

His gaze narrowed. "At least she isn't running around pretending to be someone she's not."

Yes, she was. She was running around pretending she was a size ten, but Maddie chose not to point that out in a crowded park because she *did* have a modicum of class.

Just above the noise surrounding them he said, "Not everything that comes out of her mouth is a lie."

"How would you know? You don't ever stick around long enough to get to know anyone."

"You think you know me so well."

"I do know you. Probably better than any other woman, and I'd be willing to bet that I'm the only woman you've ever really known."

Slowly he shook his head. "I don't know you."

She looked into his mirrored sunglasses and said, "Yes, you do, Mick."

"Knowing your favorite sexual position is not what I call knowing you."

He wanted to reduce what had been between them to just sex. It might have started out that way, but it had become so much more. At least to her. She took a step forward and raised onto the balls of her feet. He was so close she could feel the heat of his skin through his shirt and hers. So close she was sure he could feel her pounding heart as she said next to his ear, "You know more than whether I like it on top or bottom. You know more than the smell of my skin or the taste of me in your mouth." She closed her eyes and added, "You know me. You just can't handle who I am." Without another word she turned on her heels and left him standing there. She couldn't say that her first encounter with him had gone well, but at least he was going to be thinking about her after she was gone.

Instead of getting the hell out of the park and getting home to avoid seeing Mick again, she forced herself to take her time. She'd been down for a few weeks, but she was better now, stronger than her broken heart. She paused at the Mad Hatter stand and stopped at the Spoon Man booth. Mr. Spoon Man sold everything from jewelry to clocks out of spoons, and Maddie bought a chime she thought would sound nice on the back deck.

She put the chime in the cat carrier and made

her way out of the park. But like the pull of a magnet on a paper clip, her gaze was drawn to the beer garden and the man who stood at the entrance. Only this time Mick wasn't with Darla. Tanya King, with her little body and little clothes, stood in front of him, and his head was bent forward slightly as he listened to her every word. Her hand rested on his chest, and the corners of his mouth turned up as he smiled at something she said.

He didn't appear to be thinking about Maddie at all, and suddenly she didn't feel stronger than her broken heart.

Through the lenses of his sunglasses, Mick watched Maddie as she crossed the street and left the park. His gaze slid down her back to her butt. The memory of her legs around his waist and his hands on her behind flashed across his brain whether he wanted to remember or not. And he didn't. Hardly a day passed without something reminding him of Maddie. His truck. His boat. His bar. He couldn't walk into Mort's without remembering the night she'd arrived at his back door wearing a trench coat and one of his ties between her beautiful bare breasts. He'd like to believe that it had just been about sex with her, but she'd been right about that. It had been more than the smell of her skin and the taste of her in his mouth. At odd random moments he'd wonder where she was and if she'd gone to Boise for her friend's wedding. Or he'd remember her laugh, the sound of her voice and her smart mouth.

Are you shitting me? Jealous of a low-exception dumb-ass? If you want to make me jealous, start dating someone with half a brain and a modicum of class, she'd said, as if there were a chance in hell he'd ever date Darla. He hadn't had sex since that last night with Maddie, but he wasn't hard up. He'd never been that hard up.

You know more than whether I like it on top or bottom. You know more than the smell of my skin or the taste of me in your mouth. Seeing her and smelling the scent of her skin, the urge to feel her against his chest once again, had been overwhelming, and for a fraction of one unguarded second, he'd actually raised his hands to pull her closer. Thank God he had stopped himself before he'd touched her.

You just can't handle who I am. She was right about that. She was a liar who'd used her body to get him to talk about the past, and he'd fallen for it.

Darla wasn't the only dumb-ass.

Maddie disappeared across the street and his gaze returned to Tanya. She was talking about . . . something.

"My new trainer is brutal, but he gets results."

Oh, yeah. Tanya's exercise. No doubt about it, Tanya had a good body. Too bad her hand on his chest wasn't doing much for *his* body. He needed a distraction. His efforts to forget about Maddie, to put her out of his head and not think about her, were clearly not working.

Maybe Tanya was exactly what he needed.

Chapter 18

The night before Clare's wedding, the four friends got together at Maddie's house in Boise. They sat in Maddie's living room in front of a big fireplace made of river rock. The house in Boise was furnished in brown and beige tones, and moments earlier Maddie had cracked open a bottle of Moët. The four women raised their champagne glasses and toasted Clare's future happiness with her fiancé Sebastian Vaughan.

A little over a year ago, all four women had been single. Now Lucy was married and Clare was about to get married. Adele continued to believe she was cursed with bad dates, and Maddie had fallen in love and gotten her heart broken. Adele was the only one out of the four whose life hadn't drastically changed. Although Maddie had yet to confide to her friends about her feelings for Mick. This was Clare's night. Not a pity party for Maddie. It had been a week since she'd seen Mick in the park with Tanya, and the image still made her sick.

"My mother has invited half of Boise to the wedding. She has been in her . . ." Clare paused and leaned to the left to look behind Maddie's chair. "There's a cat in your house."

Maddie turned around and looked at Snowball, flagrantly disregarding the rules as she climbed up the satin drapes. Maddie clapped her hands and stood. "Snowball." The cat looked over at Maddie and dropped to the floor.

"Do you know that cat?" Adele asked.

"I kind of adopted it."

"Kind of?"

Lucy leaned forward. "You hate cats."

"I know."

Clare covered her lips with two fingers. "You named your cat Snowball. That's so cute."

"So unlike you," Lucy added.

Adele tilted her head to one side and looked concerned. "Are you all right? You go away for a few months and come back with a cat. What else have you been doing up there in Truly that we don't know about?"

Maddie lifted her glass and finished off the champagne. "Nothing."

Lucy raised a suspicious brow. "How's the book?"

"Actually, it's going fairly well," she answered truthfully. "I'm a little over halfway finished." The next half was going to be the rough part. The part where she would have to write about the night her mother died.

"How's Mick Hennessy?" Adele asked.

Maddie rose and moved to the coffee table. "I don't know." She poured herself more champagne. "He won't talk to me."

"Did you finally tell him who you really are?"

Maddie nodded and refilled her friends' glasses. "Yes, I told him, and he didn't take it very well."

"At least you didn't sleep with him."

Maddie looked away and took a drink from her glass.

"Oh, my God!" Clare gasped. "You fell off the wagon with Mick Hennessy?"

Maddie shrugged and took her seat. "I couldn't help myself."

Adele nodded. "He's hot."

"A lot of men are hot." Lucy took a sip as she studied Maddie. Her brows shot up her forehead. "You're in love with him."

"It doesn't matter. He hates me."

Clare, the most kindhearted of the four, said, "I'm sure that's not true. No one can hate you."

That was so blatantly untrue, Maddie couldn't help a smile, while Lucy coughed on her champagne.

Adele sat back and laughed. "Maddie Jones got a cat and fell in love. Hell has officially frozen over."

The day after Clare's wedding, Maddie packed up her cat and headed to Truly. The wedding had been beautiful, of course. And at the reception, Maddie had partied and danced the night away. Several of the men she'd danced with had been good-looking and single, and she wondered if she'd ever get to a point in her life when she would not compare every man she met to Mick Hennessy.

She spent the rest of September writing and reliving the days before her mother's death. She inserted parts of interviews and diary entries, including the very last:

My baby will turn six next year and will go to first grade. I can't believe how big she is. I wish I could give her more. Maybe I can. Loch said that he loves me. I've heard that before. He says he's going to leave his wife and be with me. He says he doesn't love Rose, and he's going to tell her that he doesn't want to live with her anymore. I've heard that before too. I want to believe him. No, I do believe him!! I just hope he isn't lying. I know he loves his children. He talks about them a lot. He worries that when he tells his wife he wants a divorce his kids will have to witness a big scene. He's afraid she'll throw things or do something really crazy like start his car on fire. I worry that she will hurt Loch and I told him so. He just laughed and said Rose would never hurt anyone.

The hardest part of the book hadn't been reliving the death of her mother moment by moment, as she'd always thought. That had been hard, to be sure, but the most difficult part had been writing the end and saying good-bye. In writing the book, she realized that she'd never said good-bye to her mother. Never had any sort of closure. Now she did, and it felt as if one part of her life had ended.

When she was through with the book, it was

mid-October and she was physically and emo-
tionally drained. She fell into bed and slept for
almost twenty hours. When she woke, she felt as
if a thorn had been taken from her chest. A thorn
that she'd never even known was embedded there.
She was free from the past and she hadn't even
known she'd needed freeing.

Maddie fed Snowball, then jumped in the
shower. Her cat had yet to sleep in the bed Maddie had bought for her. She liked the video, and
the carrier not at all. Maddie had given up on any
sort of rules. Snowball liked to spend most of her
time lying on the windowsill or in Maddie's lap.

Maddie washed her hair and scrubbed her body
with watermelon-scented sugar scrub and wondered what she was going to do with her life.
Which was such an odd question, really, when
she thought about it. Until she'd finished the book,
she hadn't realized how much of her life had been
wrapped up in the past. It had dictated her future
without her even knowing it.

Maybe she'd take a vacation. Someplace warm.
Just pack a swimsuit and a pair of flip-flops and
hit a nice beach. Maybe Adele needed a break
from her cycle of cursed dating.

As Maddie toweled herself dry, she thought of
Mick. She was thirty-four, and he was her first

real love. She would always love him even though he could never love her back. But perhaps there was something she could do for him. She could give him the same gift that she'd given herself.

Mick's gaze rose from the bottle in his hand to the woman walking in the front door. He set the Corona on the bar and watched her as she moved between the tables. Mort's was slow, even for a Monday night.

Her hair curled about her shoulders like the first time he'd seen her, and she wore a black bulky sweater that hid the wonders of her body. She carried a box beneath one arm. He hadn't seen her since Founders Day when she'd told him that he couldn't handle the truth about her. She'd been right. He couldn't, but that didn't mean he hadn't missed her every damn day. Didn't mean that his gaze didn't drink up everything about her. Trying to forget about her hadn't worked. Nothing had worked.

Above Trace Adkins on the jukebox, she said, "Hello, Mick." Her voice poured through him like warmed brandy.

"Maddie."

"May I talk to you somewhere private?"

He wondered if she'd come to tell him good-bye and how he'd feel about that. He nodded and the two of them moved to his office. Her shoulder touched his, adding need to the warm mix spreading across his flesh. He wanted Maddie Jones. Wanted her like he was starving, wanted to jump on her and eat her up. She shut the door, and the urge got stronger. He moved behind his desk, as far away from her as possible. "Maybe you should leave the—"

"Please let me talk," she interrupted and held up a hand. "I have something to say and then I'll leave." She swallowed hard and stared directly into his eyes. "The first time I recall being afraid, I was five. I'm not talking about Halloween and boogeyman afraid. I am talking sick-to-my-stomach afraid.

"A sheriff's deputy woke me up to tell me my great-aunt was coming to get me and that my mother was dead. I didn't understand what had happened. I didn't understand why my mother had gone away, but I knew she was never coming back. I cried so hard I threw up all over the backseat of my great-aunt Martha's Cadillac."

He remembered that night too. Remembered the backseat of the cop car and Meg sobbing beside him. What was the point of remembering?

"When I met you," she continued, "I didn't expect to like you, but I did. I certainly didn't expect to like you so much that I ended up in bed with you, but I did. I didn't expect to fall in love with you, but I did that too. From the beginning, I knew I should have told you who I was. I knew I should have told you a hundred different times. I knew it was the right thing to do, but I also knew that I'd lose you if I did. I knew when I told you, you'd leave and never come back. And that's what happened."

She set a Xerox copier-paper box on his desk. "I want you to have this. It's the book I moved here to write, and I want you to read it. Please." She looked down at the box. "The disk is with it, and I've deleted it from my computer. This is the only copy. Do what you want with both. Throw them away, run over them with your truck, or have a bonfire. It's up to you."

She looked back at him. Her brown eyes steady, calm. "I hope that someday you can forgive me. Not because I personally need your forgiveness. I don't. But I've learned something in the past few months, and that is just because you refuse to acknowledge something, refuse to look at it or think about it, doesn't mean it's not there, that it doesn't affect you and the choices you make in your life."

She licked her lips. "I forgive your mother. Not because the Bible tells me I should forgive. I guess I'm not that good a Christian, because I'm just not that magnanimous. I forgive her because, in forgiving her, I am free of all the anger and bitterness of the past, and that is what I want for you too.

"I've thought about what I've done since I moved to Truly, and I'm sorry that I hurt you, Mick. But I'm not sorry that I met you and fell in love with you. Loving you has broken my heart and caused me pain, but it made me a better person. I love you, Mick, and I hope that someday you find someone you can love. You deserve more in life than a string of women you don't really care about and who don't care all that much for you. Loving you taught me that. It taught me how it feels to love a man, and I hope that someday I can find someone who will love me the way that you can't. Because I deserve more than a string of men who don't really care about me." Her gaze moved over his face, then returned to his eyes. "I came here tonight to give you the book and because I wanted to say good-bye."

"You're leaving?" He didn't have to wonder how he'd feel about her good-bye.

"Yes. I have to."

Her leaving was best, no matter that it felt like she was reaching into his chest and ripping out his heart all over again. "When?"

She shrugged and walked to the door. "I don't know. Soon." She looked over her shoulder one last time and said, "Good-bye, Mick. Have a good life." Then she was gone and he was left with the scent of her skin in the air and a big emptiness in his chest. The red sweater she'd worn the night she'd come into his office wearing a white halter dress still hung on a hook behind the door. He knew that it still smelled like strawberries.

He sat in his chair and leaned his head back. He thought of old drunk Reuben Sawyer spending three decades sitting on a barstool, sad and pathetic and unable to move beyond the pain of losing his wife. Mick wasn't that pathetic, but he understood old Reuben in a way that he never had before he'd loved Maddie Jones. He hadn't picked up the bottle. He owned two bars and knew where that path led, but he had gotten into a fight or two. A few days before he'd seen Maddie in the park, he'd kicked the Finley boys out of Mort's. Usually he called the cops to deal with assorted assholes and numb nuts, but that night he'd taken on both Scoot and Wes. No one had ever accused the Finley boys of being smart, but they were fighters, and it had taken both Mick and his bartender to shove them out into the alley, where a knock-down free-for-all had ensued. The kind Mick hadn't enjoyed since high school.

Mick raked his fingers through the sides of his hair and sat forward. Since the night he'd found out who Maddie really was, he'd been in hell and he didn't know how to get out. His life seemed to be one miserable day after another. He thought things would get better, but his life wasn't heading in the direction of better, and he didn't know what to do about it. Maddie was who she was, and he was Mick Hennessy, and no matter how much he loved her, real life wasn't a made-for-TV movie on that women's channel Meg liked to watch.

He leaned forward and pulled the Xerox box toward him. He took off the top and looked inside at the orange disk and a stack of paper. In big type across the first page was written: *Till Death Us Do Part.*

Maddie said this was the only copy. Why would she give it to him? Why go to so much trouble and spend so much time doing something, only to give it to him when she was through?

He didn't want to read it. He didn't want to get sucked back in time. He didn't want to read about his unfaithful father and his sick mother and the night she'd gone over the edge. He didn't want to see the photographs or read the police reports. He'd lived through it once and didn't feel like revisiting the past, but as he picked up the lid to replace it on the box, the first sentence caught his eye.

"I promise it's going to be different this time, baby." Alice Jones glanced at her young daughter, then returned her gaze to the road. "You're going to like Truly. It's a little like heaven, and it's about damn time Jesus drop-kicked us into a better life."

Baby didn't say anything. She'd heard it before. . . .

Maddie plugged Snowball's DVD into the player and sat her on the cat bed in front of the television. It wasn't even ten A.M., and she'd had enough of Snowball. "If you don't behave, I'm going to throw you in your carrier and toss you into the trunk of my car."

"Meow."

"I mean it." Snowball was going through some sort of passive-aggressive phase. She meowed to go out. Meowed to come in, but when Maddie opened the door, she'd run the opposite way. You'd think the cat would be more grateful.

She pointed at her kitten's nose. "I'm warning you. You've just gotten on my last nerve." She rose and tiptoed away. Snowball didn't follow, for the moment transfixed by the parakeets chirping on the screen.

The doorbell rang and Maddie moved to the front of the house and looked through the peephole. Last night when she'd said good-bye to Mick, she hadn't expected to see him again. Now here he was, looking a bit rough. The lower half of his face was covered in stubble like all the times they'd stayed up late making love. She opened the door and saw the Xerox box in his hand. Her heart dropped. All that work and he hadn't read it.

"Are you going to invite me in?"

She opened the door wider and shut it behind him. He wore a black North Face fleece jacket and, beneath the black stubble, his cheeks were pink from the cold morning chill. He followed her into the living room, bringing the scent of October air and of him into her house. She loved the way he smelled and had missed it.

"Is your cat watching television?" His voice was kind of rough too.

"For the moment."

He set the box on her coffee table. "I read your book."

She glanced at the clock above the television just to make sure of the time. She'd given it to him to read and destroy because she loved him, and he'd probably skimmed it. "That was fast."

"I'm sorry."

"Don't be sorry. Some people are just fast readers."

He smiled, but it didn't reach his blue eyes or bring out his dimples. "No. I'm sorry for what my mother did to yours. I don't believe anyone in my family has ever apologized to you. We were all too wrapped up in what it did to us to even stop and think about what it did to you."

She blinked and managed a stunned, "Oh. You don't have to apologize. You didn't do anything wrong."

He laughed without humor. "Don't let me off the hook, Maddie. I've done a lot of things wrong." He unzipped his jacket, and he wore the same Mort's polo shirt he'd had on the night before. The man must have dozens of them. "Believing that just because I don't think about what had happened in the past meant it doesn't bother or affect me was not only wrong, it was stupid. If I'd truly gotten over it, who you are wouldn't have mattered to me. It would have surprised me, maybe even shocked the shit out of me, but it wouldn't matter."

But it had mattered to him. So much so that he'd cut her out of his life.

"I've been up all night reading your book. At first I didn't want to read it because I thought it would be a long laundry list of the things my parents had done, complete with grisly photos. But it wasn't."

She wanted to reach out and touch him. To run her hands up his chest and bury her face in his neck. "I tried to be fair."

"You were surprisingly fair. If your mother had shot mine, I don't know if I would have been as fair. I felt a kind of weird connection to my parents. To my life as a kid, and I understand how everything went so wrong. And I understand that you don't always get a second chance to do it right."

She wanted him to reach out and touch her. To put his hands on the sides of her face and lower his mouth to hers. Instead he stuck his fingers in the front pocket of his Levi's.

"When I saw you in the park, I said I didn't know you, but that was a lie. I know you. I know that you're funny and smart and that you're freezing when it's seventy degrees outside. I know that you crave cheesecake but settle for cake-scented lotion instead. I know you have a problem with people telling you what to do. And I know that you want everyone to think you're a hard-ass, but that you take in a bucktoothed cat and give her a home. Everything I know about you makes me want to know more."

Her chest got that familiar ache, and she looked down at her feet, not trusting the emotion expanding in her chest.

"Since I moved back to Truly," he said, "I've felt as if I were standing in one place, unable to move. But I wasn't standing still. I was waiting. I think I was waiting for you."

The backs of her eyes stung and she bit her bottom lip.

"When I'm with you, I feel a kind of calm I've never felt in my life. I'm tangled up in you and you're tangled up in me and it feels right. Like it was meant to be. I love you, Maddie, and I'm sorry it's taken me so long to say it to you again."

She looked up at him and smiled. "I've missed you."

He laughed, and his dimples finally dented his cheeks. "You haven't missed me any more than I've missed you. I've been one miserable shithead." He wrapped his arms around her and lifted her off the ground. "I've never believed that death happens for a reason," he said as he looked up into her face. "But if our lives had been different, I wouldn't have fallen in love with you." Slowly she slid down his body until her pelvis fit his. He was ready for love, and his hands slipped beneath her shirt and caressed her bare back.

He lowered his head and kissed her. His mouth was warm and wet and so welcome. Later she would take his hand and take him to her room. For now, she just wanted to feel his kiss again, and it was like walking into the sun after a long cold winter. An *ahh* that felt good clear to the marrow of her bones.

He pulled back and pressed his forehead to hers. "Ever since that first night you came into Mort's, my eyes have been on you," he said. "You were the only thing I could see, even when I tried like hell to look someplace else."

"Hmm. Look or touch? I saw you talking to Tanya in the park."

"Just look. I don't want anyone else."

She put her arms around his back and locked her hands together. "What about Meg?"

He raised his head. "What about my sister?"

"What are you going to tell her? She hates me."

"Actually, she's been too busy with my friend Steve to think much about you." He thought a moment, then said, "I don't think she really hates you. She blames your mother for everything that happened, but she doesn't know you."

Maddie laughed. "Getting to know me isn't a guarantee that she'll like me."

He shrugged. "I think she'll get over it, because ultimately she does want me to be happy. She wants me to marry someone I love. To have a wife and a family. I never thought I wanted kids, but after I've seen the way you've raised your cat . . ." He paused to look over at Snowball, who was mesmerized by goldfish. "You're a natural." He looked back at her and smiled. "Let me know if any or all parts of that plan appeal to you. If not, we'll make adjustments."

"This sounds a lot like a white wedding, picket fence, baby maker plan."

He chuckled. "Who would have thought?"

Certainly not her. She'd never thought she'd be some man's wife or that she'd be thinking about having a family. Of course, she never thought she'd fall in love or be a cat owner either. Her life had drastically changed since she'd moved to Truly. She'd changed.

She took Mick's hand and led him from the room. Maybe he was right. Maybe their lives had always been entwined and they were meant to be together. If that was the case, she'd happily spend the rest of her life tangled up in Mick Hennessy.